# THE BOOK OF THE
# PERILOUS DISHES

## BY DOINA RUŞTI

Translated from the Romanian by
James Christian Brown

Originally published as
*Mâţa Vinerii*

Published by Neem Tree Press Limited 2022

Neem Tree Press Limited
95A Ridgmount Gardens, London, WC1E 7AZ
info@neemtreepress.com
www.neemtreepress.com

Originally published in Romanian as *Mâța Vinerii* 2017 by Polirom
Copyright © Doina Ruști, 2022

Translation Copyright © James Christian Brown, 2022

ROMANIAN
CULTURAL
INSTITUTE

Support for this publication has been provided by a grant from the Romanian Cultural Institute's Translation and Publication Support program
www.icr-london.co.uk

A catalogue record for this book is available from the British Library

ISBN 978-1-911107-43-9 Hardback
ISBN 978-1-911107-44-6 Paperback
ISBN 978-1-911107-45-3 Ebook

Printed and bound by CPI Group (UK) Ltd, Croydon, CR0 4YY

# THE BOOK OF PERILOUS DISHES

## BY DOINA RUŞTI

Translated from the Romanian by
James Christian Brown

NEEM TREE
PRESS

# TRANSLATOR'S NOTE

*The Book of Perilous Dishes* is just one of a series of novels in which Doina Ruşti lovingly recreates the colourful but dangerous world of late-eighteenth-century Bucharest, a remote and exotic world to most of her readers today, though its traces can still be found here and there in the modern city if you know where to look. Inevitably, she uses words specific to the place and time, some of which, like the boyar (noble) titles *vornic*, *comis*, and *pitar*, I have kept in the translation. If readers of the book in English find them strange, it may be some consolation to know that they are equally puzzling to most Romanians nowadays too. Along with other words, including some proper names, that are likely to be unfamiliar to readers, they are explained in a glossary at the end, along with a list of characters.

A few words about the historical background may perhaps be helpful. At the time of the story, what is now Romania consisted of a number of separate territories, divided between two great empires. Braşov, where the story begins, is in Transylvania. Then a province of the Hapsburg Empire, ruled from Vienna, Transylvania was a patchwork of various nationalities, mainly Romanians, Hungarians, and Germans (known as 'Saxons'). Braşov itself was mainly a German city, but it also had an important Romanian community, in the Şchei district. In the south and east of present-day Romania, the principalities of Wallachia and Moldavia, with a mainly Romanian population, were subject to the Ottoman Empire. They were ruled by Greeks appointed by the Turkish sultan, known as Phanariots after the Phanar (Fener) district of Constantinople (Istanbul), from which many of them came. Some of these Phanariot princes were enlightened and modernizing rulers, but others were mainly interested in raising as much money as they could from taxes, both to please their Ottoman masters and for their own profit. Constantine Hangerli, who ruled Wallachia from November 1797 till January 1799, has been remembered particularly for his oppressive taxes—although he still failed to keep on the right side of Sultan Selim III, who suspected him of secret dealings with revolutionary France. It is during his short reign, in 1798, that most of the events of the novel take place.

But this is not only a historical novel; it is also a tale of the fantastic. The magical order of the Satorines bring into the story their own specific words and names, drawing on the heritage of ancient Rome. For example, Tutilina, a minor goddess of the fields in ancient times, here becomes the name of a learned witch, while Sator himself, the supreme being whose energies the Satorines seek to harness, takes his name from another Roman deity, Sator the sower or creator. It is also, as might be guessed from the title, a story about cooking. No less than twenty-one recipes are presented in the course of the story, recipes for perilous dishes with magical qualities. Some have been passed down through the centuries in Romanian tradition while others Doina Ruști has dug out of old Latin texts, hence their Latin names. Some, she assures me, are still being made and are even used in the modern pharmaceutical industry...

I hope you enjoy reading *The Book of Perilous Dishes* as much as I have enjoyed translating it.

JCB

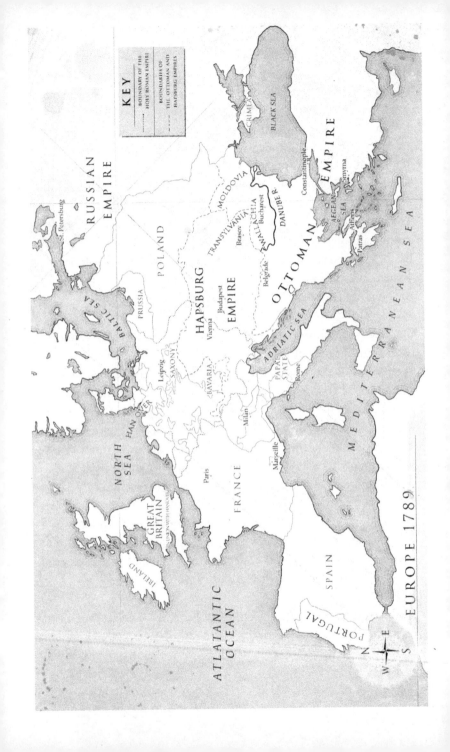

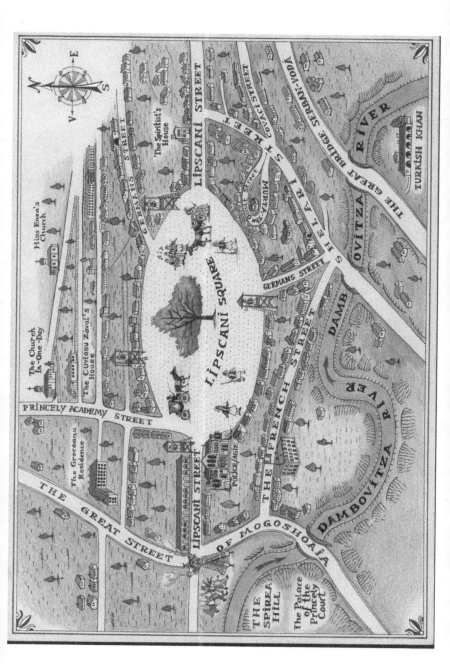

# TABLE OF CONTENTS

# CHAPTER I

# THE RED STOPPER

### My Flight

At the crack of dawn, Maxima was taken out into the square under the gaze of the scavengers sweeping around the *Walachisches Tor*. I knew what was coming. I gathered a few things and left by the back door. The butchers carrying their beef carcasses passed by me without a glance. I walked quickly to the end of the street. All around it was deserted, although I could well imagine that there were eyes pressed up against all the net curtains.

When the *Şchei* patrol pounded on some gate or other, the whole district heard it. They had batons with metal heads, specially made for hitting the little plate with the number of the house. First, they would strike a few times to attract attention, and then they would shout the name of the guilty person out loud. And it was only then that the gate would begin to rattle, as each tried to strike harder than his fellows and they all kept yelling at the top of their voices, moving on from the person's name to the reason why they were wanted. I had heard it all many a time, especially at night, but it had never entered my head that they might pound on our gate too. The city guard was for scoundrels, for robbers and for those who had killed people. And so, I didn't even open my eyes at the first blows. Our gate had a new overhang, and when they first struck it, the sound was like hail to my ears. It was only after they had shouted Maxima's name several times that I jumped out of bed, frightened to death. In the entrance hall the washerwoman stood trembling, and a few moments later Maxima too appeared. She descended the stairs in her bare feet, wearing nothing but her nightshirt.

'Get some clothes on and go out by the back door!'

'Don't for a moment imagine…!' I protested.

She took me by the shoulders, and looked at me with those eyes that left no room for discussion:

'Listen to me: don't forget your mission! In a short time the *brașoveancă* leaves for Bucharest, and you absolutely must at all cost get a place in it! I need you. Go to *Cuviosu* Zăval, who will tell you what you must do next! And until then, you know…!'

I knew: I was not to say a word about myself, not to indulge in loose talk with anyone. The first and foremost rule was never to say my true name. Even if someone should prove that they knew it, I was to flatly deny it. Not even dead was I to say it. My clothing was to be modest. My eyes cast down. Don't laugh! Never show your teeth! Smile. Don't grin and don't chuckle! Joy shows only in the eyes. And of course—I was not to deviate from my path!

Someone had already put my satchel in my hand. At the gate the guards were yelling as I put on my shoes, trembling. In the neighbours' houses, lamps had been lit.

My money was already stowed in the soles of my boots, sewn into the lining of my jacket, and hidden in various objects in my travelling bag. I was to keep only small change in my pocket. My yellow dress was stuffed with useful items.

'And don't forget, Pâtca! Make use of Sator's power when things get hard for you!'

These were her last words. She was still standing barefoot at the bottom of the stairs. I didn't kiss her. We didn't say goodbye.

I heard the gate opening, but I kept running towards the back door. From the garden, I saw them shoving her out into the street. There were three uniforms, three loudmouths. I opened the garden gate. Tears were running down my cheeks. I ran till I got to the end of the street.

And the first thing I did in my new life was to deviate from my path.

When I got to Burchioiu's house I realized that I couldn't simply walk past, especially as the wind was blowing on the veranda and the door seemed ajar. Had I had the strength of spirit, I would have cut his throat. Burchioiu was in a deep, dreamless sleep. I tarried for only a minute, my one care being that I might lose something, one of the many small things that I was attached to. All my power was contained in my yellow dress, which Maxima had made for me from nankeen and velvet, with pockets, flounces, and cuffs enough to hold the contents of a whole chest. What treasures I had tucked away in that dress! Salts, seeds, and powders, little phials of wolfsbane oil, *aqua phosphori*, the flower of death, and so many other things that a lifetime would not suffice to tell of them all. And I never went anywhere without my little box of saltpetre, in which thousands of sparks lay dormant.

Burchioiu lay on his back, snoring like a rag flapping in the wind. And that's how he remained fixed in my memory—a shadowy face, with big ears. When I was about to go, I saw one of his hats in the alcove by the door, and I stopped in my tracks. What sadness there is in clothes that no one will wear anymore!

I ran to catch the *brașoveancă*, caring nothing for the eyes that followed me. Even if I had gone at walking pace, anyone could have told that I was fleeing.

The mail coach was full, but when I got out my purse, the coachman found me a good place, a window seat. I leaned on the frame that had been polished by hundreds of elbows, and as the coach raced off, I saw for the last time the red arch of the

*Walachisches Tor*, under which Maxima was being shoved along, and beyond it, the tar-smeared gallows. I pulled down the blind, immersing myself in its lining of aging cotton. For as long as I live, the thought of her death will recall to my mind the flowers of that tapestry. And so I left Braşov behind me, its streets melting as the smoke swallowed them. Even the red gates dissolved, and with them the petrified figure of my dear grandmother.

Any flight from danger has the taste of sin about it; it turns you into a beggar. Whoever said that running away is a healthy thing was never a fugitive, only a watcher from the sidelines. My fleeing looked like a stain of phlegm that I could never wash off. Anyone could see it on me; every word I spoke was kneaded in it. But at that moment, faced with the threat of the guards and with the memory of Burchioiu fresh in my soul, it seemed to me that flight was the only way and the coach my salvation. Indeed, I even saw myself pushed from behind by Sator, convinced as I was that my grandmother had made him my protector.

In her view, there was only one place that pulsated with life, and that was Bucharest. It was from Bucharest that she had set out years before. It was there that her house was, where my father had grown up, and where I myself had first filled my lungs with air. It was in Bucharest that Cuviosu Zăval lived.

The mail coach floated through clouds of dust, raised by the breath of Sator, and I dreamed of the moment when I would find comfort in the embrace of my dear little uncle, in the city of my childhood and of all my dreams, dreams that still flowed out of Maxima's memory, even from beyond the grave. Zăval, she used to tell me, was the most important man in the city, and all the world revolved around our houses. We were the only people that counted. And when I say 'we', I mean Maxima, Zăval, and only in the third place myself, taking consolation from the thought that I already had a brilliant future reserved for me. No thought of mine ever flew out to the rest of the world. The others, the people who populated the city, bustling about in the streets, proud of their houses or their carriages, were all worthless. They did not know of the existence of Sator; they could not see where life really moved. They were no more than shadows, which I could have wiped away by raising a finger. But first I had to get to our houses, and to find the other Satorines, all of us that could draw on the power of Sator.

It was with these convictions in my heart that I approached the city, little suspecting that the real centre of the world was a renowned cook.

## The Cook

That torrid autumn, no one was talking about anything except the abducted cook. Every historical period should be judged by the events that set it alight. If I ask myself now what I remember from that autumn, it is the cook that comes in first place.

All this happened in the time of Kostas, for one of the greatest amusements of the Sublime Porte was to fool some Greek with the notion that he could make himself lord and master over the land of Wallachia for the modest price of a mere four hundred bags of loose change. No one had any idea what the price of a country should be. But it was not the real value that counted, so much as that 'yours for only…', which even today makes people restless, letting it be known that there's a bargain on offer. Once led up the garden path, the bargain hunter would hand over the money bags, and there and then he became the master of Wallachia, where he fondly dreamed that he was going to spend the rest of his days with subjects falling at his feet. A year later, however, another sucker for a cut-price offer would turn up, with another four hundred bags. Consequently, when I arrived there, Bucharest had already had the pleasure of being ruled by at least thirty Greeks, not to mention the Russian army, which made its way there from time to time, and drove out whoever happened to be the ruler, without a thought for the expense that the poor man had incurred. Fortunately, the Russian soldiers had itchy feet and they never stayed very long.

The Turks themselves showed no desire for this throne but were content to sell it to the Greeks and, of course, since they took care always to keep it occupied, that meant another four hundred bags from one of their subjects, plus gifts, gold watches, furs, and in general fine quality items, the sort of things that do good to the heart of a Turk.

The Greek who was then ruling in Wallachia, Kostas by name, was a great gourmet. And it so happened that at the time there was an expert cook living in Bucharest, namely Silică, a tiny little Gypsy with no small conceit of himself. For him, the kitchen was a sort of shrine. Every one of his dishes looked as grand as a statue on its way to being set up in Lipscani Square. He made steaks rolled in almond powder, smeared with honey and cinnamon. He was the master of hops, scalding the leaves only so he could bring them back to life again with pepper. But his favourite dish was sweet eggs. To help you understand, let me tell you with what passion he prepared them. He boiled them first in peppermint leaves. Once that was finished, he cut them in two and took out their yolks, which he mashed into cream sprinkled with cranberries and other preserved fruits, and then he stuffed this mixture back into the whites. It was right at the end that the real art came into play, when he covered the egg with a conserve of citrons and cinnamon and the thin creamy layer, whose secret is long lost, trembled under the brittle crust. He liked to make crayfish balls, especially soaked in rose or plum vinegar. And as for his sausages! No one could equal the way he matched the ingredients of the filling, especially if they included whey cheese, meats rubbed with raw garlic, liver or brain rolled in sesame, umbrella pine nuts, and other seeds that one could scarcely guess at. His walnut and fruit-juice jelly cakes would leave anyone gaping too, not just because of their taste, but also for the forms they took, like castles melting under the weight of snowfalls. And he didn't just make food for ravenous stomachs, but also for desperate souls. Here I might mention the cock-chafer beetles, soaked overnight in wine and then roasted on hot coals. He was the godfather of liqueurs, the maestro of *afyon*, and a sort of *pater veneni*, who knew elixirs against world-weariness and lassitude but also undreamed-of sauces that were good for the sicknesses of the blood.

In each dish he prepared, he would invest ten times as much energy as any other cook. Even for an ordinary nettle borscht, for example, he would scour the markets, tasting the whey himself to be sure of the right sour taste. He had become a sort of terror of the stall-holders, although they wouldn't even have passed the time of day with him if it hadn't been for Caterina Greceanu. Silică was born of a Gypsy family who bore the stamp of a great aristocratic house. For any slave has the seal of his master imprinted on his face, in his movements, and even in the way he carries the rags he wears. In Bucharest especially, it is never hard to tell who some Gypsy or other belongs to, whether he was raised in the household or bought at the market after passing through many hands. Silică looked like a pretentious little fellow, neither young nor yet old, but at an age where you could be sure that he was not going to change.

It was on this cook that the Greek, who at that moment was the rightful master of a country for which he had handed over four hundred bags of money, cast his eye. After he had been invited to dinner in the Greceanu house, Kostas, mighty prince and mighty gourmet, ordered that the cook be inventoried among the moveable goods of the Palace, thus quite simply stealing him from his mistress.

Such a thing would hitherto have been inconceivable. It was unheard of for a Gypsy who had been inherited, with a provenance as indisputable as it was in the present case, to be taken from the house of his mistress, who indeed was herself not just anybody.

And the city, which I was now approaching, had started to boil, showing the first signs of discontent with Kostas.

## Caterina's Three Steps

Caterina Greceanu, known to everyone simply as 'the Greceancă', the way one might say 'the Empress', was someone whom it would have been hard not to notice. If she appeared in the midst of a crowd, they made way for her, and if she opened her mouth, the sort of silence fell that tells you that you're in the presence of someone who will always be a cut above you. She had been married for a single night, to a rich man of the highest degree who had died on the very night of their wedding. It was put about that he had been stung by a wasp, although no one believed that someone could die of such a thing. When Caterina's carriage passed along the Princely Way, veils fluttered from its windows, and *thalers* and other silver coins were left in its wake, driving the common sort crazy. It was said that she was the richest woman in Bucharest, and that, in the end, was what determined her fate.

After Kostas, the new Prince of Wallachia, had stolen her cook, the Greceancă took what she considered to be three necessary steps. First, she sought justice from the Metropolitan Bishop, but he merely shrugged his shoulders impotently. Kostas had made out all the necessary papers for the cook, enrolling him in the category of slaves who had been abused by their masters. Indeed, there were even several witnesses who swore that his life would have been in danger if he had lingered another hour in the Greceanu household.

What was to be done? At the end of the day, the Greek was just another Greek, whereas Caterina had behind her the whole Greceanu family, all the Greceanus who had ever lived on the territory of Wallachia, and who drew their bloodline not from some wretched Greek, as one might guess from the name, but from a Romanian of long ago who had come from south of the Danube and for that reason had been wrongfully nicknamed 'the Greek'—which at least was better than if they had called him 'the wily Turk'.

Disgusted at the impotence of the Metropolitan Bishop, Caterina resorted to a second approach, and summoned minstrels. Once your deeds were on their lips, not even the waters of the Danube could wash you clean. There wasn't even any need for her to tell them what she wanted, because the whole city knew anyway.

'How would you like it, Your Ladyship? Just the story? Or perhaps with a bit of wailing for a refrain?'

'As you wish, as long as it gets into every alley!' replied Caterina, without a glance at the minstrel, who had already started to hum the immortal song that even today can still be heard in the taverns of Bucharest:

> *In Greceanu's house they weep all day*
> *The Vodă's taken their cook away...*

Anyway, when it came to the third step taken by Caterina, I was involved in that myself, even without wishing to be, on the very first night after I arrived in Bucharest. But first, I have to tell you about my arrival in the city, because right from the very start, without even knowing it, I came up against the story of Caterina's cook.

## The Showmen in Lipscani Square

Bucharest glowed like a halo of light in the dark. There wasn't the slightest breeze, perhaps because of the tall buildings, from which rounded balconies sprouted like Easter cakes. I remember being ashamed of my bonnet. In my great haste, I had snatched from the coat rack an old blue thing that had once been my grandmother's. Beneath it, on the other hand, I had a silk shawl, tied at one ear, which still made me feel exceptional. I didn't take large steps, for fear of drawing attention to myself. The road from the post house was so crowded that it was impossible not to rub against somebody. All I could do was to keep my eyes wide open and think of the feet of the beautiful Johanna. At that time, I never took the trouble to memorize numbers, the perfidy of which was doubted by no one in our family. I had to remember that Zăval's shop was beside the Church In-One-Day, at number *three*. If I kept thinking all the way about that number *three*, most likely the evils of the world would gather. It was best to have nothing in my mind except Johanna, our beautiful Johanna, the first cat that I can remember. Snowy white with a mild look. She was a cat who had been through a lot, who no longer expected anything from life. Somehow or other, in her childhood, which I knew little about, she had lost a leg. Consequently, she had only three paws, precisely the number that I had to remember. Although I knew well where to go, I had promised my dear grandmother to ask for the address, and not just anyhow, but by going into two shops. 'If a merchant tells you he doesn't know Cuviosu Zăval, it means he's lying!' Those were the words of Maxima, and for me they were the very letter of the law. The merchant who said he had never heard of Zăval was to be avoided and forgotten. She was convinced that as soon as I asked about Zăval, a whole crowd of people would be eager to lead me to his gate, and it's one thing to arrive in a town with a retinue behind you and quite another to go alone, like a pauper.

Seeing me with my travelling bag, a man with a moustache offered to give me a hand, and followed close on my heels. He wore a purple fez with two horns coming out of it. At least that was my first impression, but when he turned the other side of his face towards me, I nearly dropped my bag. The man had snakes all over his arm, sticking out their slimy tongues at me. More out of fear than as a deliberate act, I threw weeping powder in his face, box and all, and broke into a run between the carriages, seeing nothing of what had happened. In my mind, not only the moustachioed man but the snakes too were sobbing floods of tears.

The evening light was starting to fade, and I still hadn't plucked up the courage to ask about Cuviosu Zăval. I went as far as Lipscani Square. Everything made me gasp with amazement, and even now, as I write I can hardly keep myself from telling of the fabrics or of the little shoes covered with beads. They were lighting the lamps—I'll never forget it—and there was a smell of pumpkin fresh from the oven. By the post of the veranda, in front of a little booth some minstrels were singing, squeezing out tears and deep sighs. I was right at the heart of the market. Beside me I could hear the rustle of flowery silk, shalwars, and feather-light *anteris*. Although it was the beginning of autumn, it was hot, so hot, and I seemed to be the only one in the street who was over-wrapped.

I had found out which direction I had to go in, but I stopped to look at some street showmen who were talking with booming voices, accompanied by a great crowd in a state of distress and fear. Because of their hats, in fact cylinders of gold-coloured canvas, embroidered with black letters, they seemed very tall. Maxima had never let me look at individuals of this sort, whom she considered to be hypnotizers and manipulators of venom, capable of scattering over the crowd poisonous vapours and fluids that could deprive you of reason, while they kept shouting, scaring you with talk of the Saviour, or with the things that were going to happen to you when you got to the next world. All the same, I stopped. That's what I was like back then, distracted by the slightest movement in the street. Even if I had only heard a whistling, I would still rush to the gate. Not to speak of weddings, fights, or quarrels. I liked the funeral beggars best. I only had to hear from a distance how they strained to weep, begging for money for the burial of some relation or other, and there I was perched on the main doorpost or up in the tower of the house, supping with relish all the misfortunes that the deceased had gone through.

As Zăval's shop wasn't going to get up and go anywhere, I stayed to see what the fellows in tall hats wanted. One grim-faced man was yelling into a funnel: 'Onto the ramparts of the city will climb the filthy wretches from the cellars. Postilions will make the laws, and concubines will decide what joys a man deserves. Arnauts will lay down their swords, suddenly finding that the profession of teacher is much more to their liking!'

'Lord have mercy!' the people responded in chorus, full of distress, filling the whole street with their mournful voices. Then, after the wailing had died down, another voice stepped in, like a worn-out bugle: 'This very night the devilish evil and the wave-crest of the end will come over us, and its name of torment and heresy is Cat o' Friday! The bringer of death! Broken out of hell! Cat o' Friday will enter the city!'

A ball of ice passed like lightning from my brain to my guts. I was already a crushed worm when Cat o' Friday herself came down among us, a great beast going back and forth along a wall, as luminous as the day. Everyone around me was screaming, and some had fainted down by my knees, which were trembling as if they were no longer part of me. Two coils of smoke came out from between the parted fingers of that apparition, which was moving just the way a wave beats on the shore. Then it started to speak, rolling its eyes, which were no longer eyes, but jackdaws ruffled by the wind. The monster wore a variegated coat and looked like a turkey. Its disheveled hair made it look even more horrible, especially as from time to time two sharp-pointed ears pushed out of it. I couldn't understand what it was saying, or guess what language it was speaking, but from the stony sounds I had no doubt that it was a language not of this earth. It didn't matter anyway, because the three showmen were translating the terrifying words that made Cat o' Friday the most cruel of all creatures. It had been known for some time that her coming would be the beginning of the disaster. A princely head would fall right at her feet, severed by a single sword blow. The great spiritist Perticari had

12

seen her in a dream, and from his description a painter had portrayed her in the Olari Church. The showmen, who now seemed more like sorcerers to me, had invoked her shadow, which indeed seemed to have emerged out of a sort of oven. In all my life I had never seen a light like that, and I had never seen a mock figure that seemed alive.

For almost an hour I stood listening to the prophecies. The words of the showmen struck me hard, making me waste time that I was later to regret. And why I regretted doing that I shall tell you now.

### Cuviosu Zăval

On the door of the house was the proscribed number, and Johanna the cat appeared in front of my eyes for a moment. A cloak flapped past my cheek with a rustle of silk, or so it seemed, although there were no cloaks to be seen round about.

It was already dark when I finally went in through the door, calling him, so that he would know it was me.

Inside it seemed deserted; a little light broke in through the windows, coming from the yard of a church.

What hope I had placed in this man, whom Maxima had believed was a sort of god. Cuviosu—'the pious man'—had acquired the name because of his long face, whose gentleness struck you at a glance. He was known throughout the town, from children to the very old, because there was no one who had not stood in front of his great window, which occupied the whole wall towards the street. And indeed, there was something for you to look at, because it was packed with the most desirable produce, from rounds of German cheese to bottles of liqueur and walnut cakes, so that I myself, who knew them all by heart, having heard about them time and time again from the lips of Maxima, stopped in astonishment. And on the shiny glass was written in large letters *Cuviosu Zăval's*, in characters of two sorts, Cyrillic and Roman. For he was an educated man and a master of knowledge of the highest degree, who was known in all our family for deeds that surpassed all imaginings. He had lived for seven years in Lipsca, from before I was born. I remember well how he used to visit us, in a little off-white carriage with clouds of dust coming from under it. He knew a lot and imposed respect as soon as he arrived, especially as he was always dressed in the German manner, with a black bonnet worn tilted to one side over a matching thin scarf, the ends of which he twisted over his forehead, so that, seen from below, as I saw him, it seemed to me that he resembled the portrait of Theodoret of Cyrus in the entrance hall. One time he came with a goose. He always brought something, especially baskets of groceries and Latin books, and silk dresses that my mother and grandmother waited for excitedly. But most of all, I remember that goose, which seemed to have fallen asleep in the basket. I ran as fast as I could, but, when I got close enough, the bird had disappeared. 'Where's the goose?' he asked, opening his eyes wide. And I was used to such games, because Zăval, whom I called 'little uncle', often made things disappear, made curtains move, or made animals speak in the yard. And so, the goose was gone, and I was rather disappointed. 'Look in the basket,' he urged me, making me stick my nose into the velvet nest where the bird had been sleeping. At the bottom a little creature the size of a beetle was cackling. I took it and placed it on my palm. It wasn't a toy, but a real goose. I wasn't at all surprised, for Zăval could shrink anything. He had a lot of skills, and later, when I came to the Novus Oribasius, I too learned some of them, from Master Iulian, who knew almost all that Cuviosu knew, for the two were like hand and glove. They had travelled not only Europe, but also other lands, and sometimes they spoke proudly of their deeds, so I learned something more of the endless mysteries of the world, through which I had no doubt I too would wander one day.

Zăval was a lover of men, and one of the most charming. There was no man whose knees did not tremble on hearing his words.

He had the gift of the gab, and even now I can recall his voice and the soporific vapour of each word. And out of all the men who swarmed around him, his most beloved was Iulian.

From my childhood in Bucharest, I remember the last months, the time of the plague, when for a long time, which seemed to me endless, we stayed shut in the house, waiting for my little uncle Zăval to bring us food and other things, for no sickness ever touched him. And he kept coming, until one day my mother caught the infection, and Maxima flung me into a carriage, and we were off. We didn't stop till we reached the Şchei district of Braşov, where she had some houses.

My parents died in the plague, and I never set foot in Bucharest again until that evening.

I lit the lamp, and I froze in my tracks. Not far from me was death, in all its hideousness. Death and the threat of death, which lays waste to the most well-made plans.

Someone was lying on the floor. At first sight, it seemed to be Cuviosu Zăval. I didn't dare to approach him or even to move. But soon I had no doubt. I saw his little heart. It was his custom first thing every morning to draw a little black heart on his cheek, to bring him luck. Summer or winter, in sadness or in joy, Zăval would redo the outline of the heart, a tiny patch, so that, seen from a distance, it just seemed to be a little beauty spot, which heightened his charm. It was impossible to imagine my little uncle Zăval without that ornament! The tiny heart was tattooed, but every morning he refreshed it with a layer of carbon and with oils, which made it look as if he had been born with it. So it *was* him, there was not the slightest doubt, dead, with a knife thrust under his chin. Around him a pool of blood glistened.

Without my wishing it, my little uncle's life passed through my mind, not in sequence, but just a few details of it, the parts that were entwined with my own past. It was sufficient to remember Maxima's tireless mouth, my little uncle's smiling face, or the elegant men who hid behind the curtains of his carriage. That was enough. Three short recollections were all it took to convince me that my little uncle Zăval would get up from under the table, and the pool of blood would disappear without a trace.

I held the lamp close to him. The knife was his own, inherited after it had passed through the hands of all the men of our lineage. It had a hilt of agarwood, which spread a scent of culinary delights, and a silvery blade; to this day no one knows what that is made of. According to Zăval it had been brought in ancient times by some fierce hunters of Sator. This knife I had to keep. At the heart of the blade there was a sort of liquid, so that, when you moved it, you could feel its motion in your hand and sometimes even the song of those waters that terrified Sator so much, reducing him to a little lamb. Closing my eyes, I took hold of the haft with both hands and pulled with all my strength, my feet pushing hard against the chest of what had once been my little uncle.

In the yard it was dark, but not so dark that I couldn't find the apple tree. In its trunk, the blade could do its work well. For nothing is more precious in this world than a well stuck knife! Any metal will do the trick. If you are somehow assaulted by alien thoughts, stick a knife straight into the threshold! When someone threatens you, eagerly drive a knife blade into the nearest tree! The knife, more than any other object, reaches the core, gathering the currents that Magnesia scatters in the depths of the earth. It is no witchcraft. It is no mystery. A few knives can slow down the course of events around you. Have you ever felt a little gust of an ill wind under your nose? A shiver? A presence that makes you shudder? Well, such gusts exist, especially where nothing stops them.

I went back into the house. The lamp was flickering beside my nose, spreading a rich light. Without wishing to, I thought of how Zăval had bought the lamp in Lipsca. I even knew how much it had cost: 20 thalers, because we had one exactly the same.

I would have spent the whole night with my memories if it hadn't been for the matter of the stopper.

16

## The Red Stopper

I was about to put down the lamp when a shadow passed in front of the window. That silk cloak had been no hallucination. I waited petrified, given that a dead man lay at my feet. In front of the taffeta-covered glass of the veranda, someone was moving.

The time that passed before I opened the door was not long, but I have never forgotten it. There are moments like that, sometimes of no significance, that you remember more than the event that you expected.

Although I was afraid, I pulled the door open. Under the evening sky, a woman smiled humbly, immobile among the tips of the hollyhocks. "I kiss your hand, young lady,' she said by way of greeting, leaving me gaping, as no one had ever called me that before. She spoke in a whisper, which made me feel even more afraid: 'Cuviosu Zăval called me…' Around the crown of her head, the woman wore a headdress of cheap cloth.

'Unfortunately, Cuviosu has had to go away.'

The visitor knew Zăval well. 'He never goes away on a Sunday,' she said.

I looked her in the eye, but I could think of nothing but what was behind me. On the red floor, beside the table, the limbs of the dead man had probably stiffened to rods.

'What business do you have with my little uncle Zăval?' The fact that I was one of the family made her open up, and so I found out that this little woman with a big mouth was the wife of the cook that Kostas the Greek had got his hands on. Of course, at that moment I didn't know that there was any such cook. And about Kostas, even less. The woman repeated that her husband was the princely cook. I can no longer remember what her name was, even though I had dealings with her later on too. I listened to her with the lamp in my hand, keeping a foot in the threshold. Over her shoulder a breath of wind from the river reached my nose together with the warmth of the dry amaranthus in the garden.

'Then perhaps,' she said, arranging her headdress, 'you will give it to me.' I tried to delay her, but the cook's wife was very determined. 'I've paid, young mistress!'

'So? What are you going to do?'

'Well, what can I do? All I can do now is go to Captain Mârcă, under the bridge!' Her voice was raised, and her palm was pressed to her chest.

'And what were you to get from Cuviosu Zăval?'

'A flask, young mistress, the one with the red stopper shaped like a nose.'

The woman's eyes had reached as far as the table, at the feet of which Cuviosu was sleeping the sleep of eternity. If I went back to get the flask, in the short time it would take me to close the door, she was sure to see Cuviosu, and that, it seemed to me at that moment, would be catastrophic. For two long seconds the wife's eyes melted into my eyes.

Acting on impulse, I thrust the lamp in her face and asked her to hold it. Then, taking advantage of her momentary blindness, I grabbed the flask, and a moment later I was freely placing it in her arms. The red stopper, that stopper that was to enter my dreams, looked like a swollen blister full of blood.

## The Start of a Long Night

He was the first dead person in the family that I had seen close up. I didn't know what to do. A hundred beaks pecked at my soul. If I hadn't wasted time on the street showmen, perhaps I would have found him alive. I lifted the lamp and took a look around the room. Beside the coat rack lay another dead body. My hand started to tremble, and I began to fear that I would drop the lamp. It didn't take long for me to realize that there were two people, probably his domestics, a woman and a man, both with their throats cut. I couldn't even cry out. For an instant Burchioiu's face appeared in my mind, then his body stretched out, then a long line of dead people coming after me.

18

Maxima! What would she have done? I tried to imagine her—busying herself beside the dead, yelling to get everyone out of their houses. She could never do anything without witnesses, without the whole district knowing. I didn't want to think about her, but the thoughts washed over me anyway, pulling her out from the darkness of my brain, drowning out all the voices around me with her voice. A little brooding figure between the great brutes that had forced her to cross the square, passing the row of gates, shoved from time to time, abandoned by everyone, including me, who at that moment had left by the back door. I had walked out on her, instead of being there, staying with her to the last moment.

An outburst of weeping triggered, by waves of memories, brought me down beside my little uncle Zăval. His stiff arm seemed to press into the carpet. His fingers were spread out. Perhaps they had died at the same time, he and Maxima, brother and sister removed from history by criminal hands, leaving me all their duties and the burden of living with Sator. I could no longer return to Braşov. I had nowhere to go. I had to find our house, where Maxima had been born and where my parents had been cut down by the plague.

The first thing I had to do was to announce the old man's death and to do what my grandmother would have done: to make a complaint and ask for help everywhere I could think of, to seek out this Captain Mârcă that the cook's wife had mentioned, or some other captain or someone else from the authorities who would know better what was to be done.

The district was well lit, and people were still going about in the streets. Outside the Church In-One-Day, candles wept waxen tears for the living and the dead. I ran two or three paces. The city seemed quiet; I took courage. In Lipscani Square the *Agie* shone out, and on its steps could be seen the figure of a soldier of the guard. I took a deep breath. Through the windows of an inn there wafted the scent of chestnuts and coffee. A mournful song floated down from the attic of a house. I glanced at the Arnaut and got the impression that he was smiling at me. He looked like a wedding trumpet, all decked up in a big yellow fur hat and a tunic covered in tassels. Plucking up my courage, I headed towards him, but before I could say anything, he began questioning me: 'What business do you have in Bucharest, Your Ladyship?'

His words left me dumbfounded. It had never even entered my head that I didn't look like a local. Perhaps my grandmother's bonnet had given me away. And 'Your Ladyship' didn't bode well either. I didn't know how to answer, and I remembered that I had left my passport in my travelling bag. Believe me, even now I can feel the taste of betrayal just the same, like an evening breeze, in which the scent of coffee blends with the metallic movement of an Arnaut's uniform. I closed my eyes, and something struck me on the top of my head. Not physically, so much as inwardly. Minuscule droplets floated before my eyes, and my stricken mind picked up a dull scent of *Consolida regalis*. Someone's arms threw me onto a chair and hurried away with me, and before long I realized that I was going through the town like a statue carried on high. My mind continued to be active, while my every muscle was imprisoned in frozen time. Someone had blown a common paralysing agent in my face. My legs weighed heavily, but I could guess where the tips of my boots, made by Simon Schuster, our neighbour in Şchei, were. They had long shoe uppers that were fastened with two silver-plated buttons. Ugly as my situation was, I was seized with the fear that they might be stolen from me. In desperate situations, people are incapable of imagining the most bitter evil. Neither the dead bodies that I had left in the house nor the thought that I had lost Maxima and Cuviosu Zăval oppressed me as much as the possibility of losing my new boots.

Finally, we reached the Turkish inn, a run-down old building guarded by four rows of lamps.

20

The courtyard was lit, and around it rose high walls, like those of a castle. One of my kidnappers grinned in my face and I was pained to discover that he was the man with the snakes. That bandit was so talented that he could have done anything. And yet, in spite of that, he had opted to lead the most worthless of all the lives he could have chosen. His name was Cirtă Vianu. On his right hand he wore a sort of glove with snakes made in fine leather and so skilfully coloured that they seemed alive, but that night, scared to death as I was, I did not yet realize this. In the courtyard there was a monstrous figure mounted on a horse that looked as if it was on its last legs, its back nearly breaking under the weight of the bundle of pots and baskets that was tied to its saddle.

Cirtă gave his companion a questioning look, and the other replied haughtily: 'Never mind the fat man! He's nothing compared to the great Pazvantoğlu.'

The monster was not alone; beside him I could see some other individuals moving about. When Cirtă turned his eyes towards him, the fat man replied: 'Husein Pasha is arriving in Giurgiu tomorrow with some Frenchies.'

'How do you know?'

'From his son!'

Cirtă Vianu burst out laughing. 'Which one? He's got five!'

'This one!' whispered the fat man, and from one of the baskets he pulled out the head of a man, with the veins of the neck still dangling. He had been a young, good-looking man. I remember that in one ear you could still see the mark where an earring had been.

When he had got over his surprise, Cirtă flicked two of the snakes on his glove, and the head was tossed into a cauldron: 'Put some honey over it,' he ordered, 'to keep it nice!'

When I entered the building, I was sure I would never come out alive.

Although my memories of these events have faded in time like sheets laid to bleach in the sun, I can still feel the smell, I can still see the veil of smoke. The salon was guarded by a curtain-keeper.

When you hear of a dumb witness, you immediately think of a dog. But that night, I was such a witness, not to deeds of glory but to horse-trading, for I was present at Caterina Greceanu's third attempt. It was then that I found out what the abducted cook was worth to her.

## The Price of the Cook

For a while it was just me and the guardian of the curtain, an old Turk as desiccated as a wood shaving. As I waited there motionless, a woman wrapped in furs appeared. It was Caterina Greceanu. Although I was numb from the neck down, it seemed to me that I could smell a waft of perfume. The curtain was lifted, and the voice of the usher babbled something in Turkish. Through the opening in the curtain, I could see a yellow couch, rounded at one end, like a great slice of cheese, and in the middle of it a heap of silks, from which the swarthy head of a Turk barely protruded. It was Ismail Bina Emeni, a man whom from that moment on I would never be able to forget.

'*Girin!*' he said in a charming voice, for that man had one of the most perfidious voices I had ever heard.

He spoke as if it wasn't he who had opened his mouth, but a little fellow that he had swallowed, sitting in his throat and prudently pushing out the words one at a time, so that his sentences were long-drawn-out and faint, like the quacking of a moribund duck. And let me tell you why I'm focusing on this. The way a man speaks is the fastest way to tell what he's worth. When someone is all thunder and lightning, shouting at the top of his voice, it means that he's petrified. Such a man knows very well that he's a fool and that it shows from a distance. The powerful man, on the other hand, doesn't bother to ramble. His words come out smoothly, like eels slithering over wet grass.

Ismail Bina Emeni was lightly dressed, in a flowery *anteri*. He wasn't wearing a turban, and on the crown of his shaven head I could see a well-oiled tuft of hair. From time to time he took a puff on a gilt nargileh. '*Girin!*' he repeated, making a sign for her to enter.

The curtain-keeper neglected to close the curtain completely; he was, of course, familiar with his master, whose actions he followed avidly.

By the light of the salon, the face of the visitor was, as they say, like something out of a painting. She was beautiful. If I hadn't been poisoned by whatever they had blown up my nose, I would probably have sighed.

'Welcome, madam!' said Ismail Bina, with his accent of a true-born Turk. 'So, alone. Without an attendant?'

She sat down at a certain distance, on a little couch with a large cushion, and mentioned that she had left her servant outside. Ismail Bina raised his eyes to the ceiling suspiciously: 'That means that it is not just about the cook? You have secret business with me, do you not?'

'In the first place, it is about the cook, noble Ismail! Since Kostas took him from me…' Caterina stopped as if there was no point in going into details and asked in a mercantile voice: 'How long before I can get him back again?'

The Turk did not reply immediately, but when he did, his words filled the whole room: 'That depends on the price, lady…'

'You said fifty ducats…'

'For fifty ducats, you'll have him back in a month… but if you put down another fifteen, it might be sooner…'

Her voice resounded sharply: 'I'm not putting down anymore. Moreover, I want you to get rid of Kostas for me and to bring Ypsilanti to the throne! A man that steals my cook doesn't deserve to be ruler of Wallachia!'

Her words floated in the air for a time, making the usher push his fez to the back of his neck.

23

Ismail replied carelessly: 'That will cost you 400 bags, *pervane mayın!*'

Caterina fell into brooding thought. Seen from the little entrance chamber, her profile was indistinct, like melting snow.

What followed was to trouble me deeply for a long time. Even if I hadn't been frozen, I wouldn't have been able to move anyway.

The visitor took out a bag, claiming that it contained fifty ducats, and Ismail Bina held out his hand, as if it was rigid, obliging her to rise and come towards him. When she had come close, the Turk changed his position. His *anteri* fell open, and through the gap there emerged the part that I am uncomfortable naming and that only after many years I realize I did not actually see clearly. But what matters is not what you see but what is in your mind, and I was followed for a long time by that mushroom, drabber than a grey *Boletus*, not because it rose out of the folds or signalled in any way that it was thinking of rising, but because it was like an ironic comment on the bag of money! Who would expect such a man to keep to his word and to produce the cook? Certainly not me. And Ismail Bina Emeni spoke too: 'Next time come with an attendant, my lady!'

The Turk grinned, and my blood stopped in its course. Caterina, however, threw a glance towards that *caro impudica* and let the bag drop. And as she made her way to the door, quite unhurried, she reminded him: 'Don't forget that I have paid you for the cook, Effendi!'

There was a sort of mockery in her high-pitched tone, and to look at her she seemed to have no respect at all for the Turk.

It was not long before my turn came.

## My Price

The two kidnappers appeared as if from nowhere, and from the look of their greasy lips, it was clear that they had eaten well in the meantime.

Cirtă said something in Turkish, and Ismail Bina threw a glance towards me, enveloping me in a cloud of smoke. I sat motionless in the basketwork chair, probably with my bonnet at the back of my neck. Ismail Bina did not seem content, but he still had another question to ask, and the snake man forced open my lips for the Ottoman to see my teeth. On Ismail Bina's face I could read a great disappointment. It was clear that my price was very low. He wanted to say something, but he stumbled over his words. That's what happens to anyone who tries to count my teeth.

The Turk threw us out with a wave of his hand, and my two kidnappers almost ran away. In my stupidity, I thought they were going to throw me into the street, but I spent the rest of the night in a storeroom full of apples.

Before that, however, for the humiliation to be complete, the ruffians searched my pockets and robbed me of all I had. Little boxes, phials, and other items, without which I considered myself as good as dead, were relocated into their pockets.

'Weeping powder, missy? Think we're fools, eh?'

All I wanted was to see him turned into a cockroach and to hear him squelched under my heel.

'Look how much cash the little Saxon has!'

'Maybe robbed some Christian on the way.'

'Or perhaps she's a fugitive…'

A snake's head twisted itself over my cheek, giving me a sickening feeling.

'Look what she's got on her feet!'

That was exactly what I had feared! They had discovered my boots.

'Those'll make a pretty penny! And they're new too!'

The snake-man pulled my boots off while the other counted my money. On his nose he had spectacles with black wooden frames. He looked frightful, I may say.

'With those ducats we could get ourselves a carriage!'

'And what the devil would we do with it?'

'Better to buy some women. We can sell them at a profit to Ismail Bina…'

While my robbers were making their plans, I focused my mind, wishing with all my strength to get my wealth back, but of course this didn't happen, despite my belief in Sator being immense at the time. In the darkness of the night I had no one on my side. Burchioiu's eyes again pierced my thoughts. I was absolutely alone, the last living soul of all my kin.

## The Art of Denigration

Towards daybreak the feeling began to return into my fingers. Bitterness rose in my gullet. The first thing that came into my mind was the stony face of Cuviosu Zăval, the tattooed heart, the knife thrust under his chin. For a long time it was etched in my memory, and even months later, I would waken in the morning with the image of that withered face, which was no longer his face.

As is the case at any *khan*, the courtyard of the Turkish inn was bustling with people, especially with preparations for the road, for Ismail Bina Emeni was due to head south for Giurgiu with a convoy of carts, guarded by armed Arnauts. He was making his monthly journey to visit Husein Küçük, the Kapudan Pasha, on whom depended not only Ismail's position but all the well-being of Wallachia. It went without saying that he could not set out empty-handed, but must be laden with gifts and small favours, including a cartload of women.

I had rather lost my courage, but I was not the sort who just sits around waiting to die. I still had a little black powder, which I always kept in the knot of my shawl, although there was not a lot that I could do with it. An Arnaut took me out into the morning sunlight. The courtyard was noisy and heaving, with servants running back and forth about their duties. Ismail Bina was getting ready to climb into a street carriage, for which reason the gates of the Turkish inn had been opened, and that seemed a good moment to me. If I had at least had a little phial of *aqua phosphori*, I would have set fire to something, but as it was—I had no option but to run for it. When the Arnaut moved away a little, I threw myself blindly forward, running with difficulty, for all my life I had never gone barefoot. My legs were still numb. People scurried out of my way, and soon I had made my way to the gate. All I had to do now was to hide somewhere, and at that moment a heap of baskets seemed the most suitable place. I had almost escaped. I was in the street. I undid my shawl and took out the powder, but a hand grabbed me by the scruff of the neck, and moments later I was standing in front of the carriage, hanging my head like a broken hollyhock.

Ismail Bina looked at me reproachfully, and the ruffianly attendant holding me pressed his fingernails into my flesh. I remember that Ismail wore a white turban, snow-white, with a garnet glimmering among its folds. Looking back, I realize that he was a man with much charm, but at that time my standards of beauty were different! He drew a puff on his pipe and then the bluish smoke, which had wended its way through his flesh, filled my eyes with tears. The Turk didn't seem annoyed. He asked me gently why I had run away, what I had been lacking until then. I must confess that his words almost made me feel ashamed. It crossed my mind that perhaps he didn't even know that I had been kidnapped. Perhaps he imagined that those two scoundrels had bought me in the market. I had no answer prepared. And, apart from that, I could hardly breathe because of that hand gripping me mercilessly.

People had formed a circle around us, and Ismail, sensing that the crowd were expecting something from him, stretched out a gloved finger towards me and pushed my lips open, staring contentedly at the sea of bobbing heads around him: 'Aha! You're the one from last night! Ugly girls are always choosy! See what a she-boar we have here!'

The laughter round about encouraged him. Never before had anyone denigrated me in such a way. Never had anyone hurt me

27

so badly. And there was also the leather of the glove, which was still pressing my lips. The people round about seemed to approve.

I could have sunk into the ground and never come back. However, the humiliation woke me up. Out of all the supporters I had ever had, the face of Master Iulian appeared bright and clear, reminding me of one of his teachings. Strengthened, I yelled with all my power, drawing the sound from the base of my stomach and even from the starving coil of my guts: 'Ismail Bina Emeni!'

When you call to someone in the midst of a crazed multitude that is itself roaring, there is only one rule: to truly believe that you are the only speaker. Consequently, I let the words flow without haste, and after a pause I repeated his name at a higher pitch, to make him listen to me. I had nothing to say to him, but I wanted to make him look at me, to show him my teeth, for, although he had opened my mouth, he was still looking around at the crowd. Meanwhile, a voice resounded across the courtyard:

> *Ismail Bina on the road to Vidin*
> *Heeded not the Prophet's words and fell into sin,*
> *Sold his shalwar for a bottle of wine,*
> *Went on the booze and got drunk as a swine!*
> *Now of all the people round about the place,*
> *Only Ismail Bina has an arse for a face.*

There was a rustling among the crowd and a great laugh rose to the heavens. Many of them knew the song that a boy's voice had sent resounding all along the street. Some immediately joined in. The voice passed by the carriage like the ringing of a dulcimer string.

A hint of unease crept over Ismail Bina's face. In the end he looked at my teeth and couldn't find his words. The crowd had gathered closer and closer around us, and that alarmed him somewhat. The waves of smoke rose from his long pipe directly into my eyes, causing them to itch terribly, which made me grin without mercy, ignoring all Maxima's advice. From the Turk's mouth nothing came but blabbering, for there is no one that can speak normally after seeing my teeth. Some get their sentences mixed up; others forget what they want to say; and the most dumbfounded of all utter words that don't exist in any language. In that moment of stammering, a yell came from behind me and the attendant relaxed his grip. A few people were pushing their way towards us. I seized the opportunity, and confident that I would never be meeting him again, I deftly shook the powder into Bina's pipe. Then, taking advantage of the sparks that were blown all over everyone and of the resulting crush, I ran straight for a cart that was heading swiftly towards the bridge.

### Olari and the Witch

The carters had no idea what the matter was with me, but when they saw me hanging onto their cart, they asked me if I wanted to get to the Olari district, where they were going. Thankfully they weren't interested in asking questions, because I found them already engaged in a heated discussion. They were talking about Cat o' Friday, and they soon had my hair standing on end with terror. The witch who had come to eat up the joys of Bucharest was going to be caught and hanged.

'I don't believe she'll see the end of the week!' said a man with missing teeth. 'They've read a curse on her head in all the churches!'

This argument made me smile, and the man noticed.

'Don't you laugh! When the baker in Obor was murdered, the Most Reverend read from just one book! You understand? Just one! And two hours later they caught the murderer!'

What more could I say? The street showmen were just part of a long line of prophets. I felt a frisson of foreboding at the thought that the portrait of the witch was in the Church of the Olari district.

'If they don't kill her on a Friday it's pointless, because she can come back to life!'

'Seemingly on Fridays she turns into a cat and goes right to the altar.'

'The Prince's cook sells a potion that protects you from all spells!'

The men stopped the cart outside the church and urged me to go in and look at the witch.

In the porch there was a painting of hell, in the middle of which a pot of pitch was bubbling on the fire, with the head of a woman, wracked with pain, emerging from it: an old woman with bulging eyes and drooping, dog-like ears. Beside her there was Cyrillic writing, so orderly that even I could understand the words: *Cat o' Friday*.

When I left that place, I realized that I had lost my bonnet, and my shawl was almost unravelled. My cape looked more like a dishcloth, and my feet were bloody. And all that after just the first night in which I had been left alone in the world. One night had been enough for me to find out about the evils of life.

This thought was going through my head when it seemed to me that a soft breath was reaching out to me. I could sense the call; I could hear the rustle. In the movement of the city the breath and voice of Maxima were revolving. A deathly pain hit me right in the chest.

## Maxima Tutilina

Maxima had been both mother and father to me. Without her, I would have been nothing. She took me to Iulian's school and opened my eyes to life. Everything that she told me proved to be right. She had a way of saying various things that I had doubted at first, but that, reinforced over time, had become foundation stones.

'Despised love,' she used to say, 'rebounds against you, like a cannon-ball!'

How could you believe her? Especially as at that time I doubted everything.

She was a tiny woman and so agile that I couldn't keep up with her. She used to tell me things like that while running about the garden or through the rows of millet. Despised love kills you! How I laughed. And that laughter nearly killed us. Both of us.

Burchioiu lived on our street, and he was as kind as could be to everyone, I knew that, but I couldn't bear the sight of him even from a distance. He was insufferable, like a goat that wants to eat your headscarf. What do you do when you don't like someone, when you just don't, for no reason at all? You fidget, shifting from one foot to the other. You pretend you're listening to him. You pretend you're in a hurry with urgent business to deal with. That's what people do. Most people. You can't bring yourself to stop, but you can't bring yourself to tell him to his face either. I found that out in time, because back then, when I didn't like someone, I didn't hesitate to express my feelings.

I don't even remember now how he looked to me. But I didn't like him. He drank me in with his eyes and all that disregarded love was just waiting to crush me. Whether now or years later, I was condemned. It got to the point that I wouldn't go out of the house for fear of meeting Burchioiu. And, imagining myself confronted with his doughy face all through my life, I had already begun back then to think of all sorts of solutions, some bloodier than others.

Maxima called me Pâtca or Pâtculița. To this day I don't know if it means anything in particular, because every time I asked her, she just answered that it was a name for someone exactly like me. For all the love that she bore for me, sometimes I had the impression that she despised me just a little.

'Eh-hey! Pâtca, Pâtca! You have to have your ears wide open with people, because your whole future depends on them!'

31

Every time she gave me a piece of advice, her eyes filled with a pity that I can still sense today.

Maxima was the mistress of the millet field. She was called Maxima Tutilina, in honour of the goddess without a temple. It was a name that she had inherited, for all the names of the Satorines had been decided long ago, before Maxima or any of the others were born.

She knew the use of seeds and of every shoot that grew in the earth. And that wasn't all. In my memories, she lives on as the only person capable of bringing whatever she started to a conclusion. She could move anything from its place, and I don't just mean plants, which she could wrap around her little finger. Sometimes I would be talking with her and out of the blue someone would appear, a stranger who would sit down on the couch for a few moments, only to disappear again as fast as they had come. Especially at night, the occasional candle would pass through the salon, or a shawl would float by, making waves. Maxima read dreams, she made elixirs and ointments, and she could always cure me of a headache with two words that, even though I still remember them today, are no longer of any use to me. On summer evenings she would write on the gate '*Laco Fulvus*', and whoever tried to enter—because uninvited salesmen sometimes came, or the odd neighbour with nothing better to do—was scared to death by the ghost of a monstrous dog. The middle of the day was mine. She had put it into my head that I was to be a sort of guardian of the noontide.

'When you grow up,' she would say, 'you will be able to summon sleep. Especially when the sun begins to tremble, at its highest point.'

And she would make me look in the eyes of some poor wretch, the sort that would rather doze than live, until sleep came over him, heavy sleep, with dreams that made him groan or start.

'Warm up his mind, Pâtca,' she would urge me, 'and keep your eyes wide open, because the whole train of Sator is walking through that man: the snails of smoke, the imps that leap among the plum trees in the spring, and other spirits, including Lima, whom no one ever sees, because she is in between things, on the borderline that mortal eyes can never detect.'

Sometimes she would talk for hours on end, until I began to see what she wanted me to see. And in the evening, we would enter the house where we would deck ourselves out in beads and veils, to frighten the spirits resting in the mirrors or in the transparency of the windows, in the phials of poison and in the flicker of the fire that never went out in our house. Maxima had gauzes, frocks, and trinkets like no one else. How she decked herself out! She wouldn't leave the house without her pearly bonnet, which she held in place with a turban of fabric finer than a spider's web. And under it she wore her hair plaited in twelve pigtails. Sometimes she would run at night through the millet planting statuettes of Averruncus, to ward off evil, and other signs to distract Sator, but especially to show me how many means of survival there were.

Most of her time she spent on my instruction, to open my mind, so that I might hold the rank for which she believed I had been made.

'Remember, Pâtculiţa, all your power is in your teeth! Squint as they look, it is in them that the strength of our lineage lies! Their waywardness shows us that we must escape from commandments! For what is a person that does what another says? A slave! Worthy not even to be spat on!'

I looked in the mirror and I began to gain confidence. For a long time I was proud of my squint teeth, which had now so scared Ismail Bina!

Maxima had made plans for me for all the rest of my life, so much so that if I had happened to fall asleep and to wake up after ten years, I would have known exactly what I had to do.

'When I am no longer around,' she would say to me, 'make your way to our houses in Murta Street in Bucharest, houses hidden in the thick of the city, where our wealth is—chests bound shut with silver straps! There you will find dresses woven from elf hair, singing beads, enchanted greenfinch feathers, and books, including your book, which will finally open your eyes. There too are written the names of all the Satorines. Eh-hey! That will be another sort of life,' she would say, puffing herself up, 'one that you can't even dream of at present! But remember! Before anything else, you have to find Cuviosu Zăval. He is the only one able to show you the way into the old houses!'

As if it would have been a complicated matter to come by an address! The blind man found his way to Brăila, as the saying went, so surely I should have no problem finding some houses, I who at that time was convinced that everyone was stupid compared to me. Especially after I had come under the influence of Master Iulian! For years on end I had heard Maxima's words and I knew very well what I had to do. Even if I had set out blindfolded, I would still have found my little uncle's shop. Except that I had arrived late. Zăval was dead and all Maxima's advice was of no use. It had scattered on the winds. She herself was floating at that moment over Braşov, and I was unable to carry out any of the sacred missions for which she believed I had been born.

Once more I went to the church with the porch where that hag was burning in flames, and I stayed there till the tears dried on my cheek.

There was no glory left for me, no dream. Only the legend of an evil hag.

For Cat o' Friday, the hunted witch, was me.


## 1829—The Present Time

Those memories were dead, or they would have been if the man from the Austrian Post Office hadn't turned up today.

When you least expect it, along comes a morning like this one, a morning that stirs up your past. Memories are like moths hidden in your clothes. You live with them without seeing them, sometimes without even knowing they are there. Until one day, by chance, you touch something. Perhaps there is a universal force that sets in motion a whole chest of moth-eaten furs. *Impetu magis* or simply by mistake.

The letter was discoloured, and the writing partly erased. I broke the seal and unfolded the paper. The words followed one another like a wavering line of sail boats, written in thin, watery ink. There was not much writing, but it was enough to make me weep. Through the window I could still see the figure of the postman. I would have liked to reply at length, to write page after page, but it would have been a great waste of time. I looked for my boots; I almost tore my cloak from the hook. There was a time when I would have used the carriage even to go to Lipscani Square, but for a few years I have missed no occasion to walk, sometimes scuffing my feet the way I am doing now. It's one of those things that brings back the feeling of childhood.

On the Caradja Bridge I spot an old trailing cloth that is in fact Ogaru the priest. For as long as I have known him he has worn the same cassock. I stop and I say the few words that we always exchange, about donations and services, and in the end I invite him to take a fruit conserve, just as a matter of form, of course, and he thanks me in the same manner. There is an air of affliction about him that always makes of think of him as being like a fly. I don't know why, but of all the creatures on earth, it is only the fly that I cannot envisage happy, laughing from ear to ear, for example. In fact a fly is like a priest's head pressed down by his kalimavkion. Hidden under the silk hem. Frowning. With a pinched nose. Such a fly is Ogaru.

I continue on my way, thinking about what I'm going to write. I'll go into the Austrian Post Office. I'll greet them with a discreet smile, not showing my teeth. The officials have uniforms of dirty white, almost brown. Who could have chosen such a colour, one that erases you from the surface of the earth? As if they can't live because of their uniforms! The only reality that counts is the courier message. Something short. Six, up to ten words. And the name. Perhaps I should write something more personal, an endearment, a kind word. But what if he gets the wrong idea? Perhaps it would be best to make a joke.

I arrive in Lipscani Square, where a sort of stage for the shadow theatre has recently been set up. Above it flutters the portrait of a dishevelled-looking individual, and, in red letters, the words that stop me in my tracks: *The Rake of Bucharest*. How the world has changed! When I think of my first night, of the puppeteers of those days, I am struck with pity and touched with regret. I cast my eyes around and I don't even know where to begin to tell how it used to be. It was here, where this stage now stands, that I first saw the cook.

## 1798— *Thirty Years Ago*

### Meeting the Cook

One of the principles of our lineage was not to indulge in self-pity. Maxima had melted into the folds of an unseen world, and it was left to me to do many things. For a start, to get rid of the three dead bodies in the house of my little uncle. It was with these thoughts in my head that I arrived in Lipscani Square. It was the middle of the day, and the city was bustling. People were tagging along behind a little Gypsy flashily dressed in a bright green felt cape. He was grave and full of himself, as if he were at the very least a palace footman. He walked straight ahead, now and then stopping some street trader to cast an eye over what was in his basket. The stall-holders shouted after him, pointed him out or stopped to admire him: 'Silică! How's it going, Silică?'

Their friendly voices had no effect on the little fellow, of whom, not to use too many words, I shall say only that he was stuck up. He wore a yellow fez of very worn silk, decorated at the ear with a little silver brass bell. This was the cook for whom the Greceancă had given Bina fifty ducats and for whom she was ready to buy another prince, at a cost of 400 bags!

I must confess that from the start he made a bad impression on me. Although I have written and crossed out many times, in the end I cannot avoid mentioning the sour look that he gave my bare feet. Who looks down their nose at a pauper? Who swells up with contempt before a ragamuffin? Generally the rich have no time to waste on such details; on the other hand, when you meet a poor person with their nose in the air, it's best to give them a wide berth just as you would a dog. Sooner or later they're going to sink their teeth into you just because they can.

From further up the street the minstrels appeared, announcing the market; the most credible among them were Văcărescu's Gypsies. That was when I saw them for the first time. I particularly remember the vocalist, because his head was wrapped in a silk kerchief and below it his hair fell in flowing locks down to his waist. He was such a sight to see because he looked like a pedlar's display case. On every lock of his hair, tin ornaments, carved bones, beads, coins, and other trinkets rattled. The song filled the street, and I listened in amazement:

> *Starving is the Greek they say,*
> *Fruit is all he's had all day.*
> *Silică only buys the best,*
> *From Costică sturgeon flesh;*
> *Onu sells him poppy seeds*
> *And the pumpkin that he needs!*

Văcărescu's minstrels were welcomed everywhere because they never embroidered the facts. They sang every day, announcing what had been cooked at the palace, and thus all the poor wretches could know what Kostas the gourmet was stuffing himself with. The minstrels were followed by a crowd of idle spectators and various hangers-on attached themselves to the group, taking advantage of the situation to tell everyone about themselves, shouting out foolish slogans like: *Taloi's is the shop for you / Spend one ban instead of two!* These bargain-sellers kept interrupting the course of the song, raising their voices above those of the minstrels, which caused a great uproar, as angry listeners threw the most surprising things at them or jeered them, thus delaying the most important news.

The news to trump all news was Silică, whom the minstrels referred to as 'the kidnapped cook', although, to judge by the cocky manner with which he was doing the rounds of the market, he didn't seem to give a damn about that. As the hero of the minstrels' song, he seemed to be a sort of boyar's jewel.

As I listened to the gossip, the bitter odour of the previous night began to be dispelled. Only now could I truly rejoice that I had escaped from Ismail Bina, even if it meant that Caterina's hopes of recovering her cook had died with him! As far as I reckoned, he wasn't worth it anyway. To judge Silică by his face, I didn't think he could even be that good at cooking. How could a scallywag like him be worth fifty ducats? And to be blunt about it, he was a Gypsy too, and of all the races of the world, I most certainly was supposed to protect myself from Gypsies. Hadn't Maxima told me to take care? Not to talk to Gypsies, whose words are as treacherous as the wind. Not to eat from their hands, or I would forget my own name. Not to let them look me in the eye. That above all! But everybody knew about Gypsies' eyes: they can make you go mad and turn you into whatever they want!

The cook left for the Palace, and the crowd dispersed.

## Our Neighbour Burcu

In the house of Cuviosu Zăval, things seemed unchanged. The blood had clotted, and the smell of death was discreetly intensifying, mixing with that of papers and with the aroma of *cinnamomum*, sprinkled at the corners in order to trick Sator. A whiff of sulphur rose through the floorboards, which led me to believe that there was a *laboratorium* installed in the cellar, where my little uncle's secrets might lie.

The three bodies were just as I had left them. How long would it take for them to decompose? A number of skeletons passed through my mind, and with them tales of cemeteries and ghosts, and from there to Burchioiu it was only a short step. The thought of him had turned into a venomous snake, and out of all the memories, I was haunted by one particular day. It had started as one of the most relaxed, when Maxima was telling me stories in that way of hers that made you picture whatever she was recounting. Among the first of the stories she told me was the one about the twin sisters, which I had listened to so many times before that I knew it by heart. I had even learned the inflections of her voice, the pauses and exclamations that underlined every progress, every setback. Moreover, she knew that the sweet taste of the tale comes from the way in which a mouth gives voice to it. It's one thing to hear that the twins were separated by the wickedness of the world, and quite another to hear Maxima telling how Rozica came upon Anatol the Delicate, who breakfasted every morning on a salad of eyelids, collected from the eyes of the most beautiful women! And it had been my good fortune to listen to *The Tale of the Twin Sisters* told by Maxima. In short, it was all about the mysterious bonds between twins, who can pass one into the other. Rozica is saved by her twin sister, who senses that her sister is in great danger and journeys to her, into her very mind, to help her escape. And that day, while she was telling me the story as usual, Burchioiu came knocking at the gate.

Perhaps he was not a bad person. Perhaps Maxima was right. One who is rejected and cast aside sometimes changes so much that they can lose their way, messing up the lives of hundreds of individuals that they don't even know. He came into the house and sat down on the walnut bench. He was tall and his back was arched. I could see him in the light, looking like a sickle about to melt. On the sofa in the salon, Maxima was chirping between the cushions. She was merry.

'Come, Frau Massi,' he said, raising the pitch of his voice, 'and read the beans for me, because only you care for me. Have mercy and tell me what's in store for me in this world.'

Maxima, whom Burchioiu called, in the fashionable style, 'Massima', gave him a look that was full of smiles, the way she always looked at this boy, whom she considered a simpleton, trying to tame his soul and to cleanse his mind: 'And what would you like to know, Burcu? What's troubling you?'

'For example, if I'm going to get married, Frau.' He had lively eyes, which he kept casting around.

'You can rest easy on that score! A girl will turn up. Maybe not now, but in two or three years, you'll be married for sure!'

I slipped outside and I don't know what else she said to him, but a few minutes later I saw him going away, walking joyfully down the path towards the gate. He was tall and a little stooped, and on his head he wore all sorts of little hats that looked as if he had grown out of them. From the way he skipped along, it was clear that Maxima's words had cheered him. However, the joy of a fool does not necessarily bring peace to the world.

A full-scale madness had just taken hold of the Şchei district. As soon as it got about that someone was dabbling in spells, immediately they were hanged or even burned. There were all sorts of idiots that did nothing but make complaints. Not long before, Borbara Oros had complained that her neighbours, the Lăcătuş family, had turned her into a frog and that she'd had to stay that way for a few hours! Although few believed such a weird story, Mr and Mrs Lăcătuş had been hanged beside the *Walachisches Tor*. Through the summer, the agitation had continued, and some people had been burned alive—a woman who interpreted dreams and Old Coştan, who was suspected of being a *strigoi*.

The denouncers had multiplied, with foreigners in particular liable to fall prey to the disease. The people in the neighbourhood started looking askance at us, and I was convinced that Burchioiu, who was one of the few that ever crossed our threshold, had been talking carelessly in the street, though Maxima categorically refused to believe this.

Sator seemed to have faded away. One morning, somebody threw a stone at the veranda window. At one point we had thought of harnessing up the horses, but the street was guarded and all eyes were on us. The years spent in Braşov, not so many perhaps, but not so few either, no longer counted for anything. Maxima was no more than an incomer from Bucharest.

And that morning when the guardsmen knocked on our gate, I too had heard, like everyone in the neighbourhood, that it was indeed Burchioiu who had made a complaint against Maxima.

As I recalled all these things, which were not even long past, I was overcome with despair and weeping.

Through the window of the shop, I could see the silhouettes of growing numbers of customers trying the door. I had to do something with the dead bodies, who were now my dead bodies.

### The Mystery of the Red Stopper

There was no way I could go back to the *Agie* and risk bumping again into the Arnaut who had handed me over to the two kidnappers. It was clear that he'd had an understanding with them. Much later I was to find out that someone like me had no business being out in the streets at night. But at the time I was convinced that it was just my clothes that were to blame, because they immediately gave me away as a foreigner. I had to find something that would be less eye-catching, and a striped *anteri* seemed most suitable. Wrapped in that, and with my hair combed and gathered under a scarf, I could seek help in the church beside the shop.

But what if they thought it was I that had killed them? An icy flea made a rapid count of my vertebrae. On top of that, it was by no means certain that my little uncle Zăval had been in good relations with the priest. Being Maxima's brother, it was unlikely that he'd had a lot of time for churches.

The salon where the dead lay was a sort of bazaar, in which my little uncle had gathered so many things that it was difficult for me to deduce the presence of hiding places, such as would have been normal in any other house. For example, there was no cupboard set in the wall! That was incomprehensible. Who ever heard of a house without an embedded cupboard? Everyone has at least one for spices and one for papers. And in each of them there are at least a few disguised drawers, button-operated compartments, folding shelves, and other such things, where people can keep their money and their jewels safer than in chests or in the drawers under the table. Only my little uncle didn't have such a cupboard. Nothing but shelves in full view and table drawers, together with a few chests, which were unlocked anyway, as if he'd had nothing to hide.

I went through the phials on the shelves, and put a few of them in my ransacked pockets. One whole rack contained only potions of black nightshade. He'd probably had a grievance against some people's bellies. Then I came upon a little box containing some money: a few thalers and two clipped ducats. Among the objects on the table, I noticed an India rubber. Probably he had rubbed something out. In a large ledger his writing seemed fresh. The traces of the ink that he had deleted could still be made out. It was a list of purchases, principally consisting of cups and silk handkerchiefs, gloves, and ribbons, against which he had noted the name of each person who had placed an order.

On the next page was written clearly, in Latin characters: *The flask with the red stopper shaped like a nose.*

The words were underlined twice. For a moment I thought of the bulbous stopper disappearing down the streets, concealed in the skirts of the cook's wife. Then I read on, for there followed an explanation that made the hair rise up on the back of my neck. The bottle contained poison. Zăval had noted the whole process in detail: 'Around the mouth will come forth all the evils of that man, so that, after death, he will look like a giraffe of Arabia! *Cum putridis dentibus.*'

It didn't sound good. People disfigured, teeth scattered on the floorboards. How thoughtlessly I had let the bottle go! How relieved I had been to see the cook's wife disappearing! Perhaps someone had already departed for the next world. It was impossible that my little uncle Zăval would have prepared the poison for that woman. Perhaps it was she who had thrust the knife into his throat. She might have had accomplices. Perhaps my kidnappers had done away with him, which was the reason why they had tried to get rid of me. I looked for traces on the floorboards. I searched through Zăval's pockets. It almost seemed to me more important to find the bottle than to get rid of the three corpses. The red stopper was making its way towards an innocent soul!

And as I was wringing my hands in despair, my eye was caught by a wooden water barrel. If I could roll it close to Zăval, it would be the easiest way to lift him off the floor. Beside the door I found its wheels, with a new hook. But what if someone stopped me?

### The Arts of Transformation

The Novus Oribasius was but one class of the Romanian School in Şchei, where the incomparable Iulian had selected a few pupils that he believed to be gifted for medicine. And of all the priceless things that I had learned from him, most of all I had liked the arts of transformation, which included several categories, among them change of appearance. There I had learned how to make the finest of eyebrows out of dog's hair. I knew how to hide bags under the eyes. With a little piece of pumpkin peel I could lengthen the chin. I knew various recipes for mixing clay, and I was a master of painting. Of all the potions that changed the voice, most of all I liked one that produced a timbre so deep that you would have thought it came from the depths of the earth. I knew how to induce narcolepsy or to cover someone with boils, and other nasty things, as yet untested.

An hour later, I was using all my talents, everything I knew. It seemed to me that the best thing I could do was to completely change the appearance of my little uncle, so that no one would be able to recognize him. I didn't want anyone to stop me on the way.

I began by searching around for a cup, and I dyed his hair a shade of red. The skin of his gentle face had to be stretched with egg white and other pastes, and that work took me some time. But the result was worth the effort, for I managed to transform his face in such a way that even my poor little uncle seemed seized by wonder. As he was already drained of blood, all he needed was a face with an amazed expression! I had succeeded. My work had a lot that was good about it. However, it was not yet suffi-cient for my purposes. I raised his eyebrows with tweezers, but I still wasn't satisfied. So I rummaged through the drawers for a tattooing needle, which helped me to give them the imposing thickness of a merchant's eyebrows. Now the ears were no longer worthy of the new look. I worked meticulously for a long time to extend them with a little piece of sheepskin, making them a little fuller towards the neck. Only when I had got to this stage did I wrap him in a yellowing travelling rug. With his red hair and tattooed eyebrows, he looked like a clown put into storage. There was no way anyone would recognize him now. I reckoned I could take him home. My plan was to take him to Murta Street, which couldn't be too far away. At the back of the courtyard we had a house of the dead and a large oven, in which my grandfather had also been cremated. A dead man must be turned to ashes, so that he could then fly above everything.

For an hour I shed hot tears, recalling once again the Zăval who had lightened my childhood and was the beloved brother of Maxima Tutilina.

## Between Dubois and the Red Stopper

Anyway, by lunchtime the next day I was ready. I had taken care to dress modestly, so as not to catch anyone's eye, wearing the *anteri* that I had found on the coat rack, which, even after I had shortened it, was still long, and a tattered shawl. I had slippers to match, shabby old things and rather big for me.

I went out through the door of the house, pushing the water barrel, in which, hunched up just as he had died, my poor little uncle sat, covered by a nice lid painted with red poppies. I passed by the Church In-One-Day, then under the princely bridge, which linked the church to the Caradja family house. The streets were full, but no one took any notice of me. Everything ran smoothly as far as Lipscani Square, which was a kind of time machine, or a vortex of energy—at any rate, the place where I always had to start from the beginning again. I didn't understand then, but only after some time, once I had realized that all roads led to it. Lipscani Square was a sort of curse, but also the key to my whole history.

When I got there, things took a turn for the worse. Firstly, the square was full of Greeks yelling at the tops of their voices. A carriage with gilded doors had stopped right in the middle. It was the carriage of the French consul, on his way to the Princely Palace. Leaning half out of it and gesticulating was a man who made me let go of the water barrel. If I tell you he was handsome, you will understand nothing. He was a man so luminous that you'd be drawn like a magnet to him from any distance. You couldn't see his eyes. You couldn't describe any of the features of his face. He was quite simply a soul that soaked into your flesh and blood. He was like water. He was a spark struck from the heart of a coal. He was the very breath of that noontide, fixed over the city. His name was Dubois. And that meeting I have never forgotten.

And as I gaped at the carriage, into the corner of my eye, like a barb, came a sort of blood-red locust. Through the midst of the furious Greeks, the cook's wife was rushing along, carrying a basket containing two or three bottles, including the poison flask with the nose-shaped stopper. Without a moment's thought, I completely abandoned the water barrel and headed off on her trail. The woman was as black as night, and on top of her head she still wore that coiled headscarf. She walked quickly, forcing me to step up my pace too.

I didn't want to call after her, so as not to scare her. My plan was to catch up with her and to snatch the bottle from her. I could already see it shattered on the paving. To this day I cannot understand the madness that had seized me. And I don't know how I could abandon the water barrel in the square. A task begun and not finished is a recipe for disaster. All my troubles started from this point. If I hadn't gone after the stopper, the Arnauts wouldn't have caught me. That night, I experienced despair in the filthiest chamber of the *Agie*. When you are captured, it isn't the four walls that kill you but the strangers' hands sticking into your flesh. And not even those so much as the humiliation of being garbage that anyone can spit on. Prison is the end of any dream, and my dream had begun to fade from the moment I set foot in Lipscani Square.

## Chapter II

# LIPSCANI SQUARE

*1829—The Present Time*

Today Only Memories

In those days, it was wider on one side, and between the shops that surrounded it rose the foliage of lime trees. That was another reason why it was hard to get out of the square: because it looked like a fortress, even though it was really only a widening where some streets crossed. Just like nowadays, here the street named Lipscani, because of the shops of the Lipsca merchants, met the Princely Academy Street—two of the busiest in the city. Right at the crossroads stood a honey locust tree, so old that when the wind blew it creaked like a door, and when the bean pods in its crown, which no one could reach, rattled in a storm, it was like the sound of a hundred buckets.

On one side of the square stood the *khans*, with their vaults and balconies. Then it widened like a fat belly towards the Dâmbovița river, assaulted by drinking places with gardens, where the desperate and the foolish caroused till daybreak. In the same direction stood a green tower, from which a crier holding a speaking trumpet to his mouth announced the most important news. And at least once a day there would be some new gossip, which passed from one veranda to the next so that in less than half an hour everyone knew all there was to be known.

Lipscani Square was full of people, so much so that carriages could only squeeze through with difficulty. There would always be one stopped at the honey locust tree, with the coachman shouting at the top of his voice. You couldn't see any directions. You couldn't tell which way the road was taking you. Dealers and merchants went on their rounds, boasting of their goods, and in front of the shops there was always a crush of people. Lipscani Square was like a mill; it was a whirlpool. Once inside, you forgot your dreams. It was there that I forgot my little uncle Zăval, at the hour of noon, which is nowhere as dizzying as it is here, and, believe me, when it comes to that, there is no one more susceptible than me! The noontide is a honey cat padding through my soul.

When I look at Lipscani Square today, it hardly even looks like a square. A *khan* erected overnight has pushed well out into the street, so that the carriages have to make their way round it.

At the Austrian Post Office there was only one clerk, a smooth-faced youth.

'I want to send a courier message,' I informed him.

The man was kind. He took a piece of paper and signed to me to dictate. From previous occasions I knew that he didn't know Romanian very well, so I offered to write myself. I still hadn't decided what, and for a few minutes I looked out of the window at the parched gardens and the white sky. It would be best to announce my coming. The thought that I was soon to take to the road warmed me, like a glass of liqueur drunk before dinner. I had to buy myself a trunk and some spring dresses. A wig. Some white umbrellas. Perhaps shoes, although it would be better to get these in Vienna, where I would be spending a few days.

As soon as I had paid for the courier message, dismal imaginings flooded in. There could be no second thoughts now, no turning back. My words were already winging their way, announcing my imminent arrival. What a long time had passed! Thirty years. He wouldn't recognize me!

On the way back, Lipscani Square looked even sadder, especially as the sun had disappeared. A few carriages were struggling to make their way where once the honey locust tree stood, long since cut down and burned in some stove or other. An unseen breath of wind carried me back, to that day of misfortunes when I was pushing the water barrel containing little uncle Zăval.

## 1798—*Thirty Years Ago*

### The Greeks

The sun was shining overhead, and the people's faces could be seen in the finest detail. It was not one of those noontides that melt you, but nor was it the sort that seems on fire. And neither was there that heavy light that drives you out of your mind. It was a clear autumn day. Close to the honey locust tree, the Frenchmen's carriage had got stuck between other carriages, and around it the Greeks were chanting. That was what I saw at first. However, there were other things going on in the square. Dubois had stuck his head out of the carriage window, and the crowd was cheering him. Although he was merely chancellor at the French Consulate, the city folk had eyes only for him. If you had asked around what the name of the consul was, few would have known. Dubois, on the other hand, in fact Henri Dubois de Saint-Maurice, was known to everyone. And I've told you why. He was alive. When I arrived in the square with the water barrel, Dubois's head had just emerged from the window of the carriage, and from a princely veranda the powerful voice of the watchman was announcing: 'The French are going to the Palace! Make way!'

Over the square rose a song made to waken you from the dead:

*O, Basilei tou kosmou, orkizomai se Se*
*Sten inomen ton tiranon na men elton pote!*

I shall never forget the eyes of the Greeks, wide with emotion, and above all the way they raised their right arms whenever they reached the word *tiranon*, for the song was in fact a sort of oath, a fierce promise that they would never bow down before tyrants.

Dubois was waving the two silk bags containing his letter of appointment and the *berat* of the Sublime Porte. Probably he didn't fully realize what was going on, for he had not been long in Bucharest. The carriage was accompanied by Frenchmen on horseback and surrounded on all sides by men from the *Agie*, by Wallachian soldiers and officials, who looked straight ahead, completely ignoring the Greeks. From the roof of the Şerban Vodă *khan*, a young lad was shouting at the top of his voice: 'Long live France!' And a number of merchants stuck their heads out of their shops to congratulate him: 'Bravo, Codrică!'

Discussions had broken out right by my ear, and so I found out that all those Greek speakers had come out of the Academy—sons of Phanariot Greek families and of Wallachian boyars alike—to show their attachment to the French, and especially to Napoleon, whom even the Sultan saw in a good light. The song was by Rigas, and had been composed specially to offend the Turks, who, as usual, couldn't give a fez about it.

While this activity seemed to occupy the whole square, another carriage made its way through, almost brushing the Frenchmen's vehicle aside, and through the curtainless window shone the face of Caterina Greceanu. I recognized her immediately, even though I was quite a distance from her. That woman had a way of looking that was impossible to forget. She didn't smile, but her face lit up as if she had drunk up all the events that she gazed at. The square could scarcely contain the whole crowd, and because of the Greeks, who were now singing with pathos, it seemed to me that the ground was trembling beneath my feet. Thus began our French revolution, which lasted almost a month.

From the terrace of a building that reached up to the clouds, a man was watching through a telescope. He wore rose-coloured robes that caught the eye, and the immense instrument was supported on the backs of a number of servants.

It was in the middle of all this uproar that the red stopper appeared, making me leave the water barrel and run off after it. There are many circumstances in which the foot runs ahead of the mind, as happened to me. The road to the Palace was a really long one at that time, for Kostas had made his nest on Spirea's Hill. Just to describe that road would take me all day. Not to mention what happened in the Palace, where things became complicated beyond what the imagination can conceive!

## My Greatest Fear

Well, I left Cuviosu Zăval in order to recover the bottle, but just when I was getting close to it, a pair of huge hands almost crushed me to smithereens...

Through the tiny glazed window the autumn light was still trickling in, and on the other side of the thick door I could hear the hacking cough of the warder. I had seen him earlier, an old codger with a bent back, dressed in a string tunic. I sat hunched up on the brick floor, trying in vain to see my future. 'Make use of Sator', Maxima had told me. Easily said! All her advice and that of Master Iulian was now floating over the seas. In the darkness inside my head, I couldn't detect even the slightest trace of Sator! On top of that, I was still haunted by the belief of those traders in Olari that I, Cat o' Friday, was soon to be dead. Condemned to die or to destroy the wellbeing of a city!

If I stood up on the tips of my toes, I could just get a glimpse of the square. But there was nothing to see. To go by the threats of a young lad from the *Agie*, I was at the mercy of the *comis* of the guard of the Princely Court. I hadn't seen him face to face, but there was no need to, for all I needed to know could be stated briefly. He only had two punishments: either he let you go, or he threw you into the salt mines. He didn't believe in sentencing to death but considered that only the salt mines were capable of putting someone right. From the salt mines there was no way out. They were entered by a pit shaft four hundred *stânjeni* deep. And once there, you hacked away at the salt, hoping that some-one would remember you. For it was nobody's business to keep a count of the passing years. Anyone thrown into the salt mines died there.

The doddery old warder had warned me as he threw me a piece of a bread roll: 'His Highness *Comis* Dumitrache has never yet forgiven anyone! For who ends up in here? You tell me, little one! Only the scum and the dregs of the world!'

Still, my greatest worry was not the *comis*. The last few days had brought me other fears. After I entered the palace, seeking the red stopper, my eyes had been filled with so many things that, for a while, the flask, together with the stack of corpses it could leave behind it, had melted into nothingness. The palace was so full of people that, right from the moment I entered, I got bumped on the back of my head by the sharp edge of a huge tray. The banqueting hall looked like a beehive, and the tables formed a veritable labyrinth. In a raised position sat Kostas, a rather elderly and prune-like Phanariot wearing an unimagina-bly tall cap. His little face was not even a quarter the size of that pyramid that drooped over his eyes.

Out of all the mass of people chattering in the hall, the only one I really saw was Dubois. He was dressed in a white coat, which brought him even more into the foreground. His hair fell over his cheeks, which were neither pallid in tone nor olive-coloured, but looked like a piece of caramel dissolved in honey. I stared at him till his eyes met mine. I can still see him: a man who showed me his teeth, who looked straight into my eyes. In all my life up until then I had never received so much attention. With one look he told me that he was mine. I had forgotten about the bottle; I had forgotten about myself. And, melting in the euphoria of the moment, I advanced towards him. It was only then that I saw Caterina, supported on his arm. More than that, looking at her, it was not at all difficult for me to see that that woman, whom providence had brought into my path on my first night in Bucharest, was a menace. I had no doubt that the Greek had taken her cook fairly and squarely, and nor did I have the slightest drop of compassion for the treatment she had received from Ismail Bina. Before you could count to three she had become a cockroach fit only to be trodden on mercilessly. That was how I was thinking when she grabbed me by the arm and pushed a coin between my fingers.

'Listen,' she said, 'go and tell Silică to slip into the carriage!'

She talked continuously, while my hand struggled to get rid of the coin. My fury rose to my ears and at that moment I felt totally humiliated. What was that gaudy creature thinking? Why was she treating me like a servant?

I couldn't speak. I was completely silent, just like some ignorant bumpkin. Not because I had nothing to say, but because a knot had formed in my throat that Maxima used to call the knot of arrogance. People who often keep silent are not weak, not bashful. They are not drowned in emotion. Their dumbness comes from measureless pride, from the fear of being something less that what they think they are. Their fear of looking more stupid than the rest puts a lock on their lips and makes them look like idiots. That's how I was when Dubois began to speak to me. It was the first time I had heard a Frenchman, and his words sounded like sticks of candy that had come through the mouth of an old minstrel.

'He's asking what your name is,' explained Caterina, looking at me in her piercing way, like a dragon swallowing up the whole landscape.

Finally my mouth unlocked. I felt the need to praise myself, to say who I was, and so, puffing up my feathers, I uttered with a trembling voice the words: 'I am the niece of Cuviosu Zăval. My name is Pâtca!'

'And what business have you here?' the Greceancă immediately asked me. 'Did Cuviosu send you?'

Her words threw me off balance, reminding me that my little uncle was dead and abandoned in the water barrel. I would have liked to have opened my mouth, but what could I have said? A footman hustled me towards the kitchen.

In the crush that followed, some time passed. Beside the hob, Silică the cook was standing on a stool. As the seconds passed, he kept putting his fingers in his mouth and whistling, signalling to this or that servant to grab hold of a tray. The food occupied a table so long that I couldn't see where it ended. And what a spread! Roast meats with stuffing, meatballs, sauces with rose petals floating on them, little fish half emerging from cremes, bread rolls with poppy seeds, doughnuts threaded on sticks and smeared with honey, little plates of halva, Turkish delight, baklava, saraili, and other cakes drenched in syrups. And among them my eye was caught by a bowl of gut salad. A dish of that sort I knew how to make, but it wasn't for everybody, for whoever ate it would start to go a bit crazy, putting into practice their most obscure desires. It was a rare dish, also known as *errator pinniger*, because the patient's wanderings took wings, transforming dreams into nightmares. The salad is made from leaks and parsley, together with other green vegetables available at the same time, but the principal ingredient is lamb guts, heavily salted and fried in oil. Of course the cook had no way of knowing about *errator*, even though the dishes on the table were proof of his passion and knowledge. Still, for me that salad was an alarm signal.

When it was my turn, the cook gave a short whistle and signalled to me to pick up a pheasant. Perched on his chair, he was looking at me as if I were a servant, which made me deepen my voice: 'Your mistress says you are to get into the carriage!' The little cook froze for a moment, and then scrambled down from his chair. 'Here is a coin from her! She says to go straight to the stables and to wait in the carriage until she leaves!'

Once off his chair, Silică had transformed into a mere slave. Even his silky clothes had lost their shine. 'The little mistress?' he asked. 'Is she here, at the dinner? The mistress?' (His voice was trembling. In fact, I observed later that whenever he spoke about Caterina, he had the same tremor. Most often he called her 'the little mistress'.) 'I can't. Tell her I can't go. Now I'm the Palace cook!'

And with these words his voice returned to him as if by magic. He was proud of his work and believed that without him the princely kitchens would go to ruin. He had become insolent, and even during this meeting I understood that this was his true nature. And when I speak of *insolence*, I'm not necessarily referring to something base and vulgar. He was full of himself, enough to drive you mad, but somehow you would catch yourself recognizing that he was entitled to that pride, and then immediately you would kick yourself for having gone over to his side.

'And your wife?' I repeated, exactly as Caterina had told me to, reminding him that Kostas hadn't brought her to the Palace but had left her still in the Greceanu house, like something cast off.

The cook had finished with me. He took up his place again without giving me another look. 'She can manage! Let her stay there! I'm not leaving the Palace!'

While I was talking with the cook, who was preening himself more and more, I caught a glimpse of the bottle. I saw its red stopper floating for a moment through the bustle of the kitchen. Then a woman washing bowls took hold of it and stashed it away in her skirts.

The wave of porters pushed me once again into the banquet hall. I was trying to get to the Greceancă to give her the answer, not so much out of any sense of duty as because she knew my uncle. And of course I wanted to hear Dubois again. But on my way between the tables I was struck by a deathly fear.

Not far from the Frenchman, on a wide sofa, a man was lazily puffing on a chibouk. He was dressed in a rose-coloured *anteri*, which at first glance reminded me of the man looking through the telescope. Then my mind opened like a peony. The man lolling on the sofa was Ismail Bina Emeni! Alive and unharmed. I wanted to go further, but I was transfixed. I had firmly believed that he was dead! On his face not a sign was to be seen; he was smiling through the curtain of smoke. His pipe was new, and his face seemed that of an infant, due to the fact that he had been left without eyebrows. The black powder had done almost nothing!

What if Burchioiu too was alive?

A deathly horror brought me to my knees, and now, locked in the chamber of the *Agie*, this was my only fear. It was not the *comis* that I was afraid of, and nor was it punishment in the salt mines. It was the inevitable meeting with Bina, whom I could visualize forcing my mouth open with distaste so that he could laugh at my teeth. I was sure that he would flay me alive and offer me up at some banquet in Stamboul.

## Waiting

The square was buzzing with a sort of pride. I don't know why, but even without getting up to peer through the window, I could feel a confident buzz in the air, even though the news that was flowing around was increasingly bitter and dark. The guards were shouting through trumpets that the taxes had been increased, and from time to time a voice could be heard letting fly a long and richly detailed oath. In spite of that, there was not too much concern: 'Devil take the Greek! How long do you think he'll stay? Till Easter at the most!'

Kostas was raising money to reinforce the army of the Kapudan Pasha, Husein Küçük, the great liberator, who had been struggling for several months to wipe out the bands led by Pazvantoğlu, who to all Bucharest had become Pazvante the One-eyed. No one swore at the Turks, but every mouth spat curses on the head of the Greek and all his kin. Like anyone brought up in Stamboul, Kostas had learned early on how to seek the valuable things in life. The son of a doctor, he was well educated, and, in order to make his own living, he had made himself an interpreter for all the foreigners who fell ill and were calling out for a doctor. First he had learned Turkish. Then he had picked up the languages of the foreigners in Stamboul, and, as many of these were Wallachians, he had made so many friends in Bucharest that before long he was appointed an official *dragoman* of the Empire, with particular responsibility for the Romanian lands. He had married a Wallachian princess and moved permanently to Bucharest, so when he bought his throne, he knew pretty well what he was getting into. And he knew especially well that he had limited time. That was why he broke people's backs with taxes. Convoys bearing fresh payments for Husein left the city daily. A part ended up in the hands of Pazvante's brigands, who were intent on rebelling again the Turks, but not even Ismail Bina, Turk as he was, had anything against feeding the rebels. At the end of the day, no one knew who was going to win, and in life you need to keep on the right side of everyone.

While Kostas was laying tax upon tax, and the Romanians were waiting for him to be replaced, the Greeks, who in fact were mostly Vlachs from Thessaloniki, continued to talk of the Revolution in all the high-end drinking places, which resounded with rhetoric and songs.

Meanwhile, I focused all of my attention on seeking Sator, setting my mind either on getting out of the *Agie*, or on getting rid of the old fellow who kept watch, or on doing away with Ismail Bina before he got to me. I wanted to place myself in the shadow of Sator's power and to push it towards the door, then to make it go away, taking the warder into its folds too. I could see myself tricking Sator as if he were an autumn mist. I imagined myself disappearing without a trace, veiled in clouds of smoke. I told myself secretly that if I praised the Turk Bina, depicting him like an exquisite garden, Sator would be tricked and would go in search of him to the ends of the earth. And only then would I send my poison arrows, my cruellest part, my overlapping teeth, to tear Ismail Bina's heart, to rip his entrails, to deprive him of his life or at least of the revenge that I believed he was nursing.

I tried to practise on the warder, who was closest to me, thinking intensely of how to make him disappear. I imagined him veiled in the cloak of Sator, spiralling above the city in long rolls of smoke. I visualized him carried away on the wings of thought, dissolved into the sky, turned into wandering clouds, from which he would later fall like drops of rain onto some far-off town. And on its unknown streets he would be reassembled drop by drop, becoming once again what he had been. The same warder, with the same string tunic, many lands away.

This is what was going on in my mind, already half doubting all Maxima's advice, which so far had proved to be no more use than flies' wings harnessed to a cart.

And when I finished with everything, Burchioiu broke into my thoughts. I couldn't say that I regretted his death, but it had begun to gnaw at me. In a way I felt sorry for him, for he too was an orphan. Not as I was, though, because he had a father, Gentleman Ispas. He troubled Maxima too, not just me, because he was a hairy, frowning man, all the time dressed in black. When we saw him that is, for most of the time he was away. Sometimes he would turn up in the dead of night, and from his carriage, which looked like a helmet, could be heard giggles and women's voices that made all the neighbours give up whatever they were doing, even sleeping, to catch at least one word from the lips of his nocturnal guests. Sometimes we spotted a passing figure or the flutter of a cloak, and at other times we could hear heavy footsteps, like those of soldiers. Burchioiu's father was a merchant, but he was certainly up to other business, and he kept his distance from the life of the district and even from us, who lived over the fence from him. The wife of this hairy man had died long ago, which in my view was not surprising. Anyone would have given up the ghost in the company of such a man. Sometimes he unloaded into the cellar of his house long chests, coffins as they seemed to us, and on one occasion I heard sobbing coming from the darkness of the house.

Burchioiu didn't speak much about his father, and if Maxima insisted on asking him questions, he would answer curtly, red with fear. It was precisely for this reason that I thought of him as an orphan, even if he had one parent. He was older than me by three years and yet he was timid, worse than a rabbit. I had never thought about him like this until now, after his death. Indeed, nowhere do one's ideas about other people develop so much as in prison.

## The Short Road of Truth

And while I was dreaming, curled up on the brick floor of my dungeon, the dotard of a warder opened the door.

'Come on, it's your turn! Come to the interrogation room!'

I was dumbfounded to see that the warder was still there, after all my invocations of Sator. Because I had eaten nothing all day, it was hard for me to get to my feet.

'Come on, up with you,' urged the man, 'and thank your stars they're not taking you to Rahtivan Square for a whipping! You're lucky! What, you think any common robber is allowed to stay in the *Agie*? They're all taken to the prison and beaten till they shit themselves!'

At the end of the corridor there was a room with tall windows up to the ceiling. On a sort of throne with silk cushions a man as round as a bagpipe was lounging comfortably. The room was wide, with a lot of furniture, so much that I didn't know what to look at in particular. I stood in front of the pot-bellied man waiting for him to ask me something, but he gave no sign that he'd noticed me.

Through the window I could see the square, and from next door came the sound of voices. Finally, the door opened and another individual, well-groomed and with his nose in the air, entered and, talking all the time, threw himself onto a sofa with a red velvet back. Around him some servants immediately began to bustle, bringing him coffee and a tall narghileh that they placed on the floor.

'Are you ready?' he asked the bagpipe-man, who took out from among his cushions a register with seals.

'Of course, Your Honour!' the man replied. Then, fixing his eyes on me, he said as if talking to a feeble-minded person: 'His Highness *Comis* Dumitrache Banu is going to ask you questions. Give answers that are clear and as short as possible, without hiding anything! Is that understood?'

His Highness was the man with the narghileh, and he began to speak to me, frowning more and more as the discussion progressed, so much so that after just half an hour, his forehead looked like a dried plum.

'What is your name?'

This question was hard. My right foot stuck out a little in front, then froze like a post. What could I tell him? That I was Cat o' Friday? I couldn't say that even if he threatened to kill me! What would he say if I just told him I was Pâtca? Or should I tell him my name as given in my passport, which would immediately connect me to Zăval and the two dead bodies in his house? His Highness tapped his feet with impatience, staring intently at me. Perhaps it would be a good idea to invent a name. However, the *comis* opened his mouth again: 'Do not imagine that somehow we do not know! It's just procedure! If you want to say your name, fine. If not, that's your business! We move on! Are you from here or are you a foreigner?'

'From here!' I replied, for fear that he would dig further into my past, which would lead straight to the dishonourable death of Maxima and to Burchioiu, whose eyes flickered in the darkness of my mind.

'At which church do you worship?'

This was terrible. What would this frowning man say if I told him that I didn't worship? That I had never worshipped. That I had never even talked with a real priest, apart from Master Iulian, and you could hardly call him a priest!

'I want to know why I'm here,' I began, in my most polite voice. 'What have I done and why have I been locked up for so many days?'

The *comis* of the guard nearly choked on the pipe smoke, and the bagpipe-man, as red as a beetroot, signalled to me to be quiet and said: 'Here only His Highness the *comis* has the right to ask questions!'

After a few moments of silence, the great smoker asked gently: 'How did you kill Cuviosu Zăval?'

The question came like a slap across the mouth. How did he know? I thought they had arrested me because I'd had my eyes on the stopper. After the dish-washing woman had left the palace, I had run after her as far as Lipscani Square. The girl had gone into a grocer's, and I had stopped in the threshold, eavesdropping. As the thief wanted to sell the bottle, the most sensible solution was to wait and to buy it back from the grocer. She had praised the stopper and asked four thalers for it, but the grocer had only given her two. The dish-washing woman had prepared to leave. The bottle was mine! The story of the red stopper was over. I could put an end to it. But at that very moment, the square was invaded by a crowd of armed men. People were shouting. A soldier cast his wide eyes on me and picked me up like a chicken...

For a few moments I looked in the direction of the smoker who thought me guilty of the death of my little uncle and, quite unexpectedly, my tongue was unleashed. I no longer knew what I was saying, but suddenly I wanted to tell everything. I couldn't imagine how they had realized that the man in the water barrel was Zăval himself! I told them rapidly, stammering at times, how I had entered the house, how my little uncle had been lying dead, the knife in his throat, the other bodies.

I told them about the cook's wife and about the bottle of poison, which was still in the grocer's shop in Lipscani Square. I mumbled without a pause, and from time to time the smoker repeated a long word that meant nothing to me, which lodged itself in my mind like a tick:

'*Plerophorize*: what were you looking for in the house of the merchant Zăval?'

Whatever I said, he threw in a '*plerophorize*', which undoubtedly showed his displeasure. I told him the facts, but he seemed to demand more, and whenever I heard '*plerophorize*', I could see the pit getting deeper into which I had not the slightest doubt I would be thrown alive. '*Plerophorize*' became a fiery snake, an earwig two cubits long.

'Your Highness,' interrupted the bagpipe, 'the girl says she has a *tezkere* in her luggage. Where did you leave your papers?' he asked me, in the same voice for simpletons.

'In the house of my little uncle Zăval,' I answered, shifting both my arms behind my back while standing stock still with my right foot forward.

'You are a relative of his? Then what were you doing with the water barrel in the square?'

At last he had come round to the water barrel! How did he know that I had taken it there? Who else knew me? Who had noticed that I had left the water barrel? These were the questions that seemed insoluble at that time, but which today make me laugh and regret the long years spent in folly. How could

I imagine that a covered water barrel could just be abandoned in the street? Everyone's eyes must have been fixed on me the moment I entered the square! The indifferent eyes of men who couldn't stop gazing on the carriage of the Frenchmen, and the eyes of women fallen into dreaming, all the eyes of a world that seemed to be getting on with its own business were in fact on the water barrel and on me. The poppy-painted lid generally covered the good things that my little uncle transported in the water barrel, for it was in it that his servants brought plum brandy from the still, liqueurs, ice, or sometimes grapes fresh from the vine. Whatever was in the poppy-painted water barrel was going to be worth stealing! As soon as I had left it, they had started to lay their plans, taking added encouragement from the fact that, as all the on-lookers in the square had realized, I wasn't a local!

'Are you a Saxoness?' the *comis* asked me.

I had no idea what he was asking, but it could only be for the worse!

'When I arrived, there was someone there…'

'Who?'

In my soul the perverse tick of fear settled, and the door opened noisily. First came the stamping of Arnauts' boots, then the padding of slippers, and finally the rustling of Maltese silk. The smoker jumped to his feet, and the bagpipe of a man rushed to make salaams. Through the door of the office had come the tall, dignified figure of Ismail Bina.


Sator, My Saviour and My Fear

There are fears and fears in this world, and among them is the richest of all, the most frothy: *terror vanus*. Vain fear. Fright without reason. Black horror. The eyes do not see, and the legs no longer listen to the mind. The hands take on a life of their own. You no longer have an aim; you no longer care about your path. All your blood is a desperate bird, a badly injured animal. You are just you, turned into pitch that is hurrying to make room for itself before it hardens.

Such was I after my eyes had fallen once again on Ismail Bina. And the darkness that had drowned me thrust Sator into my soul. I was alone. *Expavefacta.* Full of fears. And then a firebolt of courage flashed through me, a hope of escape. Exactly as Maxima had told me. Exactly as Iulian my teacher had foretold. Sator was by my side.

My first thought was to blind Bina. I must not let passion distract me, I knew that. I must not enhance my fear. In that office packed with Arnauts, less than two cubits away from Bina, I had become a solemn statue. I did not move, determined not to open my mouth. I forced a slight smile on my face. Not to use my teeth was my first concern, whatever might happen—no teeth!

In all my pores, Sator was breathing, wallowing in pleasure. All that was needed was for Bina to attack me. I only had to let him jump at me for Sator to believe that he himself was under attack.

That little fellow in Ismail Bina's throat spoke ponderously: 'I need forty carts of pigs by this evening! And I don't have men. How many soldiers can you give me?'

The comis put aside his narghileh, caught off guard like a startled turkey, and reeled off the figures, slipping in at intervals the odd 'as Your Worship desires'. The discussion was not very long, and Bina was far too interested in the soldiers to look around him. We were standing less than a cubit apart. If I had reached out my hand I could have touched him. The Turk was left without eyebrows and, as I could now see, on one side of his nose he had a graze the size of a louse. I held my breath, in my mind following Sator, who had become the steam from a bowl of porridge.

Ismail Bina finished his business and cast a glance at the secretary, the way you might look at a dog. He was ready to leave. The Arnauts set their boots in motion and the Turk's eyes wandered around the room, stopping with perfect calm upon my face. For a moment nobody moved. Then Bina stretched out two fingers towards my mouth. Even though I had promised myself not to lose my temper, I grabbed hold of his hand and bit deeply into it. Don't try to tell me you have never felt the pleasure of sinking your teeth into someone's flesh! Of tightening their hold and grinding them a little, sizing up the resistance of an enemy through your molars!

The Arnauts rushed upon me, and Bina said in his most irritated voice: 'This girl comes with me!'

When I came out of the *Agie*, the streets were buzzing. From the balcony the voice of the watchman resounded like thunder: 'Make way! The Musahip of the Sublime Porte, Ismail Bina Emeni is passing through the square!'

From all directions, the townspeople hurried to see him close up, and the Lipscani merchants came out of their shops. I was now in the grip of an Arnaut, who kept pushing me towards the place where they had left their horses. He was intending to tie me to his saddle. Bina had reached his carriage, and a footman was bandaging his wound. I burst into tears, not particularly because of what was going to happen, so much as because Sator had abandoned me. I had felt his force within me for the first time, and I had let him go, just so I could stick my teeth into Bina's hand. In fact, to this day I do not know what happened. Perhaps he had felt a stronger pull from elsewhere. Perhaps it had just been chance. Regardless, he had disappeared like a spark in the night.

A trickle of blood was coming from my nose, and in the battering that I had been through my *anteri* had got torn too.

A voice caught me by surprise on account of its lilting tone: '*Selamün aleyküm*, noble Bina!'

The Turk turned and made a semblance of a bow, moving his hand and his head slightly. A short distance away, Caterina Greceanu was speaking, leaning against the window of her carriage, and who should be beside her on horseback but Dubois, with that face of his that made the whole square gaze upon him.

I was left gaping, not because I had seen the Frenchman, but because I couldn't imagine at the time how a woman who to my mind had been so humiliated could still exchange words with that rogue of a Turk. And what's more, she was even smiling at him as if they were close family.

'I hope you haven't forgotten what you promised me,' she said, raising her voice, and making Ismail Bina bow again.

She presented to him Dubois, who said a few words in his own language, and then in extremely faltering Romanian: 'We rejoice in the sympathy of the great Selim, Sultan of the Sublime Porte!'

'And if your Napoleon can make an end of the Austrians, we shall all rejoice!' replied Ismail, winking at Caterina, who in the meantime had turned her eyes on me.

I was sobbing loudly, while the Arnaut kept scolding me as he tried to tie one of my hands.

'But what's this I see, Effendi? What brings the niece of Cuviosu Zăval here? Whatever is that ill-bred Arnaut doing?'

Bina kept silent for a long moment, during which his eyes looked through me several times.

'Ah, Cuviosu, you say? But I thought I heard he was dead...'

'Yes indeed, and the girl has been left in my care! Get into the carriage, Pâtca!' she commanded me.

'No, *princesse*! The girl is mine! Look, she has bitten my hand! And a few days ago she very nearly blew off half my face! You have no idea what she is capable of! I'm doing you a favour if I rid you of her!'

Dubois's eyes were sparkling, a sign that he had understood. A short sentence caught the attention of the whole square, even if no one knew exactly what he had said.

'Just so, Chancellor,' agreed Caterina, raising her voice a little for the masses to hear her: 'This girl is a free person, more precisely, a child! How can someone be lifted from their home, as if they were a slave in the market?'

66

Over the world of Lipscani, expectation reigned.

'How old are you, fiend?' Bina asked me with distaste in his voice.

'Fourteen.'

From the way he looked at me silently, it was clear that he had expected me to be older.

'You are the heiress of Cuviosu Zăval,' continued Caterina. 'Once the succession is confirmed, you too will have a gift coming to you.'

### The Worthy Successor of My Little Uncle

As if age mattered! It's true, I was fourteen, but things, those things that matter perpetually, have remained unchanging through time. There are people who haven't even opened their eyes at fifty, still dozing in their cocoons, and others who at fourteen are already able to turn a world upside down. I'm not saying that I was some kind of prodigy, but I'd had the good fortune to be among people who had treated me as an adult. Perhaps in the eyes of Dubois I was no more than a child. But at least I knew a thing or two about life. Five months before, Master Iulian had died of consumption, and that had aged me by a hundred years. A few weeks later the guardsmen had come to close our school, and we had fought with them for two days. I was there when Nețu Birt put out the eye of one of them and burned his uniform in the square. All this added more years. Then there had been the week of harassment, until Maxima Tutilina had tamed Sator and poured out forgetfulness over the city. From time to time someone had been hanged or a house had been burned down. One week we had sent things to Bucharest, by the *brașoveancă*, because Maxima had a presentiment of disaster and had decided we should return home. She hadn't managed. The Burchioiu episode had put an end to my education. This thought at once made me recall Burchioiu's eyes. He had a look that always seemed to be reproaching you for something, a doleful way of looking at you, which as far as I was concerned made me feel guilty even before that fateful morning. When I saw how he moved his lanky arms or how he moistened his lips, which seemed permanently swollen with discontent, it wasn't with him that I was annoyed, but on account of my own weaknesses. All the same, what was done could not be undone. I was strengthened by the thought that I had done my duty to my family. Was I not the only one left to carry forward the burdens of our lineage? The fact that I had poisoned Burchioiu felt at the time like a sort of coming of age. Perhaps I was not fully mature, but nor was I a child anymore. I had gone into battle. I had killed a man and I had tried to do away with Bina, whom I would still have had no qualms about butchering. And don't imagine that I wasn't sorry for what I had done! For Burchioiu I tossed and turned in my sleep! And remorse weighs you down even more than any misfortune that befalls you! What are passing years compared with the bite of self-reproach?

Well, I had lived to the full at my fourteen years, so much so that I felt old, just as all people feel after their first trials. Although for some, these come later, after they have lived their humdrum lives! But then, believe me, it no longer matters any more. And nor do I take into account those who live with horror wound up in their chests. How many people are still wondering why they were born! How many people kneel in church, firmly believing that someone can hear them! How much time some lose in expectations that ruin them!

At fourteen years old, I had learned not to have expectations. I could write in Latin; I could read in Greek. Master Iulian had shown me all the secrets of transformation, and even if I didn't know how to enhance my power with Sator, at least I had never been overpowered by him.

Ismail Bina let me go, and after I paid the *comis* fifteen thalers, he gave me a break from his 'plerophorizing' and postponed the investigation for a while.

All the work I had put into transforming my little uncle had been for nothing. The tiny heart on his cheek had counted for more. He had been recognized by some servants, and some market traders who had been friends of his had started investigating. Not long after I had abandoned him in the square, the truth was out. The death of Cuviosu Zăval was an event that couldn't be overlooked. That was when I found out how many friends he had.

The house was filled with people. The minstrels sang of his death, and the guards yelled out hour by hour all the details of the news that had horrified the city. Kostas himself gave orders that the killer was to be found, and Perticari, the same spiritist who had seen Cat o' Friday in a dream, now also provided a description of the brutal murder. Thus I found out, together with the whole city, that my little uncle had been killed by some robbers, who, judging by their audacity in breaking into a house next to the church, could only be Serbs. And there was no one who didn't know at least one Serb who was intoxicated with the fumes of revenge. Even I could now describe the killer, a giant who would pull a knife on you before you had a chance to open your mouth. But why had he killed him? What was missing from Zăval's house? From somewhere or other, the rumour spread that a box full of ducats had gone.

It wasn't very clear at first whether a single weapon had been used to kill all three victims. However, the *comis* himself and his chubby secretary investigated the case of the two servants, and concluded, after much discussion, that indeed they and Zăval had probably been murdered with the same knife. The men from the *Agie* turned the house upside down in search of it, but to no avail.

Cuviosu Zăval was buried with full pomp and circumstance, and I, as his only relation, was obliged to pay for all these honours. There was absolutely no question of taking him to the House of the Dead in Murta Street! On top of that, a cohort of priests pounced on me to give me their interpretation of my little uncle's testament. The shop, houses, and money went into the hands of the metropolitan diocese, for the forgiveness of sins! Even a mill, which wasn't mentioned in any of the provisions, was taken as payment for the drawing up of my inheritance papers. The priests spoke of Zăval as of a man of great piety, although I knew very well what he really believed in!

'May the Lord forgive all his sins and set him at His right hand,' said the last priest to me, as he too came after the loot.

This was the parish priest of the Church In-One-Day, where his grave had been dug. In fact, I found out that it was my little uncle himself who had made arrangements for the construction of the tomb. This was the place of worship of barbers, apothecaries, and even poisoners, whom Saint Nicholas had determined to protect. And my little uncle had felt a sense of brotherhood with them. Or he had liked the story of the church, of which it was said that it had stood for many years without a roof, until one day—that day that had entered into legend—when someone gave orders for it to be roofed, and the work was started in the morning and completed by evening, hence the name. As happens with all things left to ripen, this too had begun to get distorted, and after a while the rumour had begun to circulate that the whole church had been erected in a single day, thus becoming a place of miracles. And for the great dedication day, which was approaching, seemingly Cuviosu Zăval had promised a pile of money, though at that moment I couldn't see where I was going to get it from. In those days, the parish priest always had a dapper air about him.

'To do honour to our devout Cuviosu Zăval, you ought to give something towards the cleaning of the tomb. It would be good if you could offer up the house in which he lived, so that our church can be enlarged. You can't imagine how useful it would be if I could extend the churchyard over the garden of our good Zăval! What need have you of the house of an old merchant, when, from what I hear, you have the houses in Lipscani Square.'

The dapper priest had made detailed plans for me!

70

'I don't know anything about this dedication day. I don't think my little uncle would have given such a sum for a barbers' party,' I said.

'It's not a donation,' he explained to me, 'but part of Gentleman Zăval's debts, and if it's not paid in full, he will have to find another tomb! The Church In-One-Day might no longer keep his sinful bones.'

At something like that, all I could do was burst out in a loud laugh. My little uncle and his debts to the church! I could have believed anything about him, but not that! The great Cuviosu Zăval, master in the art of using Sator! Among the few people who could direct his paths! *Motator Satoris*! The tamer of the great Sator had suddenly proved to be a massive debtor to the barbers' church!

# CHAPTER III

# SATOR

*Sator Omnium Bonus-Malus*

The sole reality bestowed on a person is Sator. Beyond Sator lies only death. There is no hell. There is no heaven. Only the chance to be the bearer of Sator, the beginning and the sparkling water that descends into all breath. *Hominum Sator atque deorum.*

The earth is a kind of sponge, in whose holes the drops shaken by accident from the great wave come to life. And when the first seedlets start sprouting, from the black rings of the sky there descend skeins of water, lit by millions of sparks and by the mists that make the seeds come to life. Sator is the shadow descending, the cloud in motion. He is a willow tree dancing. He is a scented vapour, counting a person's breaths and the joys of which they are capable. Sator does not hear the prayers of the world. He does not know that people have needs. Sator is but the pampered wave in every seashell, created especially for his pleasure. And his greatest delights are the hopes and longings of the soul, which feed the billions of sparks in his viscous waters. Unchecked, Sator will drive the weak to evil. For with every hope begins also the bitter struggle for its fulfilment. And the more desire becomes enflamed, the greater the multiplication of deeds required to satisfy it. 'Just let me do this, let me have that. Just this far—and I'll stop. This is my last wish! If I can only be promoted to general, there is absolutely nothing else I need. This is all I want from life!' So speaks every adventurer setting off to war. But in the reality of the struggle, in the proximity of Sator and in the recklessness of mortal blood, few know where to stop. And fewer still are capable of putting a stop to their desires. Such is man, made up of hopes, especially for the delight of the great Sator. One who does not hope is like a creature that gives up breathing for fear of being detected by its pursuers. It is a precarious situation, but, as I see it, quite a happy one, for Sator is not attracted to the fearful. Lying on your belly, with your heart in your mouth and your mind emptied of dreams is one way to keep Sator at arm's length. But what sort of life is that, just existing without a purpose, like an onion left to rot in the rain?

To live life to the fullest and yet to escape the domination of Sator, it is best to accommodate him, just as you learn to steer a course through the waves of mighty rivers, just as you learn to make your way through the blasts of winter. Just as you pass through storms. And for this there are a number of rules, which it is good for each person to know.

The first and most important of them is the rule of silence. Once you have sensed his fire, it is best to stay motionless. Sator appears like the steam that scalds, like the venom that runs down a throat. If he comes upon someone who is unsettled in some way, frightened, so troubled that his head is filled with plans and with the hope of salvation, that person is already doomed. Sator will settle deep into their soul, he will bestir their mind, filling them with monsters and with great desperation, pushing them to the most ill-considered acts, pouring into them anguish and craving to drive them to madness.

Thus the first rule is to freeze as soon as you sense his presence. To let him pass you by, as if you didn't exist. And if that hasn't worked, and you feel that he is soaking into your soul, it only remains to think as hard as you can of the place where you want to send him. Sator sniffs the trail of thoughts, hunts them.

He is like a hound, like a scandalmonger avidly seeking rumours. If you can succeed in igniting his curiosity and diverting him, he will race ahead in that direction, scattering everything before him, leaving devastation behind. On one occasion, Cuviosu Zăval drove him into the Leinawald Forest, where he knew a caravan of carts was going to pass. They were merchants he knew from Lipsca, who had done him mischief a few months previously. Zăval was not vengeful by nature, but he could not tolerate wickedness. And those individuals had made him suffer a lot. My little uncle had been crazy back then over a Turinese, and talked about him whenever he had a free moment. That was before Iulian. The Turinese was a jeweller who lived in Lipsca. Out of everything I heard, I can only remember one thing: the Turinese had a golden tooth, which in my childhood days I imagined scattering fiery stars at every word he spoke. Even I dreamed of this man that Zăval had loved. But those two merchant brothers didn't look kindly on the Turinese, or on his liaison with my little uncle. And so, to settle their score against Zăval, they butchered the Turinese one evening and, in mockery, sent my little uncle his head, wrapped in a parcel, together with other parts of his body that are best not spoken of. To show even greater contempt, they had taken out his golden tooth and turned it into an earring, which one of the brothers now wore, as a reminder of their brutal deed.

A few months later, when he had pulled himself together, my little uncle got his hands on Sator and sent him straight to Leinawald. The two murderous brothers were lifted up in Sator's vortex and whirled over the seas to the Isle of Staffa. But not just as if on a pilgrimage, for first he had deprived them of their feet and their tongues. I never knew whether this island really exists and nor could I ever verify in any way the disappearance of the murderous brothers. Zăval alone was convinced that they had arrived in that place at the ends of the earth. Around the same time, he had returned from Lipsca together with a convoy of carts, which, he said, he had found in Leinawald.

Cuviosu Zăval was a master in harnessing the power of Sator, through which he could do all that he wished. He would never have let himself be caught under the vortex, as happens to most people.

The second important rule is to extricate yourself from Sator's domination, no matter how. When Sator no longer has any use for the dry flesh of a person, he withdraws, and that person falls flat, like a cast-off glove.

And being released from Sator is such a difficult thing that only Zăval knew how to do it. He had potions that made you seem dead, powders that hid you from the sight of Sator, and a sort of crystal that made Sator vanish, if only for a short time.

When a lineage accumulates experience generation after generation, its members become more skilled in making use of Sator. So it was with Maxima, who from all her grandfathers and grandmothers, all the hoary greybeards and wise old crones of our lineage, scattered through many lands, collated drop by drop all that each family member had managed to find out. She knew very well the advantages of living with Sator.

And there is something else that it is essential to know: the hardest of all the burdens a person is destined to bear is the unrequited hope that can drive you to your death. Sometimes Sator makes his silken nest in the sorry depths of your throat, turning your life into the black water of the cruellest summonses.

## The Greceanu House

Consequently, when Father Ogaru of the Church In-One-Day ended his threatening exposition, I burst out laughing, the sort of raucous laugh that frequently lands one in trouble, and if Caterina hadn't been nearby, the meeting would probably have ended badly. She was named in the will as my protector until I married, and she was a gift from heaven. Only later, after my mind had matured, did I realize that my little uncle had chosen well. It was from her that I learned that if you want something you have to ask for it. In no circumstances do you wait, like a fool, for others to become aware of what you need. And of course asking takes many forms. With her, everything depended on how she looked at you. She had in the corner of her mouth a very fine crease that transformed any smile into an act of defiance. Whatever you might say, first she would arrange that fold, from which would emerge in turn approvals, reprimands, and promises. Some were reduced to stammering, while others were left without arguments. Few could stand up to her.

As for me, she did me a great deal of good by leaving me to my own devices. During the day I rummaged around in Zăval's house, and only towards the evening did I return to hers, a few streets away.

When I entered the Greceanu house for the first time, I was overwhelmed. It was an imposing building of two storeys, with high ceilings and countless rooms. Right at the entrance the housekeeper was waiting for us. I had never seen a servant with such grand airs. Her name was Papuc—'Slipper'—but no one ever laughed at it. When you said 'Housekeeper Papuc', all the movement in the house froze, not so much from fear as from respect, for the housekeeper was always right and may fate preserve you from such people!

'This is Pâtca, the niece of Cuviosu Zăval,' Caterina informed her. 'She needs a nice room, on the first floor, a carriage, and a woman to attend on her.'

Caterina didn't talk much with me. Not at first. But life in her house was full of joys. In the first place, my room looked like a rose, thanks to its curtains, for I passed through two sets of curtains to get to my bed. First there were those at the door of the room, and then another set that hid the bed, lace curtains with tassels. And then there were the rich drapes over the windows, which parted to reveal lace curtains falling like an icy fan, studded with sequins and edged with a string of beads.

I had a carriage driven by a young boy, smaller than me, with coffee-dark skin. I can't remember his name. And an old woman, whom I always called just that, who came after me everywhere I went. She was a Gypsy too, as were all Caterina's servants, for she had inherited from her parents over a thousand slaves, all born on her estates. My old woman was very quiet and mild-mannered. I don't know if she ever even told anyone where I took her, for I usually left her in the carriage. Any conversation I attempted with her quickly came to an end, because she always just smiled and said, 'Yes, little mistress,' as if to say, 'Never mind, you'll get over it!' After many years I understood that she didn't speak because she simply didn't want to waste her time on me.

When I think of that period, I remember Caterina climbing the stairs with a rustle I have never heard anywhere else. She always spoke in a loud voice, and sometimes she shouted to me, so I could hear her from my room: 'Well, Pâtca? Do you like it in my house?'

## Murta Street

Since my head was buzzing with properties and inheritances, the first thing I wanted to do was to see the houses in Lipscani Square, which just about everyone who was anyone seemed to know about. I had no need of Cuviosu Zăval to find them, as Maxima Tutilina had suggested. People remembered her. 'Aha, Maxima,' said Papuc the housekeeper, 'the sister of Zăval the merchant! Yes indeed, she has a pair of white houses next to Lipscani Square.' On the other hand, no one seemed to have heard of Murta Street. Either the name of the street had been changed in the meantime, as can happen, or what had remained in my grandmother's mind was some old name, which perhaps hadn't been in current use even in her day.

Lipscani Square was, as usual, packed, but from my little uncle's carriage, I got a different view of people, smaller and gentler. Between shops and gardens there were winding streets. I tried each one. None of them was Murta but the watchman had heard of it: 'It's somewhere around here, young lady. It can't be far. Maybe next to Frenchmen's Street.'

At the mention of Frenchmen, the brocade-laden voice of Dubois came into my mind. Around the Consulate there was a web of streets, numerous and short, with so many shortcuts and little cul-de-sacs that my every attempt seemed in vain.

Not far off was the Dâmbovița. Whichever way I went, sooner or later I would arrive at the edge of the river, facing a crowded bridge. What was I to do? I stopped. A man in a captain's uniform saw how lost I looked. 'How can I help you?' he asked. I blurted out what I was looking for. The house, the street, its red tower, and the cat.

'You've lodged a written request? No?' said the captain in amazement. Clearly this topped it all! How could I have set out, alone, in search of some houses, relying on the memories of unknown people with a tendency to be forgetful!

'Have you any idea how quickly these people forget? They don't even know what they ate yesterday, let alone your houses from… how many years back did you say?'

The man gave a disappointed whistle, then held out a sheet of paper that had been in his pocket for a long time. 'Very well, look, write here on the carriage window and I'll deal with it!'

'I always have something to write with on me,' I boasted, searching through my pockets for my penholder and inkpot.

It just took a minute to set down word for word everything dictated to me by the man, who already seemed like an uncle to me. It was a short text in which I requested that somebody tell me where my houses were.

'To whom do I address it?' I asked, respectfully.

'To Captain Mârcă! Write this: "To His Excellency Captain Mârcă under the bridge"!'

'Do you know the captain?'

'I am the very same!' he announced joyfully.

The man had something grandiose about him. Clearly he liked being Captain Mârcă. He took the paper, and my careful handwriting was still visible as he went down under the bridge, where only now did I notice there was a sort of hut. Before disappearing into the hovel, the captain scrunched the paper into a ball and threw it into the middle of the river.

So this was Captain Mârcă under the bridge. Whoever had a wish wrote it on a piece of paper. That was the way it went. The waters of the Dâmbovița had probably swallowed up so many letters that they had turned blue from the ink. It was only now that I understood what the cook's wife had meant! My first night in Bucharest floated out of the depths of my mind, and with it, memories of the bottle with the red stopper, which I had completely forgotten about.

## On the Trail of Poison

The grocer's shop was empty apart from one shopman, who was all milk and honey. The bottle with its nose-shaped stopper was nowhere to be seen. To be sure he wasn't lying, I blew in his face a drop of *vericola*, made from cricket's legs.

'You must remember if you sold it!'

'Just so, young lady, but I don't remember!'

'But you remember the bottle?'

'Certainly! It was a half-pint liqueur flask, with a red stopper shaped like a nose. If I get another one, I'll let you know before anyone else!'

Of course I kept on questioning him until the man lost his patience and I had to buy something in order to keep him interested. He had probably sold it that same evening, and almost a month had passed since then. The shop had filled with Arnauts, who had bought something to drink. Probably the same soldiers who had roughed me up. Some housekeepers and other servants from the district had also come, but he couldn't say exactly who. The thought that perhaps the bottle had ended up in the hands of the soldier who had gripped me by the scruff of the neck comforted me. In any case, after such a long time, the buyer ought to be already dead.

Finding the cook's wife was easy enough. Caterina was her mistress, and all the cook's family lived in a little house at the back of the yard.

'What did you want to do with the poison?'

The woman was frightened.

'It wasn't poison!'

'Had the cook perhaps asked you for it?'

'No!' she said defensively. 'How could he ask for it? Silică doesn't even know, the poor thing! It was my business! Only I knew about it!'

'And my little uncle Zăval.'

She nodded, as if it was self-evident.

'I don't believe he had any idea what you wanted to do with it!'

'Cuviosu? Of course he knew!'

'I very much doubt it! My little uncle would never have put poison into your hands!'

The cook's wife flared up.

'Oh no? Wouldn't he? He wanted him dead too!

'Who?'

She was left speechless. She hadn't expected me to be so stupid.

'The Greek! Kostas, little mistress! Who did you think?'

'And what interest had my little uncle in doing away with the Prince?'

'Who didn't want rid of him? He's wicked, young lady, as vicious as a dog! He's skinned everybody... as you should know! There's no one who doesn't wish him dead!

'And what about you? Has he skinned you? You don't even pay taxes!'

'In my case it's something else: if the Greek dies, Silică comes home! No more wasting his time at the Palace.'

It had seemed to me that Silică was proud of his work. I doubted that he would return to his family again, even if Kostas died.

'And how did you know that the bottle would get to the Prince?'

'How could it not get to him! That Greek is particularly partial to raspberry liqueur. No one at the Palace would dare to keep it from him!'

The dish-washer who had appropriated the bottle hadn't looked at all afraid.

'For that very reason,' the woman continued, 'Cuviosu Zăval gave Silică a recipe book too!'

My little uncle had only two: a red one, for the manoeuvring of Sator, and a green one that I didn't even want to think about.

'What recipe book?'

'A green one, with a cat on it.'

'The *Book of Perilous Dishes*?'

All the woman knew was that the cook had received a book. As he was such a skilled cook, I took comfort in the hope that he would perhaps not open it very often.

'And what about my little uncle? Who killed him?'

The woman swore she didn't know and that she hadn't even seen anyone.

'Apart from Father Ogaru, maybe, who was passing that way, as he often does in the evening... otherwise, nobody.'

The little woman had large innocent eyes.


Laboratorium

My uncle Zăval now appeared to me in a different light. Perhaps he had actually hired some killers, Serbs or other Arnauts, who, instead of killing Kostas had done away with him. All the same, the memory of the cloak that had gone past me made me doubt that.

As I reached the Church In-One-Day I quickened my pace, so as not to bump into Father Ogaru again, and as soon as the door of the house closed behind me I hurried down the stairs that led to the cellar. The door was padlocked, but, as I had expected, the key was on the lintel. Fumbling my way, I found the candle that had been placed nearby and then I lit the lamp. The cellar extended under the whole house and was vaulted in stone. At its entrance there were shelves of foodstuffs, oak buckets, and barrels. I didn't tarry. As in our cellar, the important things were in the last room. I pushed the wall and through the crack that opened I was hit by a well-known perfume. That was where my little uncle's sanctuary was, all his goods of great value. The Laboratorium. On the table, the tripod was still standing where he had burned something: going by the smell, it was a drop of phosphorus.

A travelling rug lay half fallen from the sofa, a sign that he had sometimes slept down there. I opened the stove, any contents of which had long been burned. Finally, there was a cupboard in the wall, with its key in the lock, and from it something was hanging, a small object. I held it up to my eyes and was struck by a poignant stab of grief, which I can still feel today, for it was a little cat made of mohair, left there specially for me. He knew I would reach this spot. My uncle's face flitted through my mind, alive and dead, especially dead, and with his eyebrows tattooed. A bitter regret darkened my eyes. *Conscientiae labes.* In the cupboard the first thing my eyes fell on was a box of money, Greek *lefta* and thalers, but also Wallachian *paras*, and on top of them, on a piece of brown paper, my little uncle had written: '*Church In-One-Day— for the dedication day.*' So he really had intended to give that sum, which had seemed enormous to me! Father Ogaru knew Cuviosu Zăval well! I looked at the handwriting with its rounded letters, exactly like Maxima's, exactly like mine. It was he who had first put the pen in my hand. It was he who had taught me to make *M*'s with arches and whirls of smoke. It was from him that I knew to round the letters, to gently turn back the *r*. My first recipe scribed with flourishes was a *pecunia* for the killers of Satorines. The list of ingredients alone occupied three pages. But it turned out to be a masterpiece, with floral borders and two drawings made by Iulian. It was only two years later that I wrote the *Book of Perilous Dishes*, which I knew by heart, for it was my ABC, containing dishes and elixirs that I had taken from other books, but especially from Maxima and my little uncle, all recipes that had been tried by them or by their parents, but never prepared by me. For who needs perilous dishes? They are just the final weapon, when there is nothing else left to be done. How many precautions Maxima had taken so that not one of the recipes might fall into some-one else's hands! And yet the *Book of Perilous Dishes* had ended up in the possession of an ordinary cook. Any dish from that book would spread suffering all around, and if a person were to feed only on those recipes, they could turn into a monster. I now knew that I had not been mistaken about the gut salad! The cook was becoming initiated in the arts of occult cuisine!

For more than an hour I rummaged through papers, most of them writings connected to Sator and to various experiences which only my uncle could understand. In the desk drawer there was a map on which he had written two words, rather hurriedly, so that it was not very clear what he had meant: *Nomen nule* or perhaps *nuble*. It was the plan of a city. It would not have caught my attention if it hadn't been in a little box with some valuable objects, among them his passport, a residence permit for Vienna, the names of banks, and a letter, Maxima's last letter, sent two days before she died.

At this point, I was suddenly overcome by all the difficult experiences I had come through, reminding me once more that I had been left an orphan and that I would never again see either Maxima or my little uncle Zăval.

My dear brother,

I have kept postponing writing to you and I still do not know where to begin. Incredible as it may seem, it is possible that I shall be accused. Not for Neţu Birt's revolt, as you might think, but for a complete fabrication. *Ridiculum!* I do not know if you still remember our neighbour Laurian Burcu Podaru. The poor thing! A boy whose heartbeat is audible. Someone has put pressure on him and made him sign a letter full of nonsense. Of all the evils of this world, none is more profound than what comes out of the unhappy mind of a fearful person. Any person suffers if they are cast aside, but greatest of all is the suffering of one who is so terrified that, given the chance they will create havoc. The more frightened someone is, the more embittered they become. Defeats are painful, but a person who is beaten licks their wounds and moves on. Not so when they are terrified by a blow that has taken place only in their own mind. For such a one, grievances are stacked one on top of the other, until they themselves become a pile of miseries. *Di averruncent!* In short, this Burcu swears that I have... bewitched him. Please do not laugh. I do not think anyone will pay attention to him. What worries me, however, is that I cannot contact Sator. He has disappeared. I would be glad of a sign from you. Perhaps we can make the dyad. *Magna diada.* I cannot see myself being picked up by the guardsmen. The governor of the city is only human. He can be bought. However if something bad happens, I shall send a rider to tell you, and I shall put Pâtca in the *braşoveancă.* Take care of her!

So I had been right after all: Burchioiu had sent her to her death. All the regret I'd been holding on to disappeared. I had no reason to be sorry. The scoundrel had deserved that drop of wolfsbane. My only regret was that I had not waited there to see him breathe his last.

## Trying Out My Teeth

During the next few days, word spread that one of the men at the *Agie* had disappeared. No one had seen him since the very day of my release. It was the same old codger who had guarded me, and my heart told me that this was Sator's work. So I had managed to do something after all. I couldn't remember what I had been thinking of, but the warder was now far away for sure. Perhaps I had sent him to some island or to the snows of the North. This occurrence made me hasten to find my houses and, above all, the list of the other Satorines.

The city was almost in a state of rebellion. The Greeks sang in their taverns, and the Prince's men lifted just about anything they could from the shops, from merchandise to furniture, but they first turned everything upside down in search of money. And at the head of the tax collectors was Cirtă Vianu, the right-hand man of Ismail Bina.

If Zăval had been out to get Kostas, perhaps Kostas had not been idle either, and if he had sent assassins after Zăval, for sure they would have been Ismail Bina's men.

One morning, Caterina took me through the market to buy me new clothes, and especially to get me new boots. I had begun to like her, but not so much that I would tell her so. She was never condescending, even though she was far above anyone else. For that very reason I wanted her to see that I wasn't just a downtrodden numbskull, but every time I tried I ended up embarrassing myself horribly.

Caterina left me for a few minutes in her carriage and I found myself face to face with that brigand Cirtă. Although he recognized me, he wanted to continue on his way as if he had never seen me before.

'Where are my boots, my dear sir?' I asked him haughtily.

I looked at him through the window of the carriage, sure of myself. Cirtă blushed like an angry turkey, and his snaky hand seemed dead. It was on this occasion that I realized that he wore a glove that seemed to be made of fine leather, while the tongues, which had so horrified me, were in fact little strips of silk and wire. He recovered quickly, however, and started joking about how I had nothing to put on my feet.

'What's the matter, young lady? Have you been left barefoot? Did I promise you something? That's life, lady. You shouldn't take the word of every ragamuffin you meet!'

But I wasn't lost for words. As Father Ogaru said, in those days 'impertinent' was too soft a word for me. I started accusing him of my little uncle's death, not listening to what he said. I called him all the names under the sun, and when I had no more to say, I showed him my teeth.

Cirtă was not like other people. Instead of stammering or mixing his words, he began to talk in Serbian, leaving me gaping. From his self-confidence and the way his eyes glazed over, it was clear that he didn't notice anything, probably thinking that he had bamboozled me. His companion, the one with the spectacles, laughed like an idiot. Cirtă had come up close to me, still mumbling words that seemed to me like tufts of pigweed, when, for no reason that I could see, he stopped in embarrassment, and then made a bow, which at first I attributed to my power, though it didn't take long for me to realize that I had been mistaken. Caterina had appeared, with that smile of hers that put everyone in their place. She didn't look at him, or even acknowledge his obeisance, but for all that, Cirtă remained bent double until she was in the carriage.

Although I had seen plainly the reason for his respect, this incident gave me confidence in the power of my teeth. At the first opportunity I reduced the *plerophorizer* to stammering and I didn't stop until his secretary had written in black and white that I knew nothing about my little uncle's death. A few days later, however, my trial was moved to the Metropolitan's Palace, so that everyone could find out what had happened. But here there was always something more important than Zăval's death, so I wasted many mornings waiting in the courtyard for my turn to come. Caterina always came with me, which made many backs bow when we appeared.

'Have you noticed what happens when I show my teeth?'

Caterina knew how to listen.

'You think it's your teeth that make them stammer?'

'Of course! Look, say something and you'll see.'

She began to tell me about the Metropolitan, and then I showed her my teeth. Her words were left floating in the air, and in her eyes I could read a joy that I had never before seen in anyone. She alone believed me.

'I believe you!' she said. 'Indeed your teeth are…'

'Squint!'

She made me explain. To this day I don't know what she really thought.

'Very well! That's what you should do! Show your teeth, but on no account grin! Do you hear? Just smile and no more!'

## The Talk of the City

Through the city, rumours had been intensifying about Cat o' Friday. Now that Kostas had added new taxes, some believed that she was a relative of his. Others bought from the baker, for a thaler, a potion that was said to protect you from all spells. These little bottles ended up in the Greceanu house too, and when I tasted one of them I realized that the baker was not a complete charlatan. There was a flavour of locusts and basil, which together help a person to maintain a state of wellbeing.

Of all the foolish tales that were in circulation, two were more intense, and even today you can find people who still remember them. The first was about a murder that had chilled the city. A woman from high society had been stabbed at the dead of night—for the most memorable murders are with the knife or the sword.

Even though the harshest laws are for poisoners, nobody keeps a count of those who die from poisoning. But if someone is stabbed and left to die in a pool of blood, not only does the whole city find out, but it veritably hums with gossip. This woman had been found in her doorway, with a dagger thrust right to her heart. The woman was still alive, and from her mouth, that of a soul at the point of death, the few passers-by, whoever they were, had heard only my name. I need hardly say that I had no connection with all this! All the same, from then on I began to wonder how the dying woman or her killer had known my name. For Cat o' Friday is not the sort of name everyone is familiar with. In fact there had been no one of that name, until I came along. Maxima had chosen it for me because I was born on a Friday. And our lineage had been protected for hundreds of years solely by cats. That was why we had one on the house too, the work of an Italian, whom Maxima's father had paid in Austrian gold. I don't remember much about it now, but I knew it was sculpted in marble. The cat on the tower. The cat that did good. Until then there had been no one to take the name, for the cat, by tradition, is connected to the day of Venus, and I alone of all our lineage was born on a Friday, and on top of that, at the hour of noon, which is also that of sleep and of cats.

Consequently I could not but wonder who knew of this name. It was certain that there were other Satorines in the city, perhaps relatives of ours.

The other event concerned Perticari, a dandy of a boyar who had various duties at the Princely Palace, including having charge of the bakeries, as *pitar*. He was the first to mention Cat o' Friday, claiming that she had appeared to him in a dream. The image of the hideous creature at Olari had come into his mind. I had to find Perticari without delay.

# CHAPTER IV

# THE BOOK OF
# PERILOUS DISHES

### Ova Mora

While I was looking for the house of the *pitar* Perticari, the street was taken over by minstrels singing the latest news of the city. And one of the hottest items was, of course, what Kostas had had for lunch. That day the whole city was humming with the news that in the market the cook had bought a beluga full of roe. Without waiting till the end to hear of all the dishes that were going to be prepared, I gave up my search for the *pitar* and headed home.

The cook had leafed through the *Book of Perilous Dishes* and had chosen *ova mora*, one of the most perilous of all. He didn't know its effects. He was an idiot. But the choice proved the level of his arrogance. Nothing disgusts me more in this world than imbeciles who choose to do things that are not only well above their level but are generally considered works of genius. The cook seemed to me to be such a vain creature. *Perturnicula!* A little bird full of big dreams.

This recipe calls for meticulousness and love. After the roe has been cleaned, it is kept in salt for a few hours. Meanwhile chilli peppers are roasted on the hob—fleshy ones, the kind that can be peeled of their skin. Drained and cut into strips, they are distributed in little heaps. They become the bed, onto which are laid little slices of sour grapes or other bitter fruits, cut no thicker than a fingernail. Only then is the butter poured over, almost molten, and modelled into a nest in which, at last, the caviar is placed. The whole little lump is wrapped in young hop leaves. Finally, when the tray is full, it is splashed all over with sweetened wine or the juice of ungrafted apricots, in which have lain three herbs, the very names of which it is better not to utter.

Swallowing a walnut-sized portion can give you self-confidence, but, if the quantity is greater, the person goes mad, whence the name of the dish: *ova mora—mad eggs.*

Whoever feeds on them loses any sense of measure and can no longer judge rightly. Cases are known in which a father has killed his children, and teachers have beaten their disciples to sausage-meat. A monk who lived in complete solitude, at Cozia monastery, came across the recipe in an old parchment book. And because he liked caviar and even more the combination of sweet and sour, he ate his fill of *ova mora*. There are some who have had enough after just two bites, while many others are not satisfied until they have swallowed a bucketful. The monk ate until he went mad. Two days later he left the monastery and got mixed up with a widow who lived very comfortably on her estate, which was worked by 200 pairs of hands. Here the *ova mora*-eating monk took a sudden interest in some children born into slavery. His plan was 'to make human beings of them', by which he meant servants touched by perfection. And the method he chose was the stick. Every morning he gathered them together behind the stables and began their education, hitting them with a cudgel, forcing them to inhale the stinging smoke of burning peppers, banging their heads against the walls, with the result that before long they began to die. And the fewer of them that were left, the greater grew the pedagogue's ambitions. His last surviving pupil made a break for it and ran off to Brăila. There he converted to Islam and soon returned to Wallachia as one of Ismail Bina's soldiers. During the day he was at the Turk's beck and call, but at night he prowled the streets in search of monks, an occupation he considered to be his one true duty. Acting on instinct, he disembowelled them and burned their entrails.

As for the mad monk, left without pupils, he passed away one day, taking with him to the next world the pain of an unfulfilled soul. His case is recorded in history, where nothing is said of the dish that took away his mind, but I found the recipe in the margin of a testament written in his own hand.

How my little uncle Zăval could have given the book to the cook I do not know, but it was very clear to me that, whatever the cost, I must get it back from him.

## My Houses

While all through the city the talk was of what a master the Palace cook was, I was looking for my houses, which seemed to have sunk into the earth. Not even Caterina could remember where they were.

'At the time when Maxima Tutilina lived in Bucharest, I was a child,' she confessed, spreading about herself an air of times long gone, like the scent of perfumes found in an old chest. Behind her eyes, which although they were fixed on me did not see me, there had grown a house from which protruded a red tower.

'And on this pinnacle a milk-white cat stretched out its paws.'

Her memories immediately became mine, recalling to my mind our house with its little tower, covered with clay tiles, which we painted twice a year, at Christmas and at Easter. It was into this tower that Maxima called her crows—I do not know whether I remember this or whether she told me of it, for my memories are misted over and strengthened here and there by her evocations. She had a rare gift for making you see what she wanted.

There were many days in which Caterina and I looked for the street and each time that Dubois came with us, my search became more of an amorous walk. Sometimes he brought along Fleury, the consul, a tiny man who would purse his lips at intervals, making a pouch of his mouth. Fleury had a very superior attitude. One time I heard him saying that in Bucharest there were no principles, just petty political deals.

Dubois, on the other hand, had taken part in a revolution in the Antilles, in Saint-Domingue, and he missed no opportunity to expound upon this theme. He was a revolutionary, firmly against trafficking in people. Every time we passed the slave market he became enraged, and one time he even bought a Gypsy so as to free him, which did no one any good, since by the evening others had taken possession of him.

But this happened later. On the day I am speaking of we were searching for Murta Street.

Whichever way we went, either more streets opened up or we emerged back in Lipscani Square. It's true, this didn't much matter to Caterina, who had eyes only for the Frenchman. Around lunchtime we came upon a cul-de-sac next to French Street. The whole length of it there was no one to be seen but an old vinegar-maker, and some way along there were steps down to what had once been a cellar, long since filled in. Beside the steps, some used-clothes traders had put down their wares. Dubois was amused that one of the men had put on a white dress, while the others were singing a wedding song to him:

> Green leaf, lily of the valley,
> Lado, Lado, little sister!

It's strange how I remember this: Dubois singing, trying to memorize the verses, while his hand touched that of Caterina, placed ostentatiously on the velvet of an old sofa.

'What is "Lado"?' he asked.

'A sort of ghost!' she said, although she hadn't the faintest idea what it meant, and indeed I don't believe anyone knows.

They were sitting in front of me, he was leaning slightly over her to see the traders. Tears were caught in my eyelashes, but I kept control of myself. In a way I was jealous, but I also found their meetings touching. They were in love and few things mattered any more, Murta Street not being among them.

## Dubois's Bad Luck

I never called him Henri, as Caterina did, but precisely what everyone called him: Dubois. He was used to stating his full name, Henri Dubois de Saint-Maurice, but out of all that the only part that was clearly understood was 'Dubois', perhaps because he always paused after it. In any case, after you had heard him saying all his three names, the only one that you were left with was *Dubois*. He had been born in the Antilles, and he had lived some time there, I would say, for he was approaching thirty, although in those days we didn't say that a man was this or that number of *years old*. For me, there were only three ages. When I saw someone, I immediately lumped them into one of these categories: either they were my age, or they were over twenty. And then there were the old people, who were just old—they didn't count. As I was saying, Dubois was still young, but the wild days of his youth had been spent in Saint-Domingue, of which he never tired of speaking. He'd had a newspaper, his own property, just as some have an estate or a factory. *Rigas's Paper*, or such other rags as fluttered around here were nothing to his newspaper. He had no need of minstrels. All the occurrences that mattered were written about and sometimes illustrated in *Le Moniteur*, as it was called. He had brought a few copies with him; they left some people astounded and awakened in me the dream of somehow becoming a newspaper writer.

After the revolution had broken out in Saint-Domingue, Dubois had returned to Paris. And it was from here that his misfortunes had begun. One day he was dozing in a café, listening from time to time to a certain Gaston, who was giving a fiery speech in a little square a short distance away.

'We are all equal,' the speaker was saying. 'There is nothing that can make one man better than another. The world of tomorrow belongs to the shoemakers, to the bakers! It is mine!'

The words were music to Dubois's ears, for he was a Bonapartist and believed in a future of justice.

Shortly after, the carriage of the marquis de Lagrange stopped in the square, and from its gilt-emblazoned door emerged first his dogs, two Labradors, from which the marquis was inseparable. It all happened very fast: the dogs jumped on Gaston, who continued speaking, while Dubois, suddenly alert, left the café and shouted at Lagrange to call back his dogs. This the marquis had no intention of doing, as right then he was advancing with small, elegant steps, oblivious to the fact that his two dogs were making a meal of the orator Gaston. Dubois whistled at the dogs, and then, in a panic, took out his pistol, intending to fire a warning shot. However, just at that ill-fated moment, a carriage went past him at high speed, and sticking out from its window was a statue of the Virgin, which struck hard against the elbow of the well-meaning Dubois. The pistol changed its target, and the marquis fell in a heap.

Horrified, Dubois leveraged all his family connections, and that very evening he was already on the road to Bucharest, with a letter of appointment as chancellor to Consul Fleury in his waistcoat pocket.

But all this I found out much later, by which time the story had reached even the lips of the traders in Lipscani Square.

### The Chest

That was also my last attempt to find Murta Street. Caterina decided to pay someone to look for the houses.

Meanwhile, *ova mora* began to take effect. Kostas got it into his head that his subjects were getting above themselves. There was not a citizen of Bucharest, he said, no matter how wretched, who did not have at least two slaves. Not to mention the boyars, with their hundreds of Gypsies! He who wished to be a master must pay! For every slave let him give the treasury twenty *paras*! Cirtă's gang prowled the city. There wasn't a front gate where you couldn't see someone who had been terrified or beaten up. And one day they entered Zăval's shop, which in any case had no master.

When I got there, my little uncle's house was a scene of devastation. The shop had been emptied, and the soldiers had gone down into the cellar. Out in the street, Captain Mârcă was calling on everyone to complain, urging them with his authoritative voice to set down all their grievances on paper, and some were actually giving him letters, as I had done.

I rushed down the stairs, yelling at the top of my voice. Some hefty louts were already rolling the great barrel of cheese, while others had just got their hands on the cask of wine. They hadn't discovered the entry to the Laboratorium, but they were going along the wall that needed no more than a decisive blow with an elbow. Caterina was angry, but had not lost her composure in the least:

'Who gave you permission to rob people? Show me your order or whatever paper you have!'

Cirtă Vianu emerged from the shadows, startling me. On his cheek he had a fresh gash, going from one eye almost down to his mouth. Caterina too was affected, even though she didn't let it show.

'It's an order from the palace, noble lady,' he replied full of respect, making a sign to his servants to show their papers, which the Greceancă pretended to read.

From the indulgence with which she treated Cirtă, it was clear that they knew one another.

Kostas had asked for a list of goods, which he wanted within an hour, and had persuaded even Bina to send him men. It was all in the name of the Kapudan Pasha, who was hemmed in by

Pazvantoğlu's forces. But I knew that it was the mad eggs that were to blame. It was these that had turned him into a tyrant, ready to put into practice the most stupid dreams. The proof was in the fact that he had employed a secretary to write down all those pleasures for which people ought to pay taxes. The secretary wrote with all his might, while an usher read what he wrote, pouring it into the ear of another servant, and from there it all went further on, to the criers with their speaking trumpets and to the balconies, so that the whole population learned that heavy taxes were to be paid for smoke drawn from the narghileh, for the dizziness brought on by wine, for the joys of the stomach, and above all for the delights of the soul in love. Anyone who wanted new clothes had to pay a small tax, nothing much, just enough to let it be known that you were pleased with them, a little tip, so that Kostas might share in the pleasure experienced by the wearer of new clothes. For what kind of joy would it be if the Prince himself didn't know about it? When you're happy, you give away money left and right, and all the more so to your master, who also deserves, poor thing, a little sweetener, just enough for him to know about your happiness and to take pleasure in it! And Cirtă Vianu was one of those who put their shoulder to this great enterprise of the former dragoman, who might not have been such a bad character after all, if he hadn't stuffed himself with *ova mora*!

Caterina's connection to Cirtă was further confirmed for me later. Towards the evening, Cirtă came to the back door with a trunk. They talked in whispers, like close acquaintances. It was a Nuremberg chest, of blued iron, the kind that the Devil himself couldn't get into. If you manage to open the lid, you come up against another lock and a box containing a key. This key has little moveable wings, and if you don't know how to position them correctly, then you may as well just sit staring at it for the rest of your life.

From the window, I could see Cirtă's trousers and the hands that were pushing the iron trunk inside. If he came out at the front, I could catch him as he left.

Out of instinct more than anything, I dashed down the stairs and for a while I waited to see where he would go. He had come in a carriage, beside which the coachman stood smoking. Cîrtă began to shout something in jest. It was only after three or four words that I realized he was speaking in Serbian. The discovery came as a harsh blow to me. Perhaps he was a Serb, and my teeth hadn't forced him to do anything. And if he was a Serb, that meant that Perticari was right: A Serb had killed my little uncle! The Serb Cîrtă Vianu. Perhaps the iron chest contained what he had stolen from Zăval's house, something of value. Caterina and Cîrtă knew all too well what had happened to my little uncle; surely they must have plans involving me too. This must be the reason for her interest in me. And I also suspected her of another unworthy deed.

## A Terrible Death

That evening another piece of news came that really shook me. The missing warder, whom I was convinced I had sent to the ends of the earth, had been found. For two days he had been sleeping in the city's rubbish pit, blind drunk.

My faith in the Satorines was beginning to totter, and with it my plans for my life. What could I do in a world in which not even Sator existed?

After supper I started questioning Caterina:

'What's in the chest that Cîrtă brought?'

She wasn't pleased, and it showed in her face that she had no intention of giving me an answer.

'What do you think?'

I didn't know if I should tell her what was going through my head, especially thinking of what we used to keep in such chests, or what I thought we did.

'Probably dresses,' I tried half-heartedly.

The Greceancă laughed as if only an idiot could think of such trivialities. She felt insulted.

'A dead man's head?'

She liked that answer.

Caterina had a large house, which I imagined must be full of chests. And it wasn't just me who thought this, all the servants talked about her riches. If she had put her mind to it, she could have bought the whole city. It was said that the man she had been married to for just one night was a slippery character who was up to his neck in all the dirty business that could enter a man's head. His father had sold Gypsies and had amassed money by supplying pleasures of the flesh, and with the money he inherited, the son of the late slave dealer had risen to be a great boyar, buying the rank of *vornic*. No one knew where he had lived. Just that one day in May, when all Bucharest was lounging in kiosks and on verandas, a convoy of twenty carriages had entered the city, guarded on either side by armed soldiers, who were neither wretched Arnauts nor the sort of young wastrels that are usually seen at the doors of boyar houses here, but each and every one of them a blond giant with eyes of fire.

Lipscani Square, as usual, was packed, and the carriages all came to an abrupt stop. Beside the locust tree the stranger's horses snorted. It was only then that the people of Bucharest had a chance to see him face to face. Before the stunned eyes of the crowd, his carriage began to unfold, exactly the way a flower unfolds, and the velvet on which its owner reclined rose up. And it was not just some ordinary sofa, but a sort of outstretched palm in which Caterina's future husband looked like a German dressed in silks and combed by a thousand hands. And this extraordinary man, who rode in carriages the like of which had never before been seen, met his death in his marriage bed. The servants said he was stung by a wasp. In the middle of the night, the whole house was awakened by the bride's screams, and the lucky ones among them actually saw him: the handsome man who had danced at the wedding, astounding the guests with his pirouettes, had become a sort of monster. His face had swollen up like the bladder of a bagpipe, and his body had grown so large that they had to break the door frame in order to take him to the cemetery.

With this story in my mind, I could never look at Caterina without seeing the corpse of her husband, whom, in my suspicious imaginings at the time, I saw her poisoning. Perhaps Cuviosu Zăval himself had prepared a mixture for her. But what poison could cause a man to swell up like that? Perhaps the venom of fear, of which I had read somewhere that it spread such horror that there was not the slightest part of a man that did not try to escape in some way. His guts would seek safety by coming out of his mouth. *Ars horroris!* Life had taught me that all the ills of the flesh come from food. Puffy faces have stuffed themselves with a lot of meat; slimy skin comes from too much bread; and when you see a really rough and ruddy cheek, you can tell that person indulges in wine every day. There are spices that make your nose grow big and potions that wipe away your shine. In a person's eyes you can always see the food they have filled themselves with. The pleasures of the gut rise like weeds to the surface.

But back then, I didn't exclude poison either. Looking into Caterina's eyes, which penetrated right into your brain, I could see the gigantic corpse of her late husband.

'What would you put in such a good hiding place?' she asked, bringing me back to the locked chest.

I thought, of course, about what Cuviosu Zăval might have put in it: elixirs, books, and artefacts whose value only he knew. And if it had been my chest, the only thing of value would have been the *Book of Perilous Dishes*. The thought of it, and of how it lay in strange and foolish hands, took away any desire to continue chatting. Other thoughts raced through my brain, making me forget the iron trunk in the shadows.

## The Ghost

Over the next few days, peace descended over the city. Kostas was exhausted. The carriers seemed thinner on the ground, and

Bina's men were no longer to be seen on the streets. Even the Greeks were less insistent on revolution.

During the day, I rummaged around Zăval's house, and the evenings I spent at Caterina's, where Dubois too was quite a frequent presence.

In the morning that I am now speaking of, I met him in the street, beside the Church In-One-Day. It was the first time that I talked at greater length with him alone. He dismounted, for that man only ever went about on horseback, as if he hadn't heard of carriages. And as soon as he touched the ground he became a sort of quicksilver that was eager by whatever means to get into my blood. As I looked at his mane of hair, beaten by the wind, I was overwhelmed by all the things that were troubling me. Such a great urge to talk came over me that I could even have revealed my name—despite the fact that Maxima had told me so many times that the point of a meeting with someone is to make *them* speak. This is the purpose of life: to listen. I knew that very well, yet in spite of that, I began to talk about the *Book of Perilous Dishes*, about the death of my little uncle, about Bina. I spoke in Romanian. He gave signs of approval, and from time to time threw in a word, as if he were following me. Most likely he hadn't understood a word of all my ramblings, but that's the French for you, nodding and smiling, pretending to be all eyes and ears. At a certain point he took my hand and said something very long. I understood that he was taking his leave of me, and I took mine of him too straight away, but it was only when I got into the house that I was able to breathe. What a state I was in!

And against the background of emotion and insecurity, after I had poured everything out willy-nilly, Sator found me again. I stood pinned to the ground by the door through which I had just come in, not daring to move. Sator was like rain soaking into my very bones with no intention of stopping. I had to pull myself together in the end and try to put him to some use. Before me stood the table at the feet of which I had found my little uncle dead. Perhaps something of the memory of his spirit still remained. If I could think only about the table, perhaps it would be easier. To move the table closer to me, to make Sator push it a little. For a short time I thought only of the joys that this table was going to give me if it would just shift a little. Sator was swaying to the rhythm of my breathing. Like a tomcat. There were just the two of us, in the house of death, where he had been so many times. If he had memories, they would be connected to certain cupboards, to the rooms he had passed through. I was hot, but I didn't move. If he sensed that I was afraid, I was as good as dead. For a moment the crystal by which Sator could be stopped flashed through my mind. I don't know how long I stood like that, but once I had emptied my mind of any thoughts, he was no longer there. He had moved further on, imperceptibly.

I was like a person through whom the wind has blown without leaving any trace. At first I kept guard at the door, for fear of disturbing him, then I went from room to room, expecting to come upon him again. In the shop everything was turned upside down, for Cirtă's men had ransacked the shelves. The big windows that used to be full were now empty. The light, which had a real autumnal quality, made everything seem gloomy. And as I looked out into the street, in that moment in which I had not yet properly calmed myself, my eyes fell on a face that gave me a shock. For a while I just stared, unable to accept what I was seeing.

He stood leaning on the window ledge. I couldn't see him completely, just part of his cheek, his nose, and the hat that cast a shadow over his eyes. A new hat, one that I hadn't seen before. The street was full, but no one looked in his direction. How could so many people go past without at least casting a glance at him? Then he turned towards me, in fact toward the window lit by the thin light of the sun. And now there could be no doubt. Leaning beside the door of the shop, alive and well, was none other than Burchioiu.

I had heard about ghosts that no eye can distinguish from the living person. Just the way they used to look, with nothing out of place. The red dog that Maxima used to put in the doorway had misty-looking fur and couldn't move from the spot: it was only the magic-lantern that made it look alive.

Burchioiu walked a little along the street again, and then made for the church. I could see him clearly, dressed in his travelling clothes, as I had never seen him before. So where was he going? Burchioiu had never passed through the gates of his hometown. If I had heard he was leaving for Bucharest, I could have bet that he would never get there alive. And yet it was him. As if to dispel my last doubts, he returned to the shop and, shielding his eyes with his hands, pressed his nose to the window pane. He could see the fallen shelves and the sugar left on the floor. It could only be a matter of moments before his eyes landed on me. I would have liked to have spoken the two numbers that bring darkness. But I was afraid. In the first place, because, once spoken, I didn't know how to dispel them. And also because I didn't know how many times I had to say them. As Maxima used to say, nothing in this world is trickier than numbers! You can never simply utter them! A number is like a key ready made for a lock. You speak, or just think one, and a thousand doors are already open!

And anyway there was no time. Burchioiu had seen me and had started to knock on the window pane.

## Dubois's Slave

My first impulse was to flee, despite the fact I hadn't thought where to. And because I was scared to death, I didn't stop till I was in the cellar, where I shut myself in the Laboratorium. A phantom can go anywhere. I had to find something to defend myself with. The cupboard was full of jars in which my little uncle had kept the most commonly used ingredients: crickets' legs, stag beetles' heads, birch bark, wolfsbane, phosphorous, and blue vitriol. To start with, I greased myself with a little goose fat and I swallowed some millet seeds. Then I looked for cockchafer powder, which is the best. It is kept shut in a box which it is prudent only to open when absolutely necessary, for as soon as you scatter a little powder, the room fills with a gas that can dissolve any ghost. It all takes only a minute, during which you must clear out of that space. If you breathe it in, it can kill you.

The mohair cat was swinging on the end of the key, giving me the shivers. I held it in my fingers, imagining my little uncle Zăval sewing it. Perhaps on that very sofa under which he was sure to have kept his sewing box. The cat had silk eyes and was made of good mohair, stuffed with feathers. Then my finger came against a little stone. There was something inside the cat.

It had turned so cold that my teeth were frozen, but I only dared light the spirit lamp, not the fire, for fear that the smoke would give me away. Anyone passing by would be able see it coming out of the chimney.

The room was quite large, without windows. If Burchioiu got in here, I would have nowhere to run to.

With difficulty I undid the stitching on the cat. Inside was a red stone, the size of a lentil. A ruby. The cat was stuffed with down. I had to keep it just as it was. A tear trickled down my nose, drawing others after it like a column of ants on the march. My little uncle had thought of me right to the very last! And in return I had tattooed his eyebrows and dragged him through the town in a water barrel.

It seemed to me that I had got warmer. My eyes fell on a painting that said so much about my little uncle! It was colourful. It made me dream and drove Burchioiu out of my mind. A water mill, half emerging from among a lot of red roofs. You could see part of a bridge, crossing a river in which a dog was frightening some ducks. In the background there rose a building with a hundred eyes, a sort of castle with a pointed roof. A basket of brightly coloured flowers could be seen over the parapet of the bridge.

Everything was peaceful, as if my little uncle himself dwelt in that picture.

Among the familiar things, I came across a jar of ladybirds, long dead. With great care I pulled off two wings, and then gave a thought to all the people, not too many, that I might try them out on.

I sat for a few hours in the Laboratorium, long enough for a lot of people to have got anxious. Caterina had searched for me all through the house and was convinced that someone had kidnapped me. I had to lie that I had been doing some tidying in the cellar, where she never went anyway. As for Burchioiu, he had disappeared just as he had come.

At the first opportunity I raised the subject of ghosts, and it was thus that I found out that Dubois was certain of their existence.

'When I was in the Antilles,' he told us, looking only at Caterina, 'I had a trusty slave.'

'A sort of Gypsy,' Caterina explained to me.

'Meaning?'

Caterina, who at that moment was nestled on a sofa with large cushions, beat about the bush: 'To tell the truth, I've no idea! Only that it's not quite the same as one of our Gypsies! I've heard that their slaves are jet black and feed on human flesh. That's why they keep them in chains.'

Dubois tried to find out what we were unclear about, but Caterina gestured to him to continue, while she translated into my ear only as much as she wanted to. I sat at her feet, on a cushion, while the Frenchman rambled on, walking back and forth in front of us. That man could only talk on his feet, gesticulating widely. The light that flashed from his eyes was like a shower of glittering darts.

'My slave,' Dubois continued, 'promised me with his dying breath that, no matter how hard it might be, he would find a way to give me news of the world beyond. After he died, I often thought of what he had promised, and sometimes I had the impression that he was still close by me. On the other hand, I didn't believe that a dead person could ever come back from there again.'

As Dubois spoke, from time to time he shook his hair, which reached almost to his shoulders, and Caterina listened to him with a smile that showed how attached she was to him. She was like those little puppies that some women carry in their arms, and he had the *benevolentia* of a greyhound.

'One night,' Dubois continued, 'I dreamed of Joseph, for that was his name. He was joyful and younger than I had known him. Happy. I myself had acquired something of that happiness. He told me that we would meet the next day, in the square. He didn't say when, but somewhere inside myself I knew that he had spoken of lunchtime, so that was when I went there. And I saw him.'

For a moment there was silence, and to this day I still believe there was a fluttering of wings in the room, which at the time I was convinced was the soul of Burchioiu.

'Did steam come from that... slave?' I asked, more because I wanted to break the spell that had gripped the two of them.

'Why?'

'Because sometimes ghosts give off a sort of steam,' I explained, thinking of Laco Fulvus, from our gate.

'How many ghosts have you seen?' Caterina teased me.

I would have thrown at her the curse of Calvus, which shuts your mouth for an hour, but I didn't know it by heart.

'There was no steam,' replied Dubois, who sometimes understood perfectly what I was saying to him. 'A child appeared,' he continued, 'a boy I didn't know, and told me that Joseph was well, not to worry. Because I was confused, he held out his arm towards the Cathedral. Then I saw him. It was my slave, just as I had dreamed about him, about three hundred metres away from me. I saw him the way you see someone in the middle of a crush of people, but I certainly saw him. More than that, he raised two fingers, to make a sign to me. He had drawn an eye on the wall of the Cathedral. The next moment he was already much further away, as if drawn by a magnet. All the same I could see his smile; his face was unmistakable. One moment he was there, and the next he had gone. Just like that: like a snowflake! Nothing was left.'

'And the child? The one that showed you Joseph?'

'It doesn't matter. In a few steps I reached the Cathedral, and on the wall, under that eye, his name was written in tiny letters: *Joseph*.'

Here the story came to a close, like all the stories that annoy me! All the same, his revelation left a chill in the room, and as for me, my tongue was itching:

'I met a ghost today.'

In a few words, I told them how he stood leaning against the door, without mentioning that he had seen me.

'And how do you know he was a ghost?' asked Dubois, looking not into my eyes but beyond them, into the inner darkness that teamed with billions of little blood-red worms.

'Because I know him. I mean I knew him because he died. He's a… a boy from Braşov.'

Caterina and Dubois exchanged looks from which it was very clear that they didn't believe me. Joseph's ghost had every chance of existing, while I had no right to any ghost!

'Perhaps he didn't die,' said Caterina.

That had been my fear too. But all the time I hid in the Laboratorium I had thought much and intensely. There was no way Burchioiu could be alive. I had opened his lips; I had poured the poison; and once it so much as penetrated his gums, he was as good as dead. I had let almost the whole flask trickle between his teeth. It was wolfsbane specially prepared by Maxima for the journey, and would have been enough to kill a whole pack of wolves.

# My Long Nose

Although I was afraid of meeting Burchioiu again, the next day I went back to Zăval's house. I was haunted by the thought that perhaps Burchioiu had been brought by Sator, restored to life just long enough to terrify me.

In the yard of the Church In-One-Day, I could see the figure of Ogaru moving, and something, like a warm breath of wind, told me that I had to talk to him right then and there. As I opened the gate, I recalled what the cook's wife had said: Ogaru had been in the vicinity the night my little uncle had been killed.

Along the edge of the path, thick brambles reached almost up to my nose. Ogaru had disappeared into the parish house, which was in fact more like a villa. I looked through the window and saw him throwing some wood into the stove. Inside, everything seemed shiny. Even the walls were papered with champagne-yellow silk. On the table there was a small box. I stood a little by the window, taking a look from time to time to see what else Ogaru would do. He was writing. I think he kept writing about as long as it would take to sign your name six or seven times. Then he put the paper in the box and locked it with a padlock the size of a man's hand. A maid had called him into another room.

There was no one about. Not even in the street was there anyone passing, so, without much thought, I went into the house. What could possibly happen to me? Wasn't my little uncle buried at that church? The room where Ogaru had been writing was at the entrance. I heard a crackling sound coming from the fire in the stove. I grabbed the box and walked out. But I only took a few steps. In the yard I came face to face with the priest.

The hand that held the little box trembled where I had hurriedly hidden it among the folds of my skirt, which I held with my other hand like a grand princess. Ogaru was preoccupied with something. His first words made no sense to me. Then he started to tell me what he had heard. Later I realized that this was from habit. These were exactly the sort of things he had talked about with my little uncle Zăval.

'May the Most Holy One forgive me, but this one's the biggest idiot of all!'

He was referring to Kostas, in comparison with the other Greeks who had taken their turn on the throne of the country.

'They all come from the Phanar! They're not even real Greeks! Just a bunch of oddities! Phanariots! When he doesn't like the food, he hits out at all and sundry. One cook, before this one of the Greceanu lady's, he threw to the dogs! He sits all curled up on a silken sofa and, when something doesn't suit him, he yells so you can hear it as far as the Armenian's bakery: *Skatá skatá sto thirío!* If you hear these words, you can be sure they come from that pig-head Kostas! The other day he slashed one of Ismail Bina's men, which might in the end be to the good, because that Turk lets nothing go unpunished.'

The face of Cirtă, with a fresh cut across his cheek, immediately came to my mind. If he was the one who had been slashed, well and good! As far as I was concerned, Kostas could carry on.

Not far off, a Gypsy boy laden with luggage smiled at me. He had probably seen how I was hiding the box. I smiled back, expecting him to tell on me.

The priest was now in full flood, telling me what had happened to Cirtă Vianu, whom he clearly liked just as Caterina did. Somehow they needed this Cirtă, the brigand who had kidnapped me and stolen the boots off my feet. Finally Ogaru asked me on what business I had come.

'I'd like to know if there's such a thing as ghosts.'

'Aha!' Ogaru took me seriously and looked at me with probing eyes. Evidently my words had touched something in his brain. He had surely had some such experience himself. What if Ogaru was one of those Satorines that I was looking for?

'You are referring to the ghost of Cuviosu Zăval?'

From his voice, it was clear that he was even more unsure than me. Ogaru's opinions were very mixed up. He didn't know exactly what to say to me, but nor did he want to admit openly that he too had met a ghost.

As I left, in fact just when I reached the gate, he asked me to wait a little and quickly returned with a shawl: 'Look, this belonged to my dear lady, the *preoteasă*, may God rest her good soul! Take it. Go on, take it and wear it! Stop going about in those rags, like some maidservant!

In Ogaru's eyes there could be read a profound pity, which much later moved me, but not then, for at that time I regarded any charity shown me as an insult. Who do you give things to? Beggars, vagabonds, slaves, and other unfortunates! I remember that I was furious, but I looked at myself in the mirror, admitting in my heart that Ogaru was right: I didn't look at all respectable. It was the mirror in the hall, in which my face was fresh and my hair had a life of its own, like the tail of a snake. I had a wild look, a general air of disorder, which I have since lost. Today I look at myself in the same mirror, and sometimes, even with the groove that time has dug between my eyebrows, I think I look better.

I hid the little box in the cupboard in the Laboratorium, where I had sworn that no one would reach, for I imagined that inside it were Father Ogaru's most awful secrets.

## Secret Meetings

Caterina was always out visiting, and wherever she went, Dubois was never absent. The market traders no longer mentioned only her. 'Caterina's going by with the Frenchman' became the standard formula. There was no question of thinking of the Greceancă as she had once been, but rather as the owner of some rare animal. Most people ran to see him, as his good looks were praised by women and men alike. But the great prestige went to Caterina, who had become a sort of keeper of this Frenchman who was sought by all eyes. So as not to miss the chance to see a bit of the world, I begged her to take me along too. I had begun to pay attention to how I looked, and among the things I bought in that period I remember a beaded *kavuk*, from which I was inseparable: a red felt fez, onto which I had sewn little pearls and beads, silver buttons and silk flowers. I plaited my hair at the back, and sometimes wore a veil over it, which made me look several years older than I was.

It was not long after that I found out why Caterina was gathering money. She wanted to buy the throne; the prize that everyone dreamed of. That was why she needed a trunk. The boyars gave money to keep on the right side of the future prince, and the Greceancă collected the bags. Back then, I couldn't understand why she didn't just pay the whole amount herself if she was so rich, but in time I learned that it wasn't the money as such that counted but getting others into the same intrigue. When rich people make an appeal, it's not out of meanness, but because they need to bring others onto their side and form a sort of retinue or even a party. Sometimes it's just a matter of the pleasure of smoking a cigar with someone, and feeling that the other shares the same interest.

The whole boyar class expected that Husein, the pasha who was fighting against Pazvantoğlu's men, grieving for the death of his son, whose head had passed right under my nose on my very first night in Bucharest, would lay all the blame on Kostas. It was he who should have got rid of Pazvantoğlu in the first place, instead of waiting for a great army of Turks! Most categorical on this matter was the boyar Dudescu, whose mouth I watched the same way I had watched the showmen in the square.

'The Greek,' he would say, 'will be banished in three months at the most, and we'll have a new prince, who will no longer remember your cook. I wager ten ducats that we are rid of Kostas by February! Who'll take me up on it?'

He had such slender fingers, the like of which I had never before seen on anyone, and when he felt in his money-bag for the 10 ducats, I had the impression that they were going to break. Caterina, however, was unrelenting: 'He has barely been appointed, honoured Dudescu! We would do better collecting money and sending it to the Sultan to have him replaced...'

'Who by? Another Greek equally ravenous!'

Dubois, like me, was just a spectator, content to sip with his nostrils the perfume of the Greceancă, who for every visit wore only dresses that had been kept in leaves and splashed with essences that he had never before breathed in, among which that of lime-tree flowers crushed together with peppermint seemed to me the most refined scent. The Frenchman flared his nostrils, while Caterina looked at him only out of the corner of her eye. And I, watching them from a distance, was starting to become a sort of accomplice in a story that was only now beginning.

The carriage of the Greceanu house continued to criss-cross the city, and at the end of each day another batch of money-bags went into the trunk.

## A Strange Man

Perticari too was numbered among Caterina's acolytes, which could not but please me. We reached his home in the evening, and Caterina was afraid that she would find the door shut, for the *pitar* was a spiritist, and at night he would shut himself in his house, where he spoke with the dead from all over Bucharest. We were lucky; he hadn't started yet.

Perticari was wearing a fine anteri and had lips so red that all the time I was talking with him I wondered if they were painted. To go by the elegant way in which he moved his chin, he seemed like a lover of men, which would have explained how he knew Cuviosu Zăval. More than that, when Caterina told him who I was, there was a flutter of unease in his eyes. First we spoke about the cook, but he gave no sign that he was interested. Caterina rambled on a bit about Kostas, whom she imagined turned into a bowl of jellied meat, while Perticari listened, smiling like a tomcat.

'I've been to Olari,' I began, to get somehow onto the subject of Cat o' Friday. 'I hear she appeared to you in a dream.'

The spiritist recounted his dream with the voice of a man who had told the story dozens of times.

'And where is this Cat supposed to appear from?' I asked, trying my luck a second time.

Something had touched him. He was both confused and, in a way, happy. He looked me straight in the eye, as if he wanted to say to me: this is something only we two should talk about. And later, when I was no longer expecting, he answered: 'From Chişinău.'

He wanted something from me, but I didn't know what. Perhaps my little uncle had told him who I was. In any case, that was his business. Not even to save my life was I going to acknowledge that I was Cat o' Friday.

'How did you know Cuviosu Zăval?'

'I grew up here, and when I was a child I knew the whole city.'

He was caught off guard, and I took advantage of the opportunity: 'All the same, you're much younger than him...'

The spiritist had seen his share of life; he changed the subject: 'If you want to speak with the spirit of Zăval, come on a Saturday evening...'

It seemed to me that he wanted to gain my trust.

Caterina got not a penny out of him, for, while I was getting ready to ask another question, quite unexpectedly Perticari simply vanished, leaving a puff of smoke behind him.

He had probably practised that exit many times. I had seen such tricks before, and I started to tell Caterina.

'Master Iulian used to send a light to the opposite corner of the room. He had a globe with little stars that he allowed to roll, and while the others were watching the glass, lo and behold, he would disappear without trace!'

'And nobody saw him?'

In some respects, Caterina's mind was incredibly obtuse. She couldn't understand the arts of evasion. A skilled person, let alone an *evasionis magister*, such as Iulian was, could not only become invisible but could completely vanish from a room and be gone. He had curtains made to fall just at the right time, and in the darkness of the room he would cover himself with a cloak, which hung down his back. Not to mention the strings and wires that would make any coat dance, as if a ghost were wearing it. And his cape of *mahut* was the best of all. The fine, fluffy black felt drew your eyes in, so that you didn't notice the conjurer slipping away. You couldn't see him anymore. He had made himself invisible. For black is of more than one kind, especially where textiles are concerned.

But Perticari had left me gaping. His vanishing act was far superior, especially as he had left behind him a fear that I could feel in my spine. The smoke was something new. We stayed on in the little entrance hall for a while, until we realized that our visit was over.

Caterina was not all that amazed.

'That Perticari,' she said, 'has been like this for as long as I've known him. We had the same Latin teacher, and during lessons he would make books or pages disappear. The man would be reading to us out of *De bello Gallico*, and in the middle of a sentence—puff! The book would evaporate!'

'How did he do it?'

Caterina raised her eyebrows in an expression of wonder. I stared at her lips, at the fine crease, and I was struck by joy. Despite the fact that I couldn't trust her either, I revelled in our being together, and that she was wasting her time with me.'

At the door, I bumped right into the cook, who was clearly not there for the first time.

'What a surprise, Silică! You don't come to see me, but you have time to visit grand houses!' Caterina was indignant, and the cook was lost for words. It was clear that meeting us was the last thing he could have wanted, but still he kept his nose in the air. He seemed to be looking at me in particular. The spiritist's yard was deserted, and the open gate swung in the wind.

'I've brought him some ladybirds, mistress! See here!'

The cook showed us a jar of dead ladybirds, which made Caterina screw up her face in disgust. And while she made a remark to that effect, the tiny little cook filled my pocket with ladybirds too.

'Take care, little mistress,' he warned me, 'for if you don't play with them this week, they'll lose their strength!'

'Leave the girl alone, Silică,' Caterina scolded him. 'Your head is full of nothing but nonsense! My cook,' she explained to me, 'on whom that wretched Greek has laid his paws, thinks he's a potion-maker too! If I told you what ridiculous things he used to make me drink, you wouldn't believe it!'

And after she had shut him up by saying she would buy him back soon, the cook went into the house, where Perticari had probably already summoned the spirit of some dead person, leaving me with the regret that I hadn't managed to ask him about the *Book of Perilous Dishes*, as I should have done. So often you stand gaping in moments when you would do better to ask the question that might change the whole story.

Caterina talked about the cook for a full hour, all the way home and then in the salon, until we got sleepy. The cook was, indeed, a master of cures, and after the death of her husband he had brought her every evening a sleeping draught that took away the pain from her soul.

'I can still see him, wearing a red jacket, turning up his nose to one side the way he does, and sighing as if he had taken upon himself all the suffering in the world. As soon as he had finished in the kitchen, he would move to the storerooms, where he had a little kitchen all to himself. There he would make whatever cures were wanted in the whole courtyard. He prided himself on his plant infusions. I believe he threw the odd dead beetle into them too, but even though they had a bad taste that made you clutch your stomach, folk came to his door in droves! People from the district or sometimes from the back of beyond, from round Dura's Lake, people without hope, for whom his old wives' potions were the only remedies left. Elixirs of love were in particular demand, and Silică, foolish as he looked, boasted that he had read them in books.'

Caterina talked with a delight that I had not seen before, and in her eyes of pure jet black the cook swanked about, decked out now in tight-fitting clothes, now in some ragged old jacket, but each time cocky and sure of every word he said. It was only when you listened to her that you could see just how much the cook meant to her.

'One summer,' Caterina continued, 'a little slip of a girl fell in love with him and, from the first crack of dawn she stood with her face pressed to the fence, our garden fence, to see Silică dashing about—you know his way—running around the courtyard with his great spoon in his hand, giving orders to the other Gypsies, whom he would beat till he got butter out of them! For—I don't know if you're aware of this—he doesn't cook just anything. He goes first thing in the morning to choose the chickens to be slaughtered, the vegetables for roasting or the flour from the storerooms. And that girl, who worked in the basement, took a fancy to him and she would either find her way from the cellars to the kitchens or follow him about wherever he went. She was the laughing stock of the all the servants, but Silică didn't even notice her! Then one day, someone, the cupping-glass woman I think, taught her to ask him for a cure! Not one to heal her suffering, but one that would serve her up her beloved on a plate. With his nose in the air, he didn't even look at her, but leapt to that little cauldron of his, stained green from the infusions, and before long he gave her a bottle, but, you know, pompously, as if he were endowing her with the biggest icon from the sanctuary of the Metropolitan Cathedral. Two weeks later he married that girl, some say because of the potion, others because he felt sorry for her.'

'What's her name?'

'To tell the truth, I've no idea, because everyone in my court-yard just calls her the cook's wife.'

For me, the meeting with the cook had meant something more. Those ladybirds were burning a hole in my pocket.

## Paparuga Mărgărița

Ogaru's box kept my mind busy. I imagined that he must have written something important. I don't know why, but I thought it was something about me or about my little uncle's house, on which he had set his eye. However, the box was fastened with a padlock that seemed hard to open. And there were some days in which I couldn't get to the Laboratorium. In the first place, Dubois's birthday came round. When I spoke of *gifts*, I had in mind jewellery, amulets, perfumes. That's what I expect from oth-ers. Even today. When I unwrap something, I hope to find a tiny object, something of silver, a crescent moon, a little key with some-thing written on it, some little thing to bring luck—for example a ladybird the size of a bean. My grandmother used to call it '*buburujă*', that is, 'spotted rose', but I prefer the name '*mărgărița*'. That's what I picked up somewhere, perhaps in my childhood. There was also a story that my mother, and Maxima, and my little uncle all told me by turns. The Red Emperor, famed for his wick-edness, had a daughter who learned the art of witchcraft. From an early age, she could bring rain and change the appearance of things, and even of people, and sometimes she would make herself invisible. Her name was Paparuga Mărgărița. And she had a brother on whom she usually tried out all her spells. When she wanted to turn someone into a beetle, she would start with her brother, as he was handiest. If she was learning to make teeth grow and recede, her brother was the best person to practise on. Perhaps she didn't mean any harm. Perhaps she liked playing and sincerely believed that he too was happy to please her by turning from time to time into a mouse, a rain-drenched sparrow, or a pair of slippers to be walked in. When her brother could take no more, *whoosh*, he cut off his sister's head with a single stroke of his sword. That's what happens with the victimized person: if he doesn't die, he turns into an executioner. But Mărgărița had been expecting this. So she was protected by a spell. I don't know how proficient she was, but instead of turning into a dragon or a bird of death, she took the form of a poor little beetle. We Romanians named her 'the moon chicken', because in evenings with a full moon she makes dreams of love come true. Her wings are good in all love spells, and wherever she appears, a young heart falls sick, yearning after the soul of another.

A ladybird seemed to me then, and still seems to me today, the most beautiful gift. You could buy little beetles at the goldsmiths', good for putting on a watch chain, for sewing onto a fez, or even hanging from your ears, and I secretly thought of buying such a gift for Dubois, but slipping two wings inside it. The cook's ladybirds seemed to me full of significance, and the way he had looked at me was like a challenge. '*Play*', he had said. Perhaps to test me. But even so, he had given me the itch. I knew that experiments of this kind were dangerous. The magic of the ladybird is with numbers, which even to this day scare me.

Caterina scoured the whole city to find a gift to match her feelings for Dubois.

'What shall we buy for Dubois? Tell me, Pâtca. What comes into your head?'

Looking at her with all her refined manners, I didn't dare tell her that my head was full of beetles.

'Perhaps some earrings…'

Caterina wouldn't hear of it.

'Look at the sort who wear such a thing!'

Indeed, they weren't exactly boyars, but mostly young men, some who had seen a bit of the world, whom we kept seeing in coffee houses, though no one knew what they lived on. Among our acquaintances, Perticari had small earrings, with little black stones like devil's tears.

In the end she got him an Arnaut costume. It was fashionable back then at parties to dress in various rather rare items, such as German clothes or wigs brought from Lipsca. Caterina had ordered a portrait of herself wearing an Arnaut fez. I never liked that costume, with all its braid and tassels. But they were precisely the reason why it was appreciated. The fez in particular was much sought after; it was bright red, with a great big tassel of black silk hanging from it. The jacket didn't look bad either. The tailors worked as if the very devil was at their heels because the embroidery over the chest took months to do. Not to mention the shin-guards, which had to have exactly the same design as the jacket. You couldn't buy them from different shops. When I saw a man in those red and black metal shin-guards, I would burst out laughing, because they looked like old people with cramp. All the same, Dubois was pleased and he even dressed up in his gift that evening, and they went all around Bucharest in the carriage, just the two of them, so that even today, when I think of them, the first thing that comes to mind is a tassel dangling by the window of the carriage and her laughter.

## Formaster Rosulentus

But these were secondary matters. In the reality that counted, I was trying to find a solution to open the padlock on the box and expecting to find out what else the cook had concocted. At night I dreamed of Burchioiu coming looking for me. Whatever my dream, sooner or later there would appear the prying eyes of our old neighbour.

When I got up in the morning, I would send for word of Murta Street, which I think the people Caterina was paying had given up looking for.

But most of all, I trembled with the fear that the cook would try another dish. I hoped that Bina would be true to his word and would give Caterina back her fifty ducats. I had begun to believe that my little uncle had wanted to get rid of Kostas. Everything started from him.

Caterina could not hurry Bina, and the cook seemed to know that he had to treasure every second. He went out with his retinue through the town, small and stuck up, like a paper hoopoe. His eyes were always fixed on the sky, as if he were conversing with God. No one on earth rose to the pretensions of this cook, who had acquired no small conceit of himself. And the minstrels had done their bit too—he was never missing from their songs. And there was plenty to listen to, for the cook made dishes that no one had ever heard of, and across the city aromas drifted that stirred your innards, for imitators had also appeared. Both cooks and people who had never stepped in a kitchen before were determined to make the same dishes that were made at the Palace or at least something reasonably similar. I would stick my head out of the window when the minstrels passed singing about every menu. The city was seized by cooking fever.

If I heard about doughnuts or hare with olives, it didn't worry me. I was unaffected by vegetable roasts or meats baked in a sheep's stomach. Mushroom stew was of no interest to me, and nor did I pay attention to locusts tossed in oils. And so the days passed, one by one, with steaks coated in almond powder, with rolled cabbage leaves and pies that gave off vapours perfumed with basil and walnut.

121

Until one day, when word went about that the cook had bought roses. It set people in motion too, because there was no one who hadn't put some petals aside to dry, mainly to put in vinegar, but also for other dishes. From roses many things can be made, especially sweets, jellies, and rich cakes, anointed with oil flavoured with petals, especially wild roses or grafted dog rose. But these cakes are of many kinds too.

When I heard roses mentioned, I decided that it was time to confront the cook directly, as I suspected that he had discovered the recipe for a cake that would give you laughing sickness. *Formaster rosulentus*: that's its name. Perhaps some of you have heard of it. Whoever nibbles a little bit laughs from morning to evening. But if you eat your fill of it, you're in trouble, for there is no way to get rid of laughing sickness except with poppy seeds and other cures, which the cook certainly did not know, or with a glass of *formicosus*, the recipe for which I had included in the *Book of Perilous Dishes*, but only at the end, and in Latin.

Laughing can be a useful thing. But laughing uncontrollably—that's a sickness. I wasn't worried for Kostas, but for myself. For the person afflicted with laughing sickness can destroy a world! Whatever you say to him, whatever you show him makes him laugh. Whatever you ask him, he'll answer with a guffaw fit to shake the house. He laughs with pathos at someone's sorrow, or even their death, and with every chuckle he spreads around him a thousand wicked little fairies who, left to chance, can infect anyone they encounter. They are born from the thrill of a mad fit of laughter. And we know too that they are invisible. Maxima described them as being like girls with green eyes, whence their name, for in Latin they are called *virgines caesiae*. They float in the air like dandelion seeds, and get into the lungs and even the blood of a living person. And all that they touch is soon turned into colonies of *caesiae*, which, once they have reached a sufficient number, make everything turn to dust, which the wind then scatters.

In the *Book of Perilous Dishes* I had noted many things, with the passion of my first studies. The recipe for the potion made of ants, which I told you I had written on the last page, I remember took me a day just to transcribe. In the same place I had a detailed description of tree-frog sauce (*liquamentum cum rubeta*), but also my favourite food, which was noontide honey, a bringer of calm and sometimes of sleep with pleasant dreams. Like all the others, eaten in excess, it is the food of death. *Mel meridiei*! Made of honey and milk, in which I sprinkled a powder made from hemp seeds, roasted and ground together with other things about which it is better to keep silent.

### The Meeting in the Kitchen

I wasn't thinking of killing Silică, but of making him understand. I entered the Palace with a basket, because no one notices a woman going about like that; it goes without saying that women must work in the kitchen, or else what would they be doing in the Palace? For the guards smoking in the doorway, one girl was much the same as another; all their charms lay hidden in their skirts.

The cook was giving orders with the voice of an emperor, moving about beside a heap of roses that filled the table. The *Book of Perilous Dishes* was not to be seen, which seemed to me even more serious, for it meant that he had striven to learn the recipes by heart. How could Cuviosu have let such a book get into the hands of a numbskull.

As soon as he spotted me, he recognized me and was startled, because for him I could be nothing other than a servant of Caterina's, sent to tear him away from his warm nest in the princely kitchen. So I laid into him straight away, whispering in his ear that I was the niece of Zăval, whom I had no doubt he had known very well. The cook was terrified:

'You killed Cuviosu!'

'Certainly not!'

'Everyone saw you with him in the water barrel!'

'Listen, I'm his niece. You have to believe me!'

'I hope you get sentenced to death and that I see you hanged in the market!'

The cook was both scared and full of rage, but for all that, he spoke in a whisper, probably all the more muted for fear that he might be seen in my company.

'You have to give up the *rose cake*! I know my little uncle gave you the *Book of Perilous Dishes*! But believe me, if the Phanariot eats from that cake, he'll be seized by the madness of laughter, which is catching! In a few days we'll all be dead.

There followed a moment of confusion, and then the cook's eyes spat hatred at me, in its crudest form:

'You want to take the book off me! Cuviosu told me! The night he called me to his place to give me the recipes…'

'My little uncle called you to his home? I don't think so!'

'Think what you like! But not the one by the Church In-One-Day. The other house, in Murta Street.'

I was left speechless. The cook knew where our houses were.

'And where, if you please, is that street?'

'He told me you'd ask!'

The cook grinned with satisfaction. He was almost as short as me and had a face the colour of young oak, more grey than black, with little spots.'

'Then you know you must show me where that street is…'

He agreed immediately. I didn't expect him to give me the book, and nor did I have the strength to ask him for it. All the same, I managed to utter half-heartedly: 'I'm not lying. If the Greek starts laughing, you have to give him an antidote that only I know how to make.'

He made a show of agreement, but it was clear to me that he didn't believe me. He threw his eyes towards the sky, and talking more for the Heavenly One than for me, he promised me that he would take me to Murta Street, and then he looked right in my eyes, and suddenly became another person:

'What have you done with the ladybirds? Did you try...?'

There was something in his words that seemed important and strange, as if it came out of another period in his life. What he knew about me was hard to guess and anyway he didn't give me time, for he disappeared into the steam of the kitchen, like a ghost.

## What I Did Then Has Caught Up With Me Today

In the meantime, we could all die. Somehow I had to get into the cook's larder, which couldn't be far off. The servants' quarters, as in any house, were situated next to the kitchen, close to the cellars and the larders. And the first thing that seemed to offer salvation would be a radical transformation. Among the people who could wander unimpeded through the Palace were the towel-bearers, who bustled about everywhere, distributing cloths and towels to anyone who needed to wipe their hands.

Thinking of the possibility of turning myself into a towel-bearer, I returned to my uncle's house and went down into the Laboratorium. The casket taken from Ogaru still sat on the table, with his initials encrusted on the lid. I hadn't yet found a way of opening the padlock and, as the days passed, I was becoming more and more convinced that in that little box I was going to discover terrible things. Moreover, every time I glanced at the iron box, I could feel the movement of Sator, which strengthened my satisfaction at having got my hands on it.

In the cupboard there were notebooks, papers, and a few books, and among these was one about the secrets of ciphers, which I had not bothered to look much into before. On the first page, my little uncle had written a warning that I had read somewhere before. It reminded me to beware of the *machagistia numeri*.

The traps of some numbers, I now know, are many and unimaginably complex, like the worm that digs into teeth. For all that, however, the book contained unparalleled promises. Two numbers united at the hour of evening could bring you the joys of the soul. For those with more brainpower, there were combinations and mixtures that could bring money. The simplest *praescripta* were at the beginning of the book, up to page 5, where Zăval had written 'this far', followed by two exclamation marks, as if he had wanted to stop me going further. One of them looked as if it would be good to practise on, especially as it involved ladybird wings. The cook's eyes had remained in my mind. I don't think I was expecting results, or in any case, that was not uppermost in my mind; rather I was driven by a great curiosity. But you know how it is: the nose of a curious person is more dangerous than all the weapons in the world.

That evening I went into Caterina's salon, holding in my pocket two ladybird wings, which, for fear of losing them, I gripped tightly between my thumb and my index finger. Standing with my hand stuck in my skirt, I must have looked rather stiff. Anyway, they weren't looking at me. Caterina was talking about the cook, with her eyes lit up:

'My cook is worth all Kostas's fortune!'

Dubois was more reserved: 'I believe that all people should be free...'

'You are referring to Gypsies?'

'Of course! Your cook, for example! He should be allowed to choose!'

Caterina thought for a moment, while I approached Dubois. Her voice sounded like rain on a clay-tile roof: 'To choose his master?'

'No! To choose what he wants to do! No one has the right to buy and sell people!'

To make himself understood better, he repeated it in Romanian. But Caterina did not agree. The fine cord in the corner of her mouth had formed itself into a half flower: 'I believe you're joking! Have you any idea what would happen to poor Silică if he had no master? He would be dead within a few months...'

'Nooo! He would sell doughnuts. Then he would open a tavern, and his children would be the proprietors of inns and so on.'

Caterina blew him a kiss with the tips of her fingers. For a moment, silence fell, and it seemed to me that I could hear the movement of the wings in my pocket. Then she continued, plaintively in a hoarse voice: 'And what about me? What will become of me without my cook?'

'You'll open a ham factory that will supply Silică's restaurants!'

I was quite close. All I had to do was to slip the wings into one of Dubois's pockets, while I counted up to three. Ah, that number! Three is the number of hypocrisy. It destroys the pair. It gives the illusion of perspective. In my view, it is a failure of a number, whose praises have been sung unjustly!

It was a hard test for me, because I've already told you about numbers: they're like water in the river. All the same, something drove me to try. I had back then a sort of devilish inclination, a sort of calling, I would say, for taking the craziest of chances. The prescription said that Dubois would make me a great confession. The person in whose pocket I put some wings would be unable to live any longer without speaking. His tongue would be unbound and his most terrible secret would be mine! In the book, it said that, if I respected everything, in three days at the most, the deed would be done. And to get there, all that was needed was one small step: to slip him those wings and to count to three. So many things Maxima had told me, and they had proved to be pointless! How she had terrified me with the thought that I wouldn't find Zăval's shop! And find it I had. The same with numbers: at a certain point I would have to try out my powers with them, no matter what. I would throw the wings, count, and then wait for as long as it took to pass the back of my hand across my brow. I would deepen my voice and say clearly: '*nunc denique!*' That was all. In three days, Dubois would come crawling to my feet, begging me to listen to him. I could even see him wearing out his knees.

And while Caterina made light of the supposed ham factory, my fingers were trembling and I was afraid I might lose a wing.

I approached Dubois and held my breath, carrying myself like a fly that nobody notices. I was very nervous but, in any case he was looking at Caterina, who was chirping away in his language, with bright cheerfulness.

I couldn't see his pocket. He was wearing a sort of blue tunic, made of Maltese shot silk. When he made to sit down on a sofa, I glimpsed my chance and let fly with the wings, which went right into the depths of a pocket so well concealed that you would need good eyes to see it. I did this while counting to three. And I swear, each number seemed yoked to a cart loaded with all the mischief of the world.

Relieved, I said '*nunc*,' and Dubois, who up until then had seemed totally absorbed by Caterina, the ham factory, and the abolition of slavery, turned to me and took the word out of my mouth: '*Nunc ipsum!*'

'No!' I protested, almost screaming.

Both Caterina and the Frenchman turned to look at me.

'I meant to say "*nunc denique*",' I explained.

I was shocked into silence. *Nunc denique* was for three days. But what the devil some other *nunc* would do, who could tell!

'Aha,' he said, 'not *right now*, but *in the end*. You know Latin?'

In other circumstances, the discussion would have emboldened me, but at that moment all the blood had drained from my face. I was standing, very close to him, with both hands in the pockets of my skirt. *Nunc ipsum* was for far off times. Sometimes it brought a change, but only after thirty years or more. And it made no difference in whose pockets I might have struggled to put wings or even live beetles.

I have told you that numbers are perverse. They are not for dreamers or for immature minds! Between three days and thirty years, the difference is negligible. A momentary lapse of attention, a slight pause or a word slipped in the wrong place can add hundreds of years and change your life and your direction! I may have doubts about everything in the world, but about this occurrence I no longer have doubts. And even if I had, they were dispelled when the man from the Austrian Post Office came calling. For thirty years have passed since the events I have told you about. A human life may be eaten up by the hypocrisy of a wretched number. I can only be thankful that nothing worse happened to me.

## 1829—The Present Time

Remembering that old mistake, I have come down into the Laboratorium, where things look almost exactly as they did thirty years ago. It is here that I have known my happiest moments. It is here that I have known my sorrows too. It is here that I have read the book of numbers from cover to cover and tried out dozens of elixirs, of salves. There is no place in all the house where I feel protected as I do in the laboratory in the cellar.

And because I am afraid of a disaster, today I have begun to write. Sometimes writing comes from the hope that you will find allies. At other times it is just the result of a vanity without limit. But, whether you believe me or not, writing is also an altruistic act: I am writing in order to pass on my secrets, for the mind capable of making use of them. My silken-covered notebook will be held in the hands of someone who wants to know what happened long before they were born, while their blood, that blood in which flutter the hopes of immortality, was flowing through the flesh of another. I am writing today, and I shall continue to write until the end of my journey. For in a few days I am leaving Bucharest.

But until then, let me tell you some more about that autumn. I shall start with the cook.

## 1798—Thirty Years Ago

### The Delights of Culinary Art

My worries regarding the cook knew no limits. Not only did I not like the man, but I felt duty-bound to recover the book.

Wherever you went in the city, either you came across him in person, buying whatever was newly in season, or you heard talk about him. And the things they were saying!

As I listened more and more to Caterina's servants, I found out facts that cast him in many different lights. Silică, whom you can find in the histories under his baptismal name, Vasile son of Andreica, had been born in the Greceanu house. He had never known his parents, who had died young. He had been raised by an old woman, whose sole occupation was applying cupping glasses. She slept during the day, and as soon as evening fell, the house filled with people. She had six beds, on which the Gypsies of the Greceanu household lay down to have their sore backs repaired. The old dear would run from bed to bed, throwing the glasses exactly where the muscle needed them, onto knots and cramps, getting at the root of the pain, and if she thought there was a swelling, she would lance it with a little knife and put a cupping glass over the wound. While her patients lay there, they would each talk of their troubles, which Silică's brain drank in insatiably, for there is nothing more useful in this world than the tales of others. The wise person does not listen to the misfortunes of strangers in order to avoid them, but because in a tale, especially an unhappy one, may be found the little details that give life its charm. And Silică had a nose for perfumes and eyes for the most hidden nuances. By listening to the cupping-woman's patients, he got his education and discovered his talents. While he was still a child, he attached himself to the kitchen, where other discoveries awaited him. The life of a cook was his road to happiness. For a dish is not just the nutrients that make the flesh grow, but a mixture of actions and aromas, a totality of time, teaming with life, with all the meetings, passions, and aspirations of a large number of people. And Silică discovered this truth all on his own.

When he beat a piece of steak for frying, the beat of his heart quickened too, and the sizzling of the pan made his blood tingle as if it was crawling with spiders. He was always looking into the distance—that was something that I too had observed. Even if he cast his gaze up into the heavens, he was taking part in events, happenings of another time and another history. With his eyes on the ceiling, he continued to be part of the lard that softened, with its sweetness, each morsel of meat. Especially after the frying pan reached that climactic moment when it was waiting to be thrown a slice. For him, looking at the whitened edge of the meat was like when a man sees a woman that he admires. As the boiling of the fat penetrated the fibres of the meat, so the knot in his soul grew bigger. For in any person there is a ball of bitterness and desire, sometimes just lightly tickling like a butterfly, but in many other cases utterly unbearable, like hot coals that scorch everything around them. Once he had turned the steak onto the other side, the madness began, as in a soul in love. Everything that followed after that, the salads, garnishes, and other accompaniments to the steak, was turned into the love letters, bouquets of flowers, and serenades by which men signal their longings. Only that Silică gave no thought to women. For him there was only the food into which he poured his energy, his breath, and his gaze. A lamb chop was like an evening rendezvous by the side of a river. And the more he adorned it with chilli powder, the more he bathed it in wine and other juices, the richer in action was his rendezvous. From a few tender words he passed on to kisses and caresses, till, towards the end, when the lamb chop lay red-faced and discreetly drunk on fat, the cook too was emptied of all desires, drained as after a night of love-making. There was no dish that he did not love and the memory of which he did not preserve in his heart. Mashed lentils were like an elderly governess, who became debauched as soon as he covered her with slivers of onion fried in butter. From the thrill he felt when he took quails in his hand, they might have been the breasts of a nubile maiden. He splashed them with honey and chillies, made them a nest of spinach, and took care to souse them in olive wine.

Once he had shut down the oven, he too fell, exhausted.

The aubergine moussaka took him down to its secret harem; the pork tenderloin, rubbed with garlic and singed on hot coals, simply dried up all his seed.

For him, women didn't even exist. He had not the slightest room left for them. And for this very reason, when Papuc the housekeeper told him that a girl in the wine cellars was keen on him, Silică replied that he would make her his wife.

Perhaps he wasn't arrogant, but just had a sort of absence. But even so, it still seemed to me dangerous. Besides the *Book of Perilous Dishes*, he had other sins too. He knew how to make potions that he sold all over the city, among which sleeping tea and lover drops were the most often bought.

The Gypsies in Caterina's courtyard, including the wife he had abandoned, called him the *Mistator*. The housekeeper maintained that it was what he called himself: 'When we praised him for some dish, he would puff himself up. "Am I not the *Mistator*? Of course the dish is good!" He had heard some word that he thought sounded like that.'

'But they say he makes elixirs too…'

'I've never fallen asleep after his teas,' the housekeeper complained, 'but you know how it is, little mistress. Most often it matters more what a person looks like than what they are able to do! Sometimes the cook looks as humble as a monastery dog, but at other times the way he carries himself you'd imagine he had a trunk-load of jewels and money to his name!'

I could talk to no one about my fears. Caterina was convinced that Bina would return the cook to her, as he had promised. And, looking back at things now, I believe her mind was no longer even on the cook.

## Scorpion Butter

And while the cook boasted of his dishes, and Kostas raked in money from taxes, I was struggling to open the padlock on the iron box. I knew various recipes for household use, from removing stains to grafting plums or getting rid of fruit moths, and among these was the extraordinary scorpion butter, the recipe for which everyone ought to know, for it is made of the most powerful venom. Few people know that the scorpion is also a fish, which at the time I thought lived only in the Black Sea. I have never seen one alive, only in drawings, which is not the same thing, for a drawing never shows you the most interesting parts. When I first came face to face with a hedgehog, I couldn't believe how delicate it was. All Zăval's drawings showed it looking puffed up and rather indignant, which had given me the impression it was a disagreeable animal. But when I saw its tender paws and the little snout in which all the fears of the world were gathered, immediately I softened towards it. I had imagined it a monster; I had no idea it was no bigger than a fist. For that reason I am prudent when it's a matter of a mere drawing.

In our bookcases in Șchei we had a great many books, including one on zoology, in which the scorpion fish, or *Scorpaena porcus*, looked like a dragon. It is a palm-sized fish, perhaps a little bigger, clothed in armour and feathers. It has a stony head and guards on its jaws that would give anyone a scare. When it gets angry, it's like a garden broom. Its mouth looks horrible. It can even swallow a crab. It's like the mouth of a lion. Because I have never seen it, it seems to me a monster.

The venom of the scorpion fish is sold in flasks so tiny that they sometimes cost more than their contents. Zăval had such a flask, on which he had neatly written the Latin name in that

133

orderly hand of his that made you respect him even if you didn't know him. The poison has many uses, some of which are no longer known. Out of all of these, I want to set one down here, so as not to forget it. Some alum, well ground, is combined with a tiny fragment of magnetite and two or three fibres of pumice, or 'horse stone' as they call it here. The powder is mixed in some deer fat and only at this point is a drop of venom added. This is 'scorpion butter', which is good for loosening locks and cleaning rust or other impurities from weapons, bolts, tableware, or jewellery. I carefully squeezed a little ball of the mixture into the two orifices of the lock and into the keyhole itself, and for a while I kept hammering the shackle. Any lock will give way in the end, especially when it is greased. Scorpion butter scalds the iron with the strength of the poison, so that anything can be unlocked with no more than a knitting needle.

With its padlock removed, the priest's casket looked like a worn slipper.

## The Bashful Story

As soon as I opened it, I regretted the effort. All that the iron box contained, guarded by the padlock that I had wasted so much time opening, was a few pages. But once I had read them, I decided that in fact it had been worth rescuing them from the mighty padlock, for in them the well-groomed and pretentious priest had related the story of the night in which my little uncle had died. In fact it was not the story itself that he dwelt on in the text, but rather his embarrassment at having been a witness. A sort of unease vibrated in his every fibre, and his greatest fear of all was that the reader might get a bad impression. His bashfulness could be seen in each word; from every verb the infection bubbled up. But even so, I must admit that as soon as I read it, I was convinced that he was telling the truth. I could see him approaching the window, looking into the house. The cook's wife had been right: Ogaru often walked around there, and on that particular evening, shortly before I arrived, he had been at the gate. Perhaps the silk mantle that had slipped away from me had been a priestly cassock. The night of the showmen had opened in another part of the city, distracting me from the place where I should have been. While I was gaping at the showmen, and Ogaru stood petrified at my little uncle's window, an unseen murderer had gone in the door. And when I say *unseen*, I am precisely quoting the priest's confession, in which he had heavily underlined the word three times. Immediately I thought of ghosts, and indeed of one in particular: the ghost of Burchioiu come after me seeking vengeance. A knife had been thrown by a hand from another world, flying first at the throat of Zăval's cook and then at that of her husband. Two short leaps, after which it floated before the horrified eyes of my little uncle, whom the priest constantly referred to as 'neighbour Zăval'. For a brief moment, just as long as it took Ogaru to count to five, his eyes had been fixed in horror on the knife. Perhaps the ghost, whoever it might have been, had spoken to him during that time. Five seconds. For nights on end I would dream of the terror in my little uncle's eyes. Then, s*wish*, the knife was thrust into his throat. It had happened something like that. What does a man think in five short seconds? Before dying? It has been said that no one condemned to death ever loses hope. When death can no longer be avoided, hope moves beyond. There is no dying person who will not say that life continues, even that they hope for a better one. And why should they not hope? Does Sator not come from that unseen realm of the world? Perhaps my little uncle's spirit continued to exist. If Burchioiu had turned into a ghost, I couldn't see why Cuviosu Zăval, who in any case seemed to me much more deserving, couldn't have done the same.

Ogaru had been too scared to knock on the door or to tell anyone. The terrible event in the house of 'neighbour Zăval' had drained the life from him. He was finished. He had stood petrified until I appeared. More than that, he had seen me bending over the body—and thus I found out that through the cloth in the window everything could be seen.

Besides Burchioiu, there were many others who might have killed him. I only had to think of how many people my little uncle knew and how many he had angered in the course of his life, and I could have put together a long list of enemies. But even so, no one was more guilty than me. Even if it was Burchioiu's ghost that had killed him, it was still my fault.

However, not long after, in fact the very next week, things began to take a different turn.

### The Trial

Despite there having been a witness, I couldn't bring myself to use his testimony, for I too was embarrassed. If I had mentioned the name of Ogaru, it would have been tantamount to admitting that I had stolen the iron box. The truth is not always your friend.

The Friday I was supposed to meet the cook, my trial began, and from the very first hearing it took a bad turn. The Metropolitan was an old man whom everyone nicknamed Nutty Zorzo, because he was fussy and rather irritable. All young people got on his nerves. I didn't realize this at the time, but deep down, in every beat of my heart, I believed that I wasn't trying hard enough, that I wasn't capable of convincing him of my merits in the world.

First he asked me what business I had in Bucharest. If I had lived for the last few years in Brașov, that was where I should stay till I was dead and buried. Then he gave a speech about his great puzzlement regarding my little uncle's shop. What need did I have of his house? Why wasn't I giving it to the Church In-One-Day, as would be only normal? Any healthy mind could see this. The shop would be ruined before I came out into the world. There could be no question of my handling Cuviosu's merchant business myself.

The other unfortunate thing about this old fellow was that he couldn't see well. No matter how hard I tried to show him my teeth, it was to no avail. Later I discovered that he was extremely short-sighted.

My luck turned though with the arrival of the Green Old Woman, who was brought before the Metropolitan by a whole retinue of people, for otherwise the orator would have rambled on till evening. In the middle of his arguments, which among other things praised Ogaru to the skies, an old woman appeared, lifted up above the crowd. Some citizens who seemed to have been suffering from snakebite were yelling in a mix of voices, maintaining that Cat o' Friday had been caught! You can imagine what a tremor I felt! The accused was a tall old woman, and her guilt was proven by the fact that she had a green face. The old woman wiped her face from time to time, but before long it was turning green again. In the face of all the Metropolitan's questions, she was mute. First he asked her where she came from. Then what business she had in Bucharest. Despite the fact that voices around the room were calling her Cat o' Friday, the Metropolitan asked her what her name was, repeating the question as if addressing a mad person. Finally the woman opened her mouth, and now it was the crowd who were reduced to speechlessness:

'I'm from Craiova, Father! That's why they call me Craiova!'

'Then why are these people saying that you are the witch Cat o' Friday?'

'I don't know, Father. How should I know? Maybe they just feel like it!'

Zorzo didn't know what to believe, and the accusers had nothing to say.

'Why are you green?'

'Someone cursed me, that's what I say! What other reason could there be?'

I would have liked to have taken up her defence, but instead I clammed up like a snail. Right after the case of the Green

Woman, two Arabs were brought in who claimed to be doctors. The Metropolitan began to question them too:

'What business have you in Bucharest?'

The Arabs replied with great difficulty that Bucharest did not interest them, but that they wanted to reach France, where they claimed they were expected. They spoke with an effort, but very sure of themselves, determined to let it be known that they were not crooks, as they had been accused of being by some traders, who had brought them to the Metropolitan Palace, pushing them with the spikes that are used for collecting rubbish.

'In that case why were you selling water as a medicine?'

The Metropolitan examined the whole chest of medicines and elixirs, and we all listened to the story of a girl who had drunk a potion from the Arabs and had died on the spot.

'She did not die because of us,' they broke in. 'Did Your Excellency not say that our medicines were nothing but water? Who has ever heard of someone dying from drinking water?'

For unproven murders and other accusations of the sort, there was only one punishment, which was applied to the Arabs and the old woman alike. All three were loaded onto a cart and taken to Giurgiu, whence, at the Prince's expense, they were ferried across the Danube and left to their own devices. Not only to the Metropolitan but to any Romanian, to be driven out of Wallachia seemed the most terrible punishment. Across the Danube was the beginning of hell, from which no one would ever escape again.

My legs were numb, and my stomach was knotted tight with waiting. By the time the Metropolitan remembered me, it was already noon.

A priest with a big nose, whom Caterina had paid, asked leave to take my defence:

'Let us not forget the charity that the merchant Zăval showed to many! The girl-child is an orphan, but she has not long to go before she finds a husband!'

Two words made me hate Big-Nose, who had actually been paid to defend me, and those were 'husband' and 'girl-child'. The first needs no further explanation, as even a bird-brain could tell he was insulting me. However, I have to say about the other that to me it seems humiliating to the very marrow. When you are a *girl-child*, you are a sort of a waste of space. You are neither an infant nor an adult. You are no longer overlooked, but nor are you big enough to be out in the world. And you are a *girl*, and consequently incapable of doing things that might be taken notice of. You can't be called 'young mistress', as the cook's wife had called me, or even 'young lady'. A girl-child is a kind of trash caught between two worlds. For that reason you feel nothing but pity for a girl-child, and if the girl-child somehow gets above herself, she becomes a 'little missy' fit only be put in her place.

The Metropolitan spoke the same language laden with sugary sweetness:

'And is there any future for this wish that it seems you nourish?'

For a long stretch of time I listened to nothing but words of this sort, casting desperate glances in the direction of Caterina and of Dubois, who had been left standing beside the door like a pair of beggars, and in the end, no longer knowing what to do, I asked straight out if it was known who had killed my little uncle, because after all that was why we were there. However, that issue seemed closed as far as they were concerned. The Metropolitan thundered at me, as they say, considering that I had no right to speak unless asked, and Big-Nose took advantage of the moment to make another remark about marriage. It was obvious that they didn't like the way my hand clung to my pocket. And probably for that reason, they started to speak about my bad character, while the Metropolitan let it be understood that the possibility was not excluded that I myself had sent my little uncle to the next world.

'Neither her grandmother nor her mother were of the best sort! What a shame for Gentleman Zăval, with such women in the family!'

In spite of my convictions and of all that I knew about Maxima, I was overcome by a shame as bitter as gall, so much so that I was unable to open my mouth. No matter how prepared you are for life, when someone derides your forebears it knocks the feet from under you!

And after this affront, the conversation sunk to even lower depths. The Metropolitan was of the opinion that it would be best if I were subjected to the ammoniac test. Only then would they see what I was.

And the trial had barely begun.

When I left the Metropolitan Palace I looked like a corpse. I asked Caterina to leave me at Zăval's house, so that I could go down into the Laboratorium.

'Perhaps it would be better not to go around alone any more. People will stare at you...'

Caterina had a sort of passion that touched even strangers, a sweetness that descended from her whole being, making me often forget that I was left all alone in this world.

'Perhaps it wouldn't be a bad idea,' she continued, 'if we talked to Father Ogaru and promised him another house in exchange.'

'I will not give up Cuviosu's house! What could he do to me?'

'Oho...!'

She was ready to launch into arguments, but her good breeding held her back:

'I won't let him take your house. Don't you worry! And there's Dubois...'

Hearing his name mentioned, the Frenchman gave a wide and benevolent smile. He was riding on horseback beside the carriage, throwing a kindly glance in our direction at intervals.

'And that ammoniac test...?'

'Ah! It's a piece of nonsense!'

Caterina wanted at all cost to avoid explaining it to me, but, unexpectedly, Dubois too had become interested.

'All right, a girl is given a solution to drink...'

'Of sal ammoniac?'

'Not exactly. It's something prepared by a pharmacist. It probably contains sal ammoniac among other things. If the girl urinates within an hour, it means she isn't pure… You see? It's nonsense!'

'And someone takes this seriously?'

Of course, there were many who believed in such tests, and at the time I thought of them with pity, considering them numbskulls, little suspecting that this belief was part of the most perverse arsenal of weapons that society, even today, puts in the hands of anyone who chooses to use them.

'These are *boissons diurétiques*,' explained Dubois, who managed the odd word or two of Romanian for my sake. 'They are as old as the world,' he told me consolingly.

While the Frenchman was struggling to explain to me the hypocrisies of the world, a noise with the sharpness of breaking mirrors rolled over the city. From the Princely Palace in waves came a great roar of laughter. The rose cake had taken effect, and Kostas was laughing like a madman. This reminded me that I had to get the book back from the cook, and in order to get into the Palace I needed all the art of grand transformations.

And, *impetu magis*, I let slip a part of my fear:

'This is the end! By tomorrow, the whole city will be full of *caesiae*.'

Caterina smiled knowingly, as if she had a clue what I was talking about, and then said in her firmest voice:

'We must get rid of that madman! As soon as possible, we'll take the chest to Ismail Bina!'


How to Steal a Book

The Palace was almost deserted, for the servants could hardly bear the demented laughter of Kostas. Even Silică had left his bowls in the hands of others. Not only did I not find him in the Palace, but the cook wasn't even in his own room. I had imagined that everyone would know where he slept. That I would go in the door and head straight to his bedside. In my mind, Silică was too stupid not to keep the book under his pillow or at the most under his mattress. And to steal such a book seemed to me a sort of child's play.

However, there was no room next to the kitchen, so I decided to scour the whole building. As I tried to disguise myself as a towel-bearer, a wretched good-for-nothing usher came upon me and started to yell, rousing the whole Palace. I had got myself into a mess of my own making and I had no idea how to get out of it, but in my fear I climbed the stairs up to the terrace, and from there, there was nowhere else I could go. Don't imagine that this happened because I was just fourteen! All my life I have gone in the direction that I shouldn't have! I was wearing only a dress, with nothing on my head, when a pair of uncouth louts grabbed hold of me. I showed them my teeth, thinking it would slow them down, but it made no difference, because they didn't speak; they were hulking brutes of the kind that say one word a day. As we went down the stairs, I began to cry out that I knew how to make a medicine to cure laughter.

'Take me to the kitchen,' I told them. 'The princely cook himself is expecting me!'

But the more I raised my voice, the more intense grew Kostas's laughter, infecting the servants and guards, till under the arches, in unseen apartments of that vast old building, I could hear the chuckling of pages, the giggling of chambermaids, the unrestrained roaring of houseboys polishing coffee spoons, and into this hotbed of laughter there came from time to time the odd whistle, the odd avid clatter, or noise of clashing teeth, for laughter too, like human nature itself, is of many kinds. Women full of longings laughed as they let out sighs, and their joy bubbled up like the lid on a simmering pot of broth. Nothing, however, could compare with the merriment of one enormous figure, left alone in the middle of a salon, a fat man, punished by having to stand

and afflicted with a furious fit of laughter! And the guards who had got their hands on me were just like a pair of giants, stopping here and there to let out another guffaw. From distant nooks of the Palace came squeaks and refrains, and from the street could be heard other voices, interrupted by whistles and the odd cough, which only served to emphasize the far-reaching hand of the laughter that had gripped the city. And in spite of the dire straits I was in, I couldn't help imagining Caterina laughing in cascades, as she answered the manly laugh of Dubois.

Shove by shove, we finally arrived in the courtyard, where they pushed me into a chamber of the cellar, a space so tight that it was impossible to breath. Only a little light entered it, through a hole close to the ceiling. I listened to Kostas's laugh, raised far above the laughter of the others, and already I could see the districts brim full of little green-eyed fairies. And the laughter continued in sleep, spread out like a wound, as was proved by the wheezy snorts and snores that made it as far as my ears.

If you ever hear someone speaking of horror, you should have in mind the hours I endured that night. At first I stood up, and then, when no glimmer of light came in any more, I fell on my knees, to my disgust, onto the soft ground on which dozens of wretched souls had left their filth. Rocked by the laughter of the Palace and the street, I fell asleep, with tears in my eyes, reciting in my mind a long *imprecatio* to my uncle, who was really the one to blame for everything.

I slept like a worm huddled on the ground, and when I opened my eyes it was already day. In the early morning, by which time in any case there was no one left untouched by the outbreak of unrestrained excess, the laughter afflicted me too.


## A Merry Encounter

My laughter was like a puppy's bark. On the other side of the door I could hear some women laughing heartily and I tried to call out in the rhythm of my barking, but it seems that no one could hear me. Even when I began to kick the door with my feet, not a soul stopped, as if the blows were just part of the great laugh.

All the same, someone knew that I was there, apart from the ruffians that had locked me up, not because it was one of those occurrences that get everyone's attention, but because, among all the laughing crowd, there was one person who was just as worried as me, which in the end was my salvation. And that was the cook.

When the door opened, all I could see was a light, but I knew that whoever it was, my best chance was to burst out with all my might, and so I did, knocking someone to the ground and tripping over bodies trembling with laughter, feeling that I was pursued.

It was only when I stopped under some stairs that the cook caught up with me, chuckling hoarsely. He had been looking for me all night, he said, laughing as if this was the best thing that could happen. He was terrified that what I had predicted had come true:

'Hi-hi, you were right about the cake! Hihi-hihi, how did you know?'

'Ha-ha, ha-ha,' came out of my mouth, and I was unable to articulate more than that.

Muddied from head to foot, I looked as if I had been pulled out of the rubbish tip.

The cook's room was in the courtyard, adjoining the barns. As soon as I was inside I dashed to the bed, and asked him about the book, in the rhythm of my measured laughter.

'It's not here,' chuckled the cook. 'I'm not so stupid as to keep it at the Palace!'

'But where is it?' I yelped back.

'It would be better if you told me about the potion you said you know how to make!'

The cook didn't want to give me the book. He had sensed its value, or perhaps now he really believed himself a sort of culinary wizard. He had plans.

'You'll give me that recipe, and then we'll see what's to be done!'

He probably wasn't even thinking of curing absolutely everyone. Not only that, he wasn't intending to let me go either.

'Tell me the recipe and stay here till I get back!'

As he stood blocking the door, he looked quite hostile, especially as his laugh, that of a hoarse person, also gave him a sort of air of cruelty. Not to mention that from time to time he threw his gaze up to the ceiling and I got a glimpse of what white teeth he had.

'First you need a bottle of plum brandy and a handful of poppy seeds, which you boil together.'

'Is that all?' said the tiny cook happily between two short chuckles.'

He went out, and then turned the key, locking me in his room, which was just big enough to contain a bed. Under the mattress there was nothing. In the pockets of his clothes—still less. I threw a ragged anteri over myself. The lock on the door was a cheap one; even a child could have opened it.

### Formicosus

During this time, Caterina had been looking for me everywhere, even at Ogaru's.

Convinced that I had stolen his precious casket, he had denigrated me without having the courage to say what I had taken: 'The maids saw her going into the salon! That girl has a habit of taking things,' he said, which meant either that he wasn't very sure or that he was embarrassed at the thought that people might find out what terrible things he had written.

I saw them in the distance talking in the churchyard. Caterina threw back her head from time to time, scattering a loud laugh all around, while the priest chortled into his beard. He looked like a sick goat. She seemed *meribibula*—wine-soused!

Anyway, I only learned all this many days later. As everyone was laughing around me, I passed unobserved and shut myself in my uncle's house. Among the flasks in the larder, just as I had expected, my little uncle had a potion made from ants, good as a cure for laughter.

When I recall the hours I spent in the house, it brings tears to my eyes. It was a time of what I might call much longed-for tranquility. Alone, listening to the laughter of the city, not for a moment wishing to go outside. Not wanting to save anyone. Nothing stirred me to abandon the peace that I could only now appreciate at its true value. I recall that in those hours of waiting I discovered the magic lantern, which today I am going to use once again. It was by the door, with some parasols spread over its support, which caused it to pass unnoticed, especially as it was older than ours, and Laco was painted in a different red, more scorching, more intense.

I made my preparations with all the little things that now seemed to make sense to me, for many of them had been part of my childhood, which had made me regard them with the contempt that you have for the things you see every day. The black chest I placed beside the table, ready at hand. I lit some candles, and distributed them around the house, and I changed the curtains on the door, the ones through which Ogaru had watched me on the night I came to Bucharest. Finally, I planted powders and salts at various points in the room. And I waited.

But, as they say, it's never who you're expecting that comes. As I waited with my eyes on the door, I didn't even notice when he came. I had the impression, at first, that I could hear a faint chuckle, but, as the whole neighbourhood was laughing, I gave it no importance. Then a man was breathing regularly behind me. At first I didn't recognize him. It was only when he sat down on the sofa that I saw that it was Perticari. He wasn't laughing. Like me, he seemed removed from the current predicament, and this detail startled me.

'Are you a Satorine,' I asked half-heartedly, fearful that he would make fun of me.

He smiled broadly, sizing me up like a walnut.

'How did you get in?'

'Aha!' he said, as if I had finally asked the right question. Do you know the *Tale of the Twins*?'

To gain time, I shook my head as a sign that I did not, but I had already begun to examine him carefully, to assure myself that he was really there in flesh and blood, and not a ghost.

'Rozica had a twin sister,' he began, and right from the first sentence I could tell that he knew the tale from my little uncle Zăval. 'She was kidnapped by a brigand, and her twin sister could no longer do anything. She didn't eat, she didn't sleep, she didn't speak. She just sat, seeking out her sister with her mind. Sometimes she could be seen at the window, flickering like a dying flame, and at other times some neighbour would come to her door and leave her food, which was never touched. For she fed on nothing but an enchanted potion. With every passing day, her figure became fainter and fainter, until one day, when someone approached the window, the room was empty. Do you know what had happened?'

Perticari smiled benevolently, imprinting his face in my mind forever, a face as smooth as a poplar leaf. He was wearing a coat pinched at the waist and trimmed with genet fur at the collar. The tips of his fingers were clothed in gold leaf, which gave him a very distinguished look.

Of course I immediately said no, although I knew the whole story.

'She had disappeared forever from Bucharest, merging with Rozica. Every part of her body became compressed, becoming not only much smaller than the egg of a flea, but also light, so that she could be carried on the wind to where her sister was. All her life, strength, and wisdom passed into Rozica, who, once she was thus strengthened, escaped from the brigand. And you,' my guest continued, 'will give me that elixir!'

I was left gaping. I had no idea what he wanted. And so he explained more precisely:

'The potion of the twins!'

He had got the wrong idea. I wanted to refuse, but he stopped me with a raised finger. From the way he was looking at me, with eyes that seemed to swallow me up, it passed through my mind that he was the killer in Ogaru's confession.

'Show me how you make yourself invisible!' I said, trying to imagine him on the night of the murder.

Probably he had asked the same thing of Cuviosu. The potion of the twins! I couldn't imagine where he had picked that up.

'And you will give me this potion if I show you?'

'Of course!'

He threw his head back, bit his lip like someone who didn't give a toss for my word, and continued:

'Show me the potion!'

From the way he moved, twisting his neck from time to time, it wasn't hard to tell that he had all his trickster's gear under his collar, concealed by the fur. Despite being an imposing figure of a man, he didn't inspire in me the horror that Bina had embedded into my very bones, nor the deadly chill of Gentleman Ispas in Braşov. He was not venomous like the Metropolitan, or cunning like the cook. He simply looked like a lot of my little uncle's friends, which made him seem almost likeable, and that was probably what had deceived Zăval. That explained the astonished look that Ogaru had described. He hadn't expected his death to come from such a charlatan.

I grabbed a flask from the rack and held it out to him, looking him in the eye. Both he and I were close to laughing. Still, he took it. And a second later he had vanished, leaving behind that puff of smoke.

I took a look around the house to make sure that he had gone. It wasn't long before I realized that the bottle of *formicosus* had vanished too. That was no longer a laughing matter! He knew more than I had imagined. The *Book of Perilous Dishes* had passed through his hands.

## Cuviosu Zăval's Precaution

Around lunchtime, the cook knocked meekly at the door of my uncle's house. He was still laughing, but there was despair in his eyes. I lifted a corner of the curtain and looked at him for a while, and I let him see that I wasn't laughing. When I thought he had got the message, I opened the door a little, pushing one of my feet forward to keep him at a respectful distance.

'Go and get the book, and then we'll talk!'

The cook gave a chortle with his head cast down, and then pulled the book from under his coat. The sight of it gave me a thrill. From a distance Father Ogaru was laughing as he watched us, so I made a sign to the cook to come into the house. As soon as he entered the salon, he froze. Of his whole being, which was nothing much anyway, all that was left was his hoarse laugh. On one wall, Laco was barking, red as fire. The cook was terrified. He had no idea that there was such a thing as a magic lantern, but he probably believed in real magicians.

I took the book and dropped it into the black chest, which seemed bottomless. Then I held out a cup and let him enjoy its contents. I no longer had the ant potion, but I had made a tea for him.

Once he was rid of the laughter, his insolence returned. Small and pushy, he made straight for the chest, where there was no longer any trace of the book.

'Where did you put it?'

He was determined to turn the whole house upside down. An artist he might be, albeit an artist of rolled cabbage leaves, but he was still a very practical man.

'You will leave now, or else…'

'Or else, what?' he grinned.

'You'll die!'

The cook was really laughing now, like a complete nincompoop, who, instead of rejoicing, uses laughter to hide his insecurity. I too was close to laughing, I admit. But the passage of time was on my side, and the tea had taken effect; the little fellow turned floppy like a wet cloth and fell asleep.

I took the book down to the Laboratorium, intending never to take it out of there again. On the cover was a drawing of a cat, but not quite as I had remembered it. I opened the book and was dumbfounded. The writing was not mine but was in the unmistakable hand of my uncle. It was a different book. No recipe was exactly as I had written it. This was a volume specially put together for that fool of a cook. Not one of the *perilous dishes* was complete all the way through. Some ingredients were missing and others were added, which made the recipes unrecognizable to me. On top of that, not even a quarter of the dishes were there. Zăval hadn't let the real book fall into the hands of an idiot cook after all. A tender rain soothed my soul. All the same, the whole city was laughing. I looked for the rose cake. The quantities were different, and among the novelties was a spoonful of goose fat, for the dough. Even so, I couldn't let it get into the hands of just anybody, especially now that I had recovered it.

I went upstairs and waited till the cook came round again.

'Hey, time to go! Be off with you!' I said, in a voice that I had deepened with the intention of scaring him. He was drowsy from the soporific and made no protest. I leant over him and, as he looked up at me with a glazed look, I had the impression that he was counting the beads on my fez.

At the door I took advantage of the situation and asked him:

'Does Perticari have anything to do with my little uncle's death?'

Drowsy as he was, that still startled him. He was afraid of the spiritist, and by the way he strove to avoid saying anything bad, he put Perticari on my list of suspects. With his conjuring tricks, Perticari could give the impression that he was invisible, especially to a timid soul like Ogaru. He would have had plenty of time to throw the knife, if not indeed knives.

# Chapter V

# Adversus

### The Ghost Speaks

In the end I made my way to Caterina's house, where I found her still throwing her head back and roaring with laughter. I had a remedy in the pocket of my dress, but I didn't get as far as pouring it into her coffee. The window of the salon gave a view of the street, and right in the middle, looking up at me, was none other than Burchioiu! I could see him clearly. And he could see me. He was dressed for travelling, just as I had seen him the last time. Probably these were his best clothes and he had been buried in them, to look good in the next world. Or in case he became a ghost and headed towards Bucharest. I wasn't afraid. Caterina was leaning against the stove in fits of laughter, leaving me by the window like a torch that had just been lit.

Burchioiu was laughing—I don't think I had ever before seen him showing all his teeth—and at the same time making signs to me to come down. Obviously he couldn't come up, for otherwise I couldn't see why he should keep on making signs. For a ghost to come into your house, you have to call it, to open the door to it. To keep ghosts away it is a good idea always to have on you a sprig of basil and the head of a stag beetle. Of course, a knife stuck in the threshold gives even better protection. This thought reminded me of my little uncle's knife, which I had left in the apple tree. All the same, Sator had found me right there, and Burchioiu had come the first time to that same place. Perhaps things change sometimes, and what stopped ghosts yesterday isn't worth tuppence today. At the bottom of one of my pockets I had some remains of stag beetle, and in my corset I kept my cockchafer powder, the best defence against ghosts. And to be on the safe side, I gripped the mohair cat; I didn't know yet what it could do, but my little uncle hadn't left it for me without a purpose. It would come in handy somehow.

One of Caterina's menservants came in, he too laughing in great fits, and informed me that there was someone who wanted to see me, a cousin of mine from Braşov. Cousin!

Between bursts of laughter, Caterina told the servant to invite my supposed cousin, who could be none other than Burchioiu, into the salon. I glanced at the window: he was waving both arms in my direction, exactly as a relative would do.

'He's the ghost,' I yelled. 'Don't on any account let him into the house!'

Caterina let out an even greater laugh, so that it was clear that now she was laughing of her own accord, and not at the whim of Kostas, who had spread laughter all through the city. And she had a truly infectious laugh, which made me show my teeth. The servant was laughing, holding onto the door for support; Burchioiu was laughing out in the street. The women in the next room were laughing as they ironed clothes. Even the doorman, a toothless old fellow, was laughing. The whole house was laughing. So much so that I too began to feel happy, and to laugh myself for no reason, unable to stop or to judge, for, unlike the laughter induced by the cake, this was really my laughter, kept safe inside, but overflowing from time to time, just like the Dâmboviţa when it rains. I laughed with all my heart, sharing in the common pleasure. And while I was laughing in spite of myself, I was struck by an iron silence: over the city, as over Caterina's house, a deathly hush was settling. No one was laughing any longer. Not even the buzzing of a fly could be heard. Caterina was wiping away her tears, and the servant had disappeared from the threshold.

Kostas's laughter had ceased, and the city had returned to its normal life. The effects of Zăval's recipe had been of short duration.

A minute later I found myself face to face with the ghost of that crazy Burchioiu.

Caterina was dizzy from all her laughing, and her eyes, at other times playful, like beads swinging over a bosom, had lost their sparkle. She spoke in a measured way, as if all her powers had left her.

'Good Lord, how I laughed! It felt as if the whole world was one fit of laughter.'

'Just so, indeed,' said Burchioiu in support, speaking much more politely than usual, which I put down to the fact that he had turned into a ghost.

'Laurian,' he added by way of introduction, explaining that he was also known as Burcu, although, as far as I knew, only Maxima had called him that, and then, continuing to set forth all the pretentions of his lineage, he boasted that he was the only son of Ispas Podaru, the great supplier, and at this point he enumerated all the richest houses in Bucharest, including, to my astonishment, the Princely Court and also the Greceanu house.

On top of that, Caterina knew who he was. I could no longer bear this. It was already more than I could take to see how she smiled at that waster Burchioiu!

'He's the ghost!' I whispered to Caterina in warning, but because she was already smiling with the most incredulous of all the faces she could show, I laid into Burchioiu: 'I know you died! You can't fool me! You've been dead since the day I left Brașov!'

He had turned redder than my fez and fell silent like a snake.

'You died,' I went on, 'because you sold Maxima!' And then to Caterina, who was no longer smiling: 'This is the snitch who sent her to her death. That's why he died!'

'I didn't sell her,' said Burchioiu defending himself. As usual he was scared of me.

Every time I raised my voice, he opened his eyes wide, light-coloured eyes that gave him an even more innocent air, with that look of his that infuriated me, the way it turned him from an utter idiot to an innocent child.

'I have her letter, in which she says in black and white that you reported her! You accused her of being a witch!'

Both Caterina and Burchiou protested at the same time.

'It was a mistake! Someone signed with my name! Would I have come here if...?'

'You came to take revenge!'

I realized that I couldn't bring up the dark episode when I had given him the wolfsbane. It wouldn't do me any good for Caterina to see the stuff I was made of. What would she say if she found out that I had killed someone? My deed was now a leech slithering across my cheek.

'What happened to Maxima?' asked Caterina, who didn't know the whole story, only what I had told her.

'She was killed because of him!'

Burchioiu nearly tripped over with the backward steps he took.

'The guardsmen lifted her,' I continued, 'after this piece of garbage wrote a letter!'

'It was a mistake!' Burchioiu protested. 'Which was cleared up the same day. If I hadn't been late waking up, it might have been sorted out faster...'

These words put up a wall that I could not cross. It's not what a word means that matters, but who it is that says it.

Burchioiu's eyes grew even wider, and his lips, which seemed to me swollen with bitterness, trembled as if he were about to weep: 'Massima sent me!'

In my mind, dark thoughts blossomed. If Maxima had sent a ghost to me, it could only be for one purpose. In an impulse of the moment, I threw the cockchafer powder and made a dash for the door. Without waiting. Without understanding.

## 1829—The Present Time

### Preparations for the Road

Thinking back to that day, I realize how afraid I was. The horror that made me tremble gave me the strength to fight impetuously. And that fever that animates the young has now gone from me. Looking at myself in the mirror, I almost don't like what I see. But how many people are pleased with their face in the mirror?

*

I am ready for the road. I arrange the magic lantern and project Laco onto the door. It's the same drawing, the same Spartan dog. Why Spartan? God only knows. That's what Maxima said: 'our Spartan dog.'

The last time I travelled it was to Stamboul. A long time ago. I haven't been away since then.

For two years I've been in mourning, and it takes more than a journey to heal my suffering.

The carriage is ready. All the chests have been tied with rope. From Lipscani Square I'll take Ismail Bina's Arnauts—ten ducats now and the same when I come back. If I come back. But Bina knows how to take a risk. He's a man of his word, after his own fashion. Years ago, he used to lend money. When you were in difficulties, you would knock at Bina's door. He had a eunuch who would look down at you from his extraordinary height as if you were a grain of pepper and ask you what you wanted. Then he would pass the message on to his master, and if the Turk agreed, he would come out onto the balcony and look at you, sizing you up. I never heard of any bad debts or of Bina taking revenge on anyone, the way the money lenders do. You were simply afraid of what he could do, and that was enough. Come to think of it, that Turk was never involved in any scandal.

I have a long journey ahead of me. Three weeks, at best. If I don't come back, at least I will leave these notes. They are my secrets, now become so many old rags that I am sorry to throw out. Memories sometimes have the taste that takes you back to what you once were. A song that, at one time made me fall over laughing, sounds more and more in my ears. It's a melody—I can now say—*of olden times*, sung by a group of minstrels whose faces I still hold in my memory. The whole song was a dialogue between a young man and an old woman. In the refrain, she told of her dream, which was a sort of summary of past lives, out of which I can only remember two lines, as foolish as they are persistent: 'I saw my days of youth pass / In my little thin dress.' Not only can I see her, I can feel her presence, moving shamelessly in the midst of men pained by desire. That little dress works on me, gives me suicidal thoughts, brings back to mind those noontides that saddened me for no reason, wasting my time.

But who is not sometimes struck by a sense of futility? Almost everything I did back then came to nothing in the end, and so it was with the cook too.

## 1798—Thirty Years Ago

### Plum Pie

Before so much as three hours had passed since people were released from laughter, in the Palace kitchens other *perilous dishes* were in preparation. Silică had learned all the recipes or had made himself copies, and, although my little uncle had reduced its power, the food continued to arouse Kostas's innards and turn his blood. Word went about that the Phanariot was demanding nothing less than bustard, boiled till the meat was so tender that it fell off the bones. The cook had become a sort of regular client of the minstrels, and lately so had his assistant, a snub-nosed pie-maker whom he sent to the kitchen window. People gathered in front of the Palace and gaped at this snub-nosed youth, because he reported every movement in the princely kitchen. The min-strels drank in his words with their ears and immediately trans-formed them into songs, which everybody learned, and so in the grander houses exactly the same dishes were cooked as at the Palace, thus infecting dozens of people.

I too stopped to listen to the pie-maker, although in my mind I was going over my meeting with Burchioiu, breaking it down into bouquets and blades of grass, which awakened many ques-tions in me. Maxima had sent him! I couldn't forget those words. Out of all he had told me, only those words continued to trou-ble me. But I was out of my mind and I couldn't understand whether she had sent him from the next world or from the Şchei of Braşov! After throwing the cockchafer powder I had rushed outside.

As I listened to the princely pie-maker yelling in the window, in my mind I went over the possibilities, which were not so many.

'The bustard meat has been thoroughly boiled,' the snub-nosed fellow was saying, 'and right now Gentleman Silică is kneading spices, raisins, and fresh dill into it!'

The cook pressed the stuffing into peppers, and the lad yelled in the window: 'His Highness Prince Kostas eats only chilli pep-pers, of the kind known as "crabs"!'

And while the cook was roasting the peppers, just a tad, I could see Maxima freed from the noose. Hadn't that fool said that it had all been sorted out? That meant she had been saved! But if that was so, then why hadn't she come herself? Why send a numbskull? And above all why would his father let him go?

That dismal man! He was a real tyrant! He would never have permitted his son, who he knew all too well was a buffoon, to set off madly in the direction of Bucharest!

The crier in the Palace window was telling how the cook had arranged the peppers like the petals of a flower and covered them with sweetened wine. A sigh of pleasure issued from the gathered crowd, and a violin bowed a poignant chord over the city. By the time Silică was preparing to pour the paste of turnip and ground walnuts, I had already made up my mind to look for Burchioiu again. But what if he had dissolved in the mist of cockchafers? By the time I had contemplated this, the cook had already grated the cheese and put everything in the oven, and the whole story of the peppers had passed from mouth to mouth all through the city. Without my wishing, my mind was being filled with whatever was stuffing Kostas's belly!

Only that the cook was not content with just this. The sun flickered faintly through the patchwork clouds, and its feeble light made my presentiments multiply. As I was getting ready to go, the babbler in the window loudly shouted out the recipe for a plum pie, which made me stop in my tracks, for to go by the ingredients, it could be nothing but *strena*, almost exactly as I remembered it. Whoever eats of it begins to be interested in the future to such an extent that they no longer do anything all day!

And my fears proved well-founded. Immediately after lunch, Kostas called to the Palace all the visionaries in Bucharest, among them Perticari, who was appreciated because he talked with the dead and who stayed till morning in Kostas's chamber.

## The Witch of Stamboul

Among the women whose renown has spread in the world, one who surely has a place is Syrka. Born in Skopje, she grew up and learned the joys of life in a neighbourhood of Stamboul. From an early age, she showed inclinations towards magic. That woman could soften anyone's will. No one could refuse her. If she had sent some unfortunate to pick flowers on the Moon, he would have flown there or died in the attempt. And apart from that she knew how to make cures for a lover. When a man fell into *accedia* or just profound revulsion, Syrka prepared a pill for him to get him back on his feet, a little cake, the size of a finger-nail, made of cornflowers and crickets' dreams. What things that mixture could do! After the first swallow, the colours of the world changed. Lifted high above the world or floating over the waters, any man was capable of imagining with his own mind what Paradise was like! Women, even the most pretentious, were mown down, hanging for hours on the tail of such a man. Caressed, desired, called by women! There was no man who had not wished for such a thing. Syrka's pill had come to be the most sought-after preparation. And among the men who desired it was a doctor in Therapia, none other than the father of Kostas.

In those days, let it be understood, Kostas was not a prince; he had not gathered together the four hundred money bags, but was a mere interpreter. For this reason his father sent him to find Syrka. As may be imagined, already before reaching her, Kostas was infatuated, and when he saw her, he lost his bearings completely. But the girl liked the look of him too, for in those days he didn't resemble an olive that's past its best. Everything went perfectly. In the light of Stamboul, provided by the moon and the stars, the Greek and the Macedonian became one being. They opened their hearts, confessed their little indiscretions. They tasted together of the sweetness that each was keeping for the other. It is well known, however, that there are things in this world that should be avoided. Especially where there is a fear. For the Greek was not fully happy, knowing that his father was waiting for him, and nor was Syrka completely at ease with the idea of having fallen in love with a Greek, which wasn't the done thing for one of pure Macedonian blood. The witch's powers began to melt away, like a drop of water that falls on flint in the heat of the sun. Men no longer listened to her desires, and her pills no longer worked. Her beauty faded, and with each moment of happiness her flesh lost its consistency. In the end, all that was left of Syrka was a cloud of smoke and Kostas's pain. At first sight. For in the undercurrents of history the recipe of Syrka's wonderful pill lived on, a recipe that I noted in the *Book of Perilous Dishes* and which it is worth your while to know:

Take cornflower petals, about two bowls full, and immerse them in a batter made of milk, wheat-flour, and a few eggs. Into the resulting mixture, which is no thicker than cream, put spices, honey, and finally some crickets' dreams. These are collected during the day from crickets sleeping, many of them with astounding abandon, under the odd burdock leaf or by a stalk of common mallow. Of course this is an art that not everyone has the gift for. Beside the sleeping cricket, a skilled mouth whistles the 'Song for Dreams', known especially by Macedonians and Greeks. The melody is like the branch of a fig tree tapping the window in the cool of autumn, when the wind is starting to pick up its strength. It is not an easy song. Some get it wrong precisely because they do not have a feeling for its true value. It just takes one note falling flat and it's all over! It's no longer worth a penny. But if the singer is good, then out of the tail end of the cricket so many dreams start to pour freely that a mere human being could not dream them all in a lifetime. And this is where the great art comes in. A true magician knows that crickets' dreams are always attracted by peppermint water. If you hold a flask containing a little infusion of mint, the whole flood of dreams is sure to come to rest in it. And this solution is the last ingredient needed for the dough, which, once baked in the oven, becomes a cake suitable for sharing with the enfeebled. For Syrka's pill is for men struck by sorrow, for flesh that has gone soft. It awakens desires and revives hope. The man you thought was a flaccid weakling rises from the dead. The only disadvantage is that it leads to dependency. And what kind of life is it in which you depend on the dreams of some crickets?

Perticari invoked her spirit, and for a whole night the only language heard in the Palace was Macedonian. Those who knew that language maintained that the witch, such as she was, a mere spirit brought back from the other world, had described a future made up of swords and corpses.

'Ah, my love, it will not be long! I will wait for you under the vault of foam, where the souls of lovers and of those wrongfully killed take their pleasure! But until then, you would do well to find my good sister, who is Cat o' Friday!'

These words, borne from one to another, came to my ears too, and served to strengthen my suspicion that the slippery spiritist with his fine tastes knew things that I had no idea of. How could my name be known to a witch from Stamboul, not to mention one who had passed to the next world?

This madness about premonitions lasted for two days, during which time no one spoke about anything but the Greek's dreams and the bloody signs that announced a bad end either for him or for the people of the city. But all this stir had its good side too.

## Freedom

As for me, as soon as I heard about the plum pie, even before everything else transpired, I went straight back to Caterina's house, and I ran so fast that when I entered the salon I startled everyone. And there were a lot of people. For Caterina had called her friends, who were not exactly friends, but comrades in the matter of the money chest, determined that evening to conclude the deal with Bina. With one raised finger she directed me to bed, but, as the air was already vibrating with plans, in a few moments I had found a place where I didn't get in anyone's way. They were all smoking pipes, including Caterina, throwing up swirls of smoke that made the room seem like a pot forgotten on the stove.

Dubois, sitting in a very dignified position, was explaining something, throwing in the odd Romanian word too.

163

'Bonaparte will free the Christian world,' he was saying.

'Others have made such boasts!'

The same doubt came from all mouths.

'Then why have the Turks put all their hopes in him? I have heard from someone worthy of trust,' said Dudescu, twisting those incredibly slender fingers of his, 'that the Sultan has made a pact with him, to crush the Germans. In the first place the Germans with pigtails!' (By that he meant the Austrians.)

Dubois lent forward, pursing his lips and, from time to time, shaking his hair like a dog just emerging from the water.

In the middle of the discussion, not all of which I could understand, Bina appeared, which set my heart beating twice as fast. The Turk was decked out in a mantle of fine silk, as green as a tree frog. He was accompanied by two of his men, who smelt of tobacco. In fact the whole group seemed to have been preserved in tobacco leaves and coffee.

'You didn't tell me you had so many guests, my lady,' he said to Caterina, who made a sign to him to be seated.

'Last time, you advised me not to meet you alone, noble Bina!'

Apart from Caterina, no one made a sound, and so it remained until the end of the visit, which in any case was quite short.

Ismail Bina accepted the chest containing four hundred bags. He didn't count them, which showed that he trusted her. He won't count the ducats that I'm going to give him today for the Arnauts either. That's the way he is, and that's how he has always been. In recent years, when many Turks returned home, Bina chose to remain here and to lead exactly the same life that he led back then, when he was the envoy of the Sultan himself.

On the evening of the chest, Ismail Bina spoke just a few words, but they were exactly those that the whole crowd of guests were waiting for:

'Tomorrow I leave for Stamboul, and a month from now it is possible that you will have a new ruler.'

'Bring Ypsilanti, noble Ismail!'

'Ypsilanti, if you say so! Or Moruzi,' said Bina in that voice that seemed to be nestled deep in his throat.

The murmurs of approval showed that the second proposal wasn't bad either.

Bina's ruffians seized the chest, and the Turk made a sign to Caterina to go outside.

In the darkness of the courtyard, someone was wriggling, and when the torch-bearers lit up the alleyway, I saw that it was the cook, securely tied up. At last he had got his deserts.

'Here is the cook, my lady! I have kept my side of the bargain,' said Bina. 'Now it only depends on you.'

'And the papers?'

'What need have you of papers? Once the Greek has gone, no one will ever ask about the cook again!'

The Turks left, and Caterina gave orders for the cook to be untied, while she overwhelmed him with her words and lavished welcomes on him as if he were the prodigal son returning.

In the rising mists of the autumn evening, it seemed to me that I could see at the gate a white carriage, which reminded me of my little uncle Zăval. Everybody seemed content, until the cook, who in the meantime had been untied, destroyed all the peace: 'I'm going to complain to the Palace, mistress! Have you any idea how many different dishes I should be cooking tonight?'

And he started to list them so fast that no one could stop him, until, coming upon me, in the narrow space between Caterina and the housekeeper, he threw a question at me, equally hurriedly: 'Have you ever eaten cockchafers, my little mistress?'

And imagining that I hadn't understood, he added: '*Melolontha*, young lady! Now do you know?'

Caterina, full of tenderness, thought the cook hadn't understood clearly or that he was scared to death: 'It's all over, Silică! Finished! Now you're home! To hell with the Greek!'

But he wasn't who the Greceancă thought he was. To start with, he threw his eyes up to the eaves of the house, as was his style, and then he explained, with plenty of self-flattery, as if he wanted to repair the damage that Bina had done him: 'Not so, mistress! Now I'm a princely cook! With or without that Greek, I'm staying at the Palace! It says so in papers!'

He looked her up and down, rather brazenly. Caterina reminded him of his wife and of his duties as an inherited Gypsy, who had been born and raised in the Greceanu household. However, the little fellow didn't even let her finish, but, after giving me a furtive wink, so I wouldn't forget what he had said, he headed for the gate and was off, leaving nothing behind him but the tinkle of the little bell on his fez.

You could see from Caterina's face that she hadn't expected this. She didn't even send a servant to bring him back. She who had believed that he was being tortured at the Palace, who had paid Bina and ordered songs from the minstrels, had finally seen the true face of this little man full of grand airs. The housekeeper, who had never thought much of him, was quick to speak out, and what she said seemed fair enough to me: 'Can't you find a cook, ma'am, when every estate has two or three just like Silică? To hell with the fool! That Greek has put another pair of horns on him!'

I doubted that the Greek was to blame. The cook had mentioned cockchafers, which weren't listed in the *Book of Perilous Dishes*. Of course I had eaten them. I didn't get the point of the question, and yet I felt he had wanted to tell me something. Cockchafers kept in wine and seared on hot coals are a delicacy for the most refined people. They are eaten hot, with salad and beer. They restore faith in the past, which also repairs the sufferings of the present. For the past is like a dog that never stops snapping at the seat of your breeches, while the present is a scruffy tyke that tricks you into taking it in your arms, making you forget the future, and as for the future, that, needless to say, is an Afghan hound.

Perhaps the cook had just wanted to boast of his recipes. All the same, it was me he had asked.

For a good while, in Caterina's salon there was no talk of anything but the cook. They had forgotten about Napoleon and about the bags given to Bina. The cook, whom they believed had been inveigled away by Kostas and made to prepare poisons, had become a mystery without bounds. Apart from Dubois, who argued as usual for the abolition of slavery, the other guests saw in the cook the most inexplicable of the mysteries of Bucharest:

'Whoever heard of a slave betraying his mistress for a Greek incomer, who, they say, sleeps with his sword in his hand!'

'Perhaps he promised to free him,' said Dubois tentatively, looking all around.

But his opinion was not worth taking notice of. No one could imagine Silică managing without a master.

*

As soon as I got the chance, I asked Caterina what had happened to Burchioiu, whose ghost might now be droplets of rain water or specks of dust scattered in the gardens. I hadn't even managed to ask him all my questions. That's how it is with ghosts: by the time you've come to acknowledge them—they've disappeared without a trace!

'What ghost? You made a mess of everything in the salon! I even had to change the curtains, and as for the poor boy, you ruined his clothes!'

'Didn't he dissolve?' I was amazed, and I can tell you I was really upset.

Caterina looked at me with her restless eyes, as if to say I should get my wits together.

'He's coming for lunch tomorrow. He wants to tell you something.'

167

The meeting the next day wasn't easy. Burchioiu turned up smiling, so I didn't ask any more about his clothes or if he was dead.

'The day Massima was arrested, I got up late. In fact my father woke me, coming home unexpectedly.'

For a good while he told me about that dismal father of his, who, from his lips, took on a different perspective. That ape, whom I found it hard even to say good day to, had found out somehow what had happened to Maxima and had taken Burchioiu straight to the town prison. At this point in the story, the storyteller no longer mattered to me. In my mind, I could already see Maxima, wrapped in her travelling cloak.

'And where is Maxima?'

Burchioiu turned red. After a long silence, I understood that the news was not good. But I wanted to hear it.'

'Massima is dead.'

Having given me hopes, he had dashed them again.

'Did you kill her?'

'No! I got her out of prison! Father did actually. He arranged everything!'

'Your father...'

There was no point in saying what a bad opinion I had of him. All the same, I did say. For a few minutes I unburdened myself of everything, from my conviction that the man was corrupt, to the details of those nights when women's laughter could be heard coming from black carriages.

'My father isn't the way you see him. He has friends. Both men and women. That's all. Massima died after we left the prison building. I really was the one who got her out. As I was saying, it was an accident. The street was full, because it was a market day. I didn't see who killed her, but I can tell you she knew she was going to die. Before it all happened, just before, she told me to look for you and tell you something. And the next moment she died.'

'How?'

'Stabbed. I swear! I didn't see who. The street was packed…'

The story seemed suspicious to me. A revulsion had grown in my throat that I can still feel today. My little uncle murdered by an unseen killer. Maxima stabbed in the same way. Things don't just happen like that in life. And if they do, then there's an explanation. The causes are always simple.

'And where was your father at that moment?'

'At the Governor's. He wanted to thank him. My father has nothing to do with it.'

Maxima had been buried the next day, and our house was locked up for the time being.

Burchioiu had been connected with her death. Part of me believed him guilty. But then why had he gone to the trouble of getting her out of prison? It was all rather murky, and I was convinced that he wasn't telling me everything. The fact that I hadn't killed him gave me a pain in my soul, not because he had gone unpunished, but because it meant that Maxima hadn't put wolfbane in my bottle. She had lied to me. To make sure I wouldn't look for other poisons, that I wouldn't make other potions myself. Perhaps she knew where I would make my first stop. My life was, as I have said, planned down to the smallest details.

Burchioiu continued in a voice full of reproach, as if he wanted to bring to my attention that, in spite of my disbelief, he had continued to do his duty to the end: 'Shortly before she died, she told me you should look for the houses…'

Of course! The houses that only the cook had seen lately!

'She said there's a plan, a sort of drawing of them somewhere in her brother's shop. That's what she told me.'

The shop that Cirtă had ransacked.

'How exactly did she tell you? Can you remember word for word?'

Burchioiu remembered the crush on the street. Evening was falling. Someone went past them with a lantern. He remembered what shoes Maxima was wearing! And that she had insisted, telling him twice not to forget and to set off for Bucharest to look for me.

'Why you? She didn't trust you, or your father!'

'Of course she did! Massima was very fond of me!'

Burchioiu, pettish and moody as he was, looked earnest. I didn't trust him, but part of my antipathy towards him had melted.

'She said there's a map,' he went on.

The map in the Laboratorium was of a town. In any case, if there was a map of the houses, that was where I had to look for it. All I had to do was to find Strada Murta.

'And please,' added Burchioiu, with that same face of a bashful peacock, 'call me *Laurian*! I've never liked *Burcu*. Only Father calls me that.'

'And Maxima.'

# Chapter VI

# The Spiritist

### The Turkey

Despite all that had happened the night before, Caterina was convinced that Silică was being held at the Palace by blackmail. Although she had heard with her own ears, she doubted, just as lovers doubt when they are told that everything is in their own minds. She set his wife to follow him in the street, for the cook passed almost every week in a cart that the whole city knew, transporting all sorts of good things for the princely kitchens. I remember a morning in which he had bought a turkey. He had been out in Bragadiru or somewhere thereabouts, where he had acquired, perhaps by extortion, some barrels of wine and this bird, whose neck he kept stroking with the cruel pleasure of a crazed executioner. He had a boy with him, who looked on him with respect. The cook's wife took hold of the harness, but he didn't protest as he usually did. I went out to the gate to have a look.

'This turkey is fed on nothing but millet,' the cook explained to us. 'Look what shiny feathers she has!'

'As if we were going to eat it feathers and all,' said his wife mockingly, ready to pick a fight.

'Eh-hey! When the bird's feathers are ugly, so is the taste of the meat. If you see one with ruffled and ragged feathers, it's sure to have lice, and lice suck away its life and rot its blood. The meat of a hen with lice tastes like piss…'

'A good thing you care about the turkey,' his wife laid into him again, 'since you've forgotten me!'

'I'm busy! What do you want me to do? Have you any idea how much work I have to do?'

'That's a lot of shit! You just make grub, you don't build palaces, you scoundrel! Who do you think you are? Stick three hunks of meat in the pot and they boil themselves!'

'Food calls for more much than that,' he boasted. 'If you just leave it to boil, woman, all you get is stock! Go home!'

However, his wife turned to threats: 'Never mind, she'll buy you back, the mistress will, and we'll see then what you have to say for yourself!'

The cook was startled. I could see on his face that the idea of being bought back scared him, so he began to talk to me, as if only I was capable of understanding him.

'Cooking is difficult work! What do people know? You have to caress a steak, talk to a broth. Sweets need pampering like a child, and hors d'oeuvres have to be adorned and arrayed like a bride! Sometimes cooking can even kill you! Is that not so, little mistress?'

His question sounded like a threat, and from his tone I could tell that he was still trying out recipes from the *Book of Perilous Dishes*. But what was left? At that moment it seemed to me that he had made them all!

### Crumilla cum Animis

Of all breads, the only one that I really like is bread with mushrooms. It has sweetness. It gives lightness in your innards. But of course, here too, there are breads, and then there are breads, and among them, the one that sighs is bad. The 'bag of spirits'—in Latin *crumilla cum animis*—is the bread of the most admirable impulses, but also the enemy of all moderation! It is kneaded from a mixed flour of millet and wheat, left to rise for an hour, no more. A stuffing of mushrooms, greens, and chicory powder is buried in the soft dough. When it is ready to be put into the oven, all that remains is to break an egg and brush it well over the whole surface of the loaf, which is large, about the size of a cartwheel. Here and there it is covered with horseradish leaves. Sator also likes velvetleaf. Those who know this bury a seed-case right in the middle. No one knows why it attracts Sator, but he turns up as if out of the ground. The loaf thus prepared is baked under a cloche and it is good to leave it for a long time, till it develops a crust. Ah! What pleasure it gives me to crumble that crust between my molars! It has the taste of roasted seeds, of dried grapes, and the smell of fulfilment and repose that everyone yearns for.

*Crumilla* brings to the surface all the better qualities of a person, and that, you may say, is a good thing. Generosity, love, forgiveness, and fraternity are laudable attributes. But imagine how a person looks when they throw away the coat from their back! Those who give up their coat for another are often well spoken of. But deeds like that can result in ruination and disgust. Generous people are praised in books, but in everyday life they have nothing to show for it. The more grasping a person is, the wider doors open for them. No one loves the generous! They are admired for their praiseworthy deeds, and if they give you something, you accept it gratefully. But that's as far as it goes. You don't waste your time with a giver. You don't go for a drink with them. You don't make a philosophy of their gesture. And you don't include them in your list of friends. Such a person is only good as a guarantor—the one who's ready to stump up.

The merciful are weak people, as often as not fearful or sick. They feel guilty because they are not capable of enjoying their belongings or the good fortune that appears in their path. They are not made for happiness. And they do not carry their quests through to the end.

For this reason, *crumilla cum animis* is a delicacy that I partake of only once in a blue moon. And whenever I feel its taste on my tongue, I recall the evening in which Caterina got married, causing me such a great pain that at the time I could not imagine that I would ever get over it.

## The Feast

That evening I was making plans to look for the cook again. There was a great banquet at Caterina's, from which no one who was anyone in the city was absent, not even Kostas, who came in a convoy of ten carriages. It was then that I saw him close up for the first time. When he smiled, his great heavy eyebrows stretched, and in his ear he had a sapphire that seemed to hang by magic, ready to fall at any moment, which made me get close to him to see how it was attached. Caterina had invited him for the sake of the French consul, who, not knowing that Kostas's days were already numbered, had insisted on seeing him. And as the consul had rather rigid ideas, she hadn't argued with him, but had invited Kostas with all the pomp due to his rank.

Dubois, dressed in a turquoise jacket, had become very stuck up that evening, and had almost forgotten about me. But I didn't give him much thought either, for, in the enthusiasm of the party, Silică himself had been brought to the kitchens, in a gesture that showed Kostas's desire for reconciliation. Perhaps he had heard of the kidnapping. Perhaps he had no doubt about the loyalty of his cook, and this disposed him to be generous. Whatever the reason, that evening Silică was preparing the food in his old kitchen, where he had spent a good many years.

After examining the stone in the Greek's ear and seeing that it was held by a slender wire, I went down to the kitchen. There was food all over the tables, and the cook was even more full of himself than usual. He was waving a big spoon over everyone's heads and bellowing out commands as if he were the Kapudan

Pasha himself, for this time he had climbed onto a table, so as to be able to supervise everything.

'I hope you're not making something else out of the *Book of Perilous Recipes*,' I said, tugging at his shirt tail, and he looked down at me as if I were an enemy about to be conquered.

'And why not?'

From the way he smiled, I realized that for him it had become a game. He didn't know what each dish could do, and for that very reason he wanted to try them out. I glanced around to see what he had chosen, because I had no doubt that he had already cooked something. In the middle of the table, steam was rising from a pot of blue shellfish broth. Then there were steaks and roulades, endive salads, and the most commonplace sweets, especially doughnuts with acacia sherbet, sweet eggs, a thick compote of plums, and walnut cake. There was nothing out of the ordinary to be seen. I made for the door, but just as I was about to leave, the little bell on the cook's fez gave a tinkle, because he had turned his head towards an immense cloche suspended on a chain. I spun round and hoisted it up. Under it, on a huge baking tray, the bread was browning. There was nothing abnormal about it, except that it was sighing, which indicated that it was stuffed. And the 'bag of spirits' began to rise to the surface of my memories!

This really was the end. While I was trying to recall what effects *crumilla* had, I heard a familiar voice and I went up to the salon.

## The Man of the Dead

It was the spiritist, whom I had ranked in third place among the supposed murderers of my little uncle. But perhaps I ought to say something more about him. I never knew his real name, because everyone called him Perticari, generally with his boyar title of *pitar*. He was quite a young man, like Dubois, but, unlike Dubois, he had a childlike quality that made it easy for me to relate to him. And he had a beauty that you didn't see everywhere. He was tall and delicate, with the face of a generous man. The painted image of Jesus in icons might have been modelled on him.

His connections to the dead had begun early. On his return from Florence, where he studied philosophy, he had made a name for himself by announcing that darkness would come over the city.

'Tomorrow,' he promised, at the hour of noon, everything will turn dark!'

'Eclipse of the sun,' said some, who had seen such things before.

'Oh no,' smiled Perticari, disappointedly. 'Tomorrow's darkness is the work of a wizard thief! A master in the magic of numbers, who knows how to spread darkness over the earth. He is coming for the *Book of Solomon*, which is kept in the Enei Church, in the sanctuary!'

No one knew of the existence of such a book, still less what was written in it. But Perticari maintained that he had talked with the dead. The whole cemetery behind the Enei Church had come to complain to him!

The Metropolitan sent his people, who immediately searched the sanctuary and proved that Perticari was right.

'After we die,' the Metropolitan read from the book, 'our body will turn to ashes, and our name will perish. The end is without return! No one comes back from the dead! A man's only duty is to experience all pleasures. Look not in the mouth of the righteous and have no pity on the widows and the poor.'

Silence fell over the group, and the Metropolitan's mouth turned to a goat's belly. Horrified by such a vision, he would really have liked the book to disappear, but the fact that it was the wizard who wanted it strengthened his resolve to protect it, lest somehow it fall into heretical hands.

The next day, the church was full of respectable clergy, and guards stood at the entrance. Despite this, the book disappeared out of the very hand of the Metropolitan, and no one ever saw it again. And Perticari had secured his reputation as the most renowned spiritist. Since then, he had never spoken with so many dead people at one time. However, he did have dreams and he did see the future.

And he had a great passion for books, as is clear not just from this story, but from his connection, which was still obscure to me, with the potion in the *Book of Perilous Dishes*.

### Gaining Perticari's Trust

All the same, he was not so very clever, for he had tasted the potion that I had given him as a present. Perhaps he had trusted me. Or perhaps he had just sized me up and found me rather foolish. He didn't look so very wicked, but not quite decent either. A few boils had appeared beside his nose, and his hands were discreetly gloved, a sign that they could no longer be shown to the world. My first thought was to make fun of him. He had seen me and pushed through the crowd of guests, looking for a place on a sofa apart. As soon as he sat down, I was beside him.

'Did you kill Cuviosu Zăval?'

Perticari looked at me wide-eyed, and the boils on his nose made him look humble.

'Be careful what you say!' he whispered. 'Shouldn't you be fast asleep at this late hour? I don't imagine Lady Greceanu knows that you are hanging around here!'

He had rather struck home, and for a few moments we looked at each other without my knowing what to say. As I sat, the fez I wore in those days, which I think I have told you was bright red, could be seen on the wall much larger than it really was. That shadow has no importance for the story, but I remember it perfectly. I didn't know what to say, and the black hillock on the wall swung slowly, like a sheep-bell. And of course I kept my hands in my pockets. I was dressed in my yellow dress, which protected me from all his malice.

Then I guessed what his weak point was. From the way he shifted his eyes around, I realized that he didn't want to attract attention.

'You've got those boils because you're guilty! Caterina knows about your deeds too!'

The spiritist was astonished. If he wanted to trick me into believing he was innocent, he had succeeded: I had never seen anyone as shocked as he was.

'I have nothing to do with Zăval's death! You made me ill with that poison!'

'I didn't tell you to drink it!'

Perticari wanted to make peace with me.

'Look, I'll tell you what I know, but give me something to get rid of the boils!'

In spite of the fact that the guardian in my heart told me the man was full of secrets, I felt sorry for him. I took from my dress a little box of ointment; to tell the truth I had no idea what effects it had, but I reckoned that his spots would go in a day or two anyway, as they generally do.

'All I know,' said Perticari, 'is that he wanted to leave for Braşov! He seemed worried about something.'

'All the same, you entered his house and took things. You stole from him without remorse, didn't you?'

The spiritist smiled, as if he wanted to tell me that I was not going to force him to make confessions.

'You took a green book, with a drawing of a cat on the cover. You see that I know?'

'I didn't take anything!' he said, with that air of commanding eloquence with which adults deceive the intuitions of children and weaker people.

Then, thinking again, he said quickly: 'He told me that Cat o' Friday was coming from Chişinău. To wait for her off the mail coach.'

'And?'

'She didn't come. Do you know her?'

178

I knew how to change the subject too: 'But you knew about the potion! That means you stole the book!'

'We were friends, I told you!'

I didn't believe him. Perhaps I could have got more out of him, but at that moment everyone fell silent and I found out the purpose of the party: Caterina was getting married to Dubois. Judging by their faces, it was clear that the guests knew what they were there for. I was the only one left out of the secret. It was partly because in the last few days I hadn't been home much, but even so, the fact that I hadn't been told was a betrayal.

That night I couldn't get a wink of sleep. I liked Caterina, but I liked Dubois too, and in my dreams a faint longing for the Frenchman had taken shape. In those days, a married man was lost to me. He could no longer be of any use. Even if he got divorced, it didn't count, he was like a used coat. For this reason, I didn't pay attention to the other events of the evening, even though I stayed a long time in the salon, watching with indifference the mouths guzzling the various dishes, including the bread with mushrooms, and waiting for it to bring to the surface the little ghosts hidden in their souls.

### The Brothers

In the chill of the autumn morning, with the weather deteriorating, I woke up with thoughts of death and disaster. There was no one in the house. The frost on the windows looked like butterfly wings. In Zăval's house it was cold. I usually went in the morning, lit the fire, and then went back to the Greceancă's for a few hours.

My trial was progressing with difficulty. I didn't even know what it was about any more. And as for the houses—what can I say? They still hadn't been found, and I don't think the cook really had a clue. I wasn't fulfilling the potential that Maxima had dreamed of. It was abundantly clear that I would remain a person of no significance, and that my real name would be covered with shame. It was a good thing no one knew who I was!

That morning some merchants whom Caterina knew well presented themselves at her house: *Fraţii*—'The Brothers'. In fact their name was Frăţila. They were respectable and they had known Zăval. One of them had a son whom he envisaged being married to me. Caterina was optimistic, and told me not to worry:

'As long as I live, no one's going to take you from here!'

On the other hand, I didn't much feel like sharing the house in which she would be living with Dubois.

Burchioiu had stayed on in Bucharest, because his father hadn't finished his business, and in my depressed state at that time, he had become the only person with whom I had anything to talk about.

As I was saying, the Brothers were in the house, and they were being very nice to me, although we all knew that it was not about me, but about Zăval's wealth and the houses in Murta Street that I had not been able to find. The Brothers had the faces of sick hens.

'The girl can come round to our house some day, for us to get to know one another,' they were saying, as if I wasn't even present.

'She might choose a dress from our shop, something a bit more...'

'More what? What's wrong with my dress?' I started asking one of the brothers, who looked at me out of just one eye, the way hens do when you feed them.

My yellow dress was my dearest possession. Not even Caterina had managed to make me replace it. In fact, in the course of time, I have had two dresses that I loved: a striped one, without which I never set out on a journey, and the yellow dress, which I have already told you was a sort of vestimentary labyrinth. When I took it off, I was like prey, like a little chicken swept away by the wind. Without it, I was no one. And I still have it after all this time. Nowadays I put it on in days when I am sad because its velvet still pulsates with my confidence back then, my dreams and above all my desire for life. Consequently, there was no question of my choosing another out of the shop of those sleepy Brothers.

So, in the morning the Brothers came to visit, and shortly after I made my escape and almost ran to Zăval's house.

The door was open, and it was cold inside. Through the window I could see Father Ogaru, walking around the yard of the Church In-One-Day. It passed through my mind to call out to him, but the fact that I didn't like his face weighed more than my fear. I knew there was someone else in the house. I could see that the papers on the table had been disturbed. I looked around the salon and intended to go into the shop. I could feel the breath of Sator all around. I sensed that something wasn't right. Then I fell.

### Suicidal Revelations

That day, the whole of Bucharest was turned upside down by good deeds, for the *crumilla* had taken effect. Of the displays of generosity, many have gone down in history. Kostas took a great liking to Cirtă Vianu, perhaps because he was the first person to cross his path as he left Caterina's feast. He remembered that he had slashed his cheek, and this act, which, it is true, was not in the least laudable, began to weigh on his conscience, impelling him to redeem his guilt. Kostas embraced the guard, and that very night he gave him the sapphire that he wore in his ear. The next day he sent him gifts and money. On top of that, he took off his sable fur, from which he had been inseparable, and sent a deputation with it. Every hour someone knocked on Cirtă's door to bring him another gift from the Princely Palace.

Whoever had tasted of the *bag of spirits* did the same, giving away their most precious belongings, praising their enemies, basically seeking one way or another to show fraternity towards others. And among them, Dubois came off worst of all. Overcome by remorse and by the desire to escape his guilt, he confessed to the consul about the death of the marquis: the unfortunate combination of circumstances, the statue of the Virgin, the accidental discharge of the pistol. The story spread rapidly, especially as Dubois, full of regrets, was continually weeping and endlessly repeating the tale, omitting nothing. What had happened to him was unlucky. Perhaps that Gaston, whose defence he had taken, was a bearer of ill luck, a bringer of disaster. Perhaps Sator had come upon him. Basically, it was clear that it had been an evil hour, and there was no point in speaking of such a thing. For that very reason, no one could believe that poor Dubois was to be sent back to Paris, for the killing of the marquis.

Consul Fleury was a narrow-minded man, incapable of understanding the immensity of an evil hour. A few days later we went to the Consulate. Caterina chattered away in their language, while Burchioiu and I watched it all from a distance where we could get a good view of what was going on.

I can still recall today how we waited. In a window in the hall, our figures appeared in a fragmented way, so that it looked as if it was just my fez talking with his black hat.

'Whoever heard of punishing a man who has simply been unlucky?' I asked in wonder.

Fleury kept his face rigid. Caterina spoke and the consul gesticulated categorically, keeping his lips pursed.

'In the first place, the bringer of the bad luck should be sought,' Burchioiu whispered in my ear. He had heard the story for the first time and was convinced that there must be a guilty person somewhere.

And I thought he was right. There is always someone who brings unfortunate events in their wake, like a magnet. Sator himself comes to such a person, as to a nest of delights.

'I know a bringer of bad luck like that,' Burchioiu began.

Nothing tells you more about what someone is like than the story they tell you. The way they get into the story, the way they

182

raise their eyebrows bring to light not just who this person is, but *how* they would like to be. It shows you what their character is. A storyteller who wets their lips is vain, just as one who rolls their eyes so as not to lose a single listener is sneaky, believe me. And nor do I like storytellers who fix their eyes on one point, on the ceiling, for example, like the cook, as if begging for mercy. They act timid, but you have no idea what they are capable of! They want you to keep your eyes on them, making you believe that they will open some sort of door for you. Burchioiu was an honest storyteller, and I listened to him with pleasure. He might have been telling the story for me, not for himself, so at the end I had no idea whether he had wet his lips, where he had cast his eyes, or any of that. His bringer of bad luck was a little man with short legs, and as he described him, I felt I was beginning to like the man. But, because he carried a curse, the district turned against him, and drove him with stones to the edge of the town, from where some shepherds chased him further away, and in the same way he was mobbed from all directions, until he fell off a crag.

'All the same,' I remarked, 'why should you kill a man when it's not his fault he was born like that?'

'That's just what I meant!'

Burchioiu's face lit up with a beauty I had never seen in him: 'Massima,' he continued, 'used to say that there are foods that take away your bad luck. When someone is a bearer of bad luck or ugly for no reason,' he said, fixing his eyes on me, 'that shouldn't become a matter for others. He should take care of himself!'

'How?'

'By chewing horseradish roots!'

To judge by the way he was looking at me, that was what he had done. He was changed. I could already see the effects of the horseradish, which it would take a whole lifetime to tell you about. All I will say is that Burchioiu was right. Horseradish melts wickedness, heals guilt, and makes you loved, sometimes too much, for I have heard that its effects may be felt at two hundred *stânjeni*! He no longer seemed disagreeable to me.

While we were talking, Caterina was trying to break down Fleury's resistance, but, as I have said, the consul was incapable of changing his mind, and he had decided to send Dubois to Paris, to be thrown into some salt-mine or sent to the galleys. I never liked that Fleury. That's why I think he deserved his fate. Not even when Caterina had tried to explain the meaning of bad luck was he willing to understand. He was a mule.

## Crowned

The morning in which Dubois made his confession was the same morning I was knocked down.

Perhaps I hadn't lain for long on the floor. But when I came to, I was scared. In the house I could feel the breathing of Sator, and from my temple there was a trickle of blood. I was afraid to move, not that I didn't have the courage to fight with a thief, but lest I attract the attention of Sator, who was hovering over my little uncle's table like a raven. I knew for sure that it was him. In my blood a sort of bed of thorns had grown, which filled me with sorrow, and with restlessness. You must remember that Sator has no idea about all this; he just passes on his way, not realizing that all he touches is filled with weakness and distress. For this reason, if you feel a sorrow that seems to have fallen from the sky, don't attempt explanations! Don't take medicines! Don't lay the blame on imaginary lovers! You'd do better to get to work and gather the little wings that flutter around you, grab at least a few of them and harness them without scruples to your own needs. Sator doesn't know. He has no *soul*, and nor has he eyes for you. He is just a draft horse, a fly carried on the wind!

For an hour, perhaps longer, I remained motionless, until Burchioiu came in the door. I was lying on the floor, just as I had fallen, with one leg numb. When he knelt beside me, Sator disappeared, and in time I realized that my neighbour from Braşov, whom for so many years I had been unable to bear, this new Burchioiu, who looked at me with eyes of blue waters, had become not just bearable but reliable, which raised him to the dignity of the name of *Laurian*. For what is a name if not a sum of feelings poured over someone's head? There are so many people whose names you can't bring yourself to utter! You see them and you are filled with, for example, contempt, before you understand the delicate fabric woven out of the tenderness, the sorrows, and the worthlessness that lie at the foundations of any person.

In the thrill of that moment, after Sator had gone, I kissed for the first time. Laurian, the horseradish-eater, was my first love.

## The Many Faces of the Truth

It was not long before I was knocking on Perticari's door. I was convinced that it was he who had struck me. But the spiritist was sleeping. It was obvious that I had wakened him. He too had been touched by the *crumilla*.

'I haven't a penny left! I've paid all my debts!'

He was annoyed. Like all the others, he regretted his generosity. But in spite of that, he didn't seem bothered by our visit. He didn't know Burchioiu, but from the way he looked at him, I realized that he valued him for some reason.

'This is Laurian, from Braşov.'

The spiritist smiled. Taking advantage of this pleasantness, I got straight to the point: 'Very well! You weren't in Zăval's house, but you have been several times!'

He seemed impressed by the blow I had taken, which had left a lump. He had all sorts of salves, which made me think he was obsessed. Among them were those that I had given him. We both knew that he wouldn't use them again, but he kept them there, in a cupboard. He massaged the lump, then he brought us a bag of jellied fruit. He was eager to talk. He had known Zăval well, but he was not inclined to give details. It was his secret. From the way he drew in his coat, he seemed nervous. Or so I interpreted it.

'How did you know that the potion of ants cures you of laughter?'

At first Perticari didn't answer. Laurian was tucking into the jellied fruit.

'He told me about the *Book of Perilous Dishes*. I knew when he wrote it for the cook,' he admitted.

'But why?'

'He thought it might hasten Kostas's departure.'

'And he left the book with you?'

'No. He just told me what the remedies were. I really have no idea who killed him! But from the way things have turned out... it could be the hand of Kostas.'

The spiritist had in his eyes the look of a man in love. Today he still has the same look, which makes you believe him, and even more, love him.

'There is a witness who says that the killer was invisible,' I insisted.

Laurian, who sometimes still reminded me of Burchioiu, put down the bag with a little involuntary laugh, and the spiritist had a look of great confusion on his face. From the way he looked at me, it was clear that he had taken it as a joke.

'Only you are able to make yourself invisible!' I said accusingly.

'Ah, and for that reason you believe...'

Perticari swore that it had not been him, but that he was unwilling to tell me the secret of his trick.

Laurian had become curious and began to beg him. As I have said, Perticari had a sympathy towards him, which made him give way. In the end he gave a demonstration.

'This is for Laurian,' he said, as though I was only there to fill the space.

In the end he admitted that he had a cape made of Indian cloth, which, for a few moments, until the eyes grew accustomed, seemed one with the light in the room. And some slender sticks, which could smoulder sometimes for minutes on end.

After that visit, I could no longer suspect him of murder.


## In the Streets

I didn't find out about Dubois until the evening. Because that day, when good deeds were sprouting up all over the city, to the point of becoming a sort of threat, I set out to look for Murta Street, dragging the cook along with me. Two ducats was the price. When I showed him the money, Silică abandoned his pots and pans.

He wasn't really a bad man, just filled with a sort of arrogance that perhaps only I was irked by. He believed himself not only a good cook, which he was, I must admit, but the very lord of the cooking pot. When someone gets such ideas into their head, rust starts to show on their face. Whatever they may do, whatever talent they may have, they are left without followers, and before long people avoid them like some old object. In short, Silică was irritating, and not only did I bear with him all day, I even paid for the privilege.

He remembered a street near Lipscani Square. The worst of it was that he was absolutely sure of himself. We walked along various streets, each time stopping at some yellow houses. He swore with curses on himself and all his family that that was where the street was. We both knew that his family consisted only of his wife, which considerably reduced my trust in him.

'Perhaps if you tell me something more about Cuviosu's recipe book, I'll remember…'

'What more could I tell you, when you've already found out everything?'

Indeed the cook had tried all the recipes, and now he had questions. He wanted to know what *crumilla* did and above all to understand Kostas's generosity towards Cirtă Vianu. In a way he was trying to ingratiate himself with me, but he was also rather condescending:

'What did you do with my ladybirds, little mistress? Did they help you with anything?'

'I threw them away,' I said, checking out of the corner of my eye whether he realized I was lying.

The cook walked proudly, casting a glance up to the sky from time to time.

'So, do you still eat cockchafers, sometimes?' I teased him.

'I have no need, little mistress! But you most certainly have!'

The cook's whole face had changed. Exactly like the last time, when he had mentioned cockchafers, he was gentle, almost pleasant. All the same, I couldn't forget that he was the cook who prepared *perilous dishes* and who had locked me in that room! And now he wanted two ducats for a street that he boasted my little uncle had asked him to show me.

'Do you know where those houses are or don't you?'

The cook whispered to himself by my side, and at every movement the little bell sewn on his fez rang. It was clear that he was well-intentioned, but he couldn't remember. All the same, it was with him that I found Murta Street! We had been walking for a long time on it, a long street that cut behind some shops. The place had changed recently, because some blacksmiths had moved in. The houses were no longer there; you could see the site thoroughly cleared. The Covaci brothers, the owners of the smithies, proved quite happy to tell me all they knew: 'When we moved in here, Cuviosu Zăval had some carters at work. They were loading rubble into their carts.'

'But did you see him knocking down the houses?'

'I've told you, lady! When we came, whatever had been here was already demolished!'

The yard was wide and empty. There was not even a trace to be seen of fruit trees or vines. It was a waste ground. At the back of the yard, beside the fence, there was a lot of danewort, and for a moment I thought I saw the tail of a coat. But it was only a dog.

In the meantime the cook had disappeared, as if it was no longer worth his while to waste time with me, but a little later I heard the tinkle of his bell. He had reached the end of the street and I called to him. Beside him was a whitish carriage. The carriage from the night of the banquet. He could see me out of the corner of his eye—I could tell from the way he moved—but then a hand from inside the carriage opened the door for him and he climbed in. I was too disappointed at the loss of the houses to analyse any further, and I imagined that the cook was only interested in any clue that would lead him to the secrets in the *Book of Perilous Dishes*. For a moment it passed through my mind that perhaps he too was a Satorine, but I found that possibility... *ridicula*.

## 1829—The Present Time

### The Striped Dress

The rest of that day I had spent in the laboratory. The few objects in the room had lost their mystery, because I no longer had expectations. The mohair cat was Cuviosu's last gift, a ruby hidden in the belly of a cat. It wasn't even Sator's stone or something else of value. But even so, this was my only inheritance and I have always worn it. One year I lost it, and I ransacked the house. It had slipped down the back of the sofa in the salon, and when I found it, I was so afraid of losing it again that I sewed it to the pocket of a dress without which I never go on any journey.

Every time I put it on I feel complete. It gives me a good feeling, a feeling of being someone that everybody takes notice of. When I bought the silk, I knew almost all there is to know about Sator. I could wind him round my little finger, as the saying goes, for I had discovered his weakness for order and for straight lines. In olden times, some people used to draw a circle on the ground to defend themselves from danger. They believed in its magical power, not knowing that it is lines that Sator respects. When he comes upon a line, he stops, hypnotized. He feels it. I don't know why, but it's as if I can hear the beat of his heart for a moment. Although that's absurd! Sator has no heart. But he has a way of sniffing, of feeling things, and among these things, lines simply paralyse him. He stops motionless, like someone who has to catch their breath. And if he comes upon a circle, he moves for hours round its edge, like the little thread of air left after a whistle. He is a gentle breeze, a dance of smoke.

My dress, of good silk, is crossed by stripes, which form part of the weave. Although they are thin, these lines give firmness to the material, for they are of linen and cotton. Especially because of the linen, the cloth seems stiff. When I discovered it, Sator was already snoozing in its stripes. The sunlight fell on the shimmering silk, and the merchant had been hunting me down with his eye even before I crossed the threshold.

Perhaps the straight line provides Sator the illusion of perspective. It promises him something. Otherwise why would he remain thunderstruck like a snake lying parallel to the threshold? Curves make him curious. But when he comes upon squares, he falls into a state of powerlessness that I call sleep. If I shake the folds, Sator is an alert dog. I can make him go to one side or the other just by twirling my skirt. If the lines crinkle or break, he loses interest; he's gone. But most of the time I don't bother him. We go walking together. He is of no use to me. He doesn't help me, but nor does he attack me—as I used to think in the old days he might. He is just the shadow in my skirt.

This morning I have put on my striped dress. I am ready for the road. It has two wide pockets, in which I can hold a lot of things. On one of them I have sewn the mohair cat, which, despite the passage of time, is still woolly and soft. Perhaps it is no longer as white as it was at first, but its green eyes still shine, the way a drop of water glimmers on a mulberry leaf. It is a cat ready for a fight, with its back arched and its tail raised. I have always liked mohair because it is light and silky. In comparison with cashmere, it is better aired. It lets the wind pass through it, but only just enough to cool you on a summer evening. My little uncle edged it with silk thread, in such a way that the mohair is widened on the paws, making room for the stuffing. Sometimes I stroke my cheek with it, to remind me of Maxima's hand or the even more distant hand of my mother. This cat has for many years guarded my pocket like a janitor. Whether by chance or not, Sator has never gone into it. When he reaches the cat, he disappears as if someone had swallowed him. I know, I could be mistaken, just as I have been mistaken so many times.

The striped dress holds Sator as if he were a perfume.

In Lipscani, I pick up Bina's Arnauts and signal to the coachman to set off. My first stop will be at Braşov. But until then I have my memories. Where was I? At Murta.

## 1798—Thirty Years Ago

### Dreams

I no longer had anything to look for. Our houses were no longer there. But why should my little uncle have demolished them? Perhaps somewhere in the yard there was still a trapdoor opening into some cellar, some tunnel. Or perhaps Zăval had used Sator to move them somewhere or other, to the ends of the earth. But how could I believe in such madness, when I was proving unable to do all that both he and Maxima had promised me?

At the first opportunity I asked Ogaru if he knew anything about my little uncle's carriage. The priest no longer had time for me since I'd stolen his little box, but he still hadn't asked me outright if I was in any way guilty of the theft. All the same, if I started a conversation with him, he would chat away, for he was one of those people who need to keep talking or they fall sick.

He hadn't seen my little uncle's carriage for a long time.

'He might have given it away.'

'But how did he go about town?' I insisted.

'In it.'

'Perticari, the *pitar*? Did he visit him often?'

Ogaru looked suspiciously at me, to oblige me to beg him, but, when he saw that I wasn't going to give up, he answered: 'The *pitar* doesn't go out much. More often others visit him. There are always plenty of carriages in front of his house.'

Perticari's house is in Lipscani Square, not far from Murta Street. Indeed there are carriages in front of the gates. It intrigued me back then what great trust some people put in his words. If the *pitar* dreamed something, everybody knew. But for this to happen, he had to tell someone! How did everyone find out so quickly? It seems to me that a person capable of filling the city with rumours is someone of great value. They are a creator. Their words move at matchless speed. And don't imagine that they just spread from ear to ear! Such a person chooses a few, not very many, whom they pretend to consider the most trust-worthy, in order to pour a capital secret into their funnel. And this forger of History always has a public mask, someone with a story of their own, someone like Perticari. But as to who the great rumour-monger was behind the spiritist—I had no idea!

Not long before, Perticari had dreamed about the killer of my little uncle, which had caused a great stir. On the basis of his description, a man had been caught. The principal detail was his broad face! For all the feebleness of the description, no one had doubted that the criminal had been captured, and after a night in the town prison, he had confessed to fourteen murders. He wasn't actually a Serb, as Perticari had said at first, but he had been an Arnaut at one time, and that weighted the scales against him.

I went into the courtyard. Perticari's gate was never closed, and his house had a number of entrances, so that there was no way you would meet his other guests. His courtyard was paved with stones, like a ballroom. In the stables could be seen a blue carriage, with the spiritist's blazon, a golden circle. He received me in a small salon. He was in a hurry.

'How come you dreamed of the killer?'

'I dream sometimes,' he replied with that beguiling smile.

'Do you take something?'

Perticari's eyes continued to sparkle with happiness.

'And what are you able to do?' he asked me.

He wanted to know more about me, because Zăval had praised me. And he had questions.

'What is your Satorine name? Are you Rozica?'

Fortunately I had the answer prepared, or I wouldn't have known what to say. Maxima had thought of a meeting like this.

'I am merely a *vigilax* of dreams. I haven't managed to learn very much.'

'So that's why you're interested in my dreams!'

He seemed relaxed, but also disappointed. That day he had painted his nails red, which gave him a slightly sensual air. Perhaps he was not all that clever, but he was a very sensitive man.

'Do you raise crows like your mother?'

I immediately nodded, and my mind was filled with black wings. In my childhood, our houses were covered with crows. Their hearts are good for first class dreamers, who after every night grow younger instead of fading away. Of course, not just any crow is good! Only those that have been fed on wheat that has lain for forty days in fruit brandy. And not just any fruit brandy either, but only one made from sweet ungrafted apricots, in which all sorts of herbs have been kept, from plantain to melilot, plus a sprig of thyme, which lifts any tiredness from the chest. Once the crows have got used to this drunken wheat, their hearts are taken out while they are still alive. How many times have you seen a crow lying dead in the fields with its feet in the air, but not known that its heart was missing from its little breast? For after it has been cut out, this bird that lives only to watch over the darkness enclosed in the mind of man, this delicate bird, so eager to speak, is thrown without its heart out in the sun, sometimes on a side ridge or on a wide field. It is for this reason that I hate crows' heart stew, although Maxima made me enter it in the *Book of Perilous Dishes*, in memory of my mother, she said, whom in the meantime I had forgotten anyway.

'What happened to Zăval?' I asked, making my voice gentler. 'I don't believe he was killed by that man you said you dreamed about.'

Perticari was ready to accept this too. It didn't interest him anymore: 'I don't know, Pâtca! I dreamed about him. More than that I don't know. Perhaps you want to wait by me, to be *vigilax* for me.'

'Do you know other Satorines in the city?'

Perticari shook his head, and then admitted: 'Sometimes I even doubt the existence of Sator!'

'Haven't you ever met him?

'Never!'

All the same, I could feel his presence.

# CHAPTER VII

# THE RED CAPE

### Sator Exists

Sator returned to me that very evening, and then day after day for several weeks on end, and they were the toughest days I had ever experienced. All my efforts to control him with my thoughts achieved nothing. When I heard about Dubois, I thought all night about how to get him out of the Consulate, where I imagined him bound in chains or even being beaten. Every time Sator passed through me, he found nothing but this thought. And you know how it is: when you think a lot about something, it changes everything about you, even your blood.

That was when I began to tell Caterina about Sator. She listened to me in her refined manner without commenting.

'Do you believe me?'

Not only did she believe me, she began to talk to me, the way you would reveal yourself to an equal: 'When my father died, I was your age. And as he left a fortune, robbers jumped out from all directions. And not just common thieves, Pâtca, but the sort who go around with their noses in the air, covered by papers and most of the time indignant at the existence of theft, refined people from high society, cultivated and full of moral principles.

Sparks leapt from Caterina's eyes. I can still see her: she sat on the sofa covered with a travelling rug, like a furious child.

'Important people, from the princely retinue, had decided my fate for me, and they considered that the best place for me was a nunnery.'

For a few minutes, Caterina gave me a sketch of life in the nunnery. I would have imagined anyway that it was hard, but after she had described it, the blood in my head filled with locusts. Snakes slithered through the cells, and the nuns breathed flames from their noses.

'To cut a long story short, the Metropolitan had already signed the papers. The fortune came under the management of some crafty swindlers, and as for me, someone was going to take me off to a nunnery in Vâlcea. That was when Cuviosu Zăval turned up. The carriage had gone out through the gate, and it was the month of May in Bucharest. The streets were laden with cherries and peonies, and I was weeping enough tears for three pairs of eyes. When I turned my head, there was Cuviosu sitting on the seat of the carriage. You remember him! With those eyes of his that approved good deeds. 'You're not going anywhere!' he assured me. 'Don't worry! Did your father tell you about Sator?' That's exactly what he asked me. I couldn't remember ever having heard anything of the sort. I was astonished, and I think out of fear I said he had. 'Very good,' he smiled. 'Now you're going to see him put to work for the first time!' Cuviosu took out a knife and threw his head back. We went like that almost as far as the Mogoşoaia Road. I must confess that, seeing him like that, with his eyes upside down, I was scared to death. But after a few minutes, the carriage turned round, although he said nothing to the coachman. For a moment I had visions of being sold to the Turks, but it was not long before we returned to the same courtyard that we had left. When we stopped beside the stable, Zăval seemed like another man. On his face I could read his happiness. He smiled at me, opened the door of the carriage, and made a sign to me to get out. 'No one will upset you again,' he said, and that was how it turned out. The documents the Metropolitan had signed and that I had seen with my own eyes had, quite simply, disappeared. A wave of forgetting passed through the minds of the former thieves. When I met one of those who had wanted to rob me, he just beamed at me, remembering nothing. Zăval was my guardian until my marriage, but he never did anything without asking me. One winter's evening he told me that my father had been an adept manipulator of this Sator. He knew I had lied to him, but he did not reproach me, and he never mentioned it again. In my mind, Zăval remained the most significant person for me. He was a wizard, I realized, but a high-class one. Perhaps he had God on his side, but he most certainly had the Devil!

Caterina's testimony did me good and left me with many questions. Her father had been a Satorine, but he had said nothing to her, probably because he wished to protect her from a life that he surely couldn't have liked. Why else? Or perhaps not everyone was made for him.

'Have you ever felt Sator?'

Caterina didn't really know what I meant. She thought Sator was a kind of demon, to which wizards prayed.

'And you think your father was a wizard?'

She was convinced that the fortune of the Greceanu family came from ancient times, when a spirit had shown them the site of a treasure.

That night Cîrtă came looking for her, and I realized that she wanted to pay some soldiers to take Dubois to her estate. It remained to be seen if he would agree. Probably that was the way. Although I had not one drop of trust in Cîrtă. How can you entrust your safety to a bandit? On top of that, Dubois didn't seem the type to spend the rest of his life on an estate, where you could be sure the lice would bite!

Two days later, Cîrtă brought a letter from Dubois. I went down to the hall and I caught a few words that gave me pleasant dreams:

'Tomorrow we'll take him to the estate. No one will look for him there!'

So he had agreed. I could already see Fleury, with his tight little snout, flying into a rage.

### The Séance

My meetings with Perticari were more and more frequent, and, contrary to his custom, he came to see me in Zăval's house, where, he said, we might invoke his spirit.

'We must go down into the cellar,' he said one day. 'Zăval had a room there with a secret entrance.'

I couldn't tell him about the Laboratorium. But, in my foolishness at the time, I agreed we could call up his spirit, despite the fact that a significant part of me doubted the existence of any spirit. Moreover, the cook turned up by my ear one day, whispering, in his very mysterious way: 'How are you with numbers, little mistress?'

As soon as I heard mention of numbers, it made me think about the ladybirds and the experiment I had been unable to carry to its end. But in spite of that, I did what the spiritist wanted. I was glad to have Laurian by my side.

Perticari lit five candles—not just any candles, but ones that I myself had moulded from wax and viper's bugloss, which makes you dream of the future. Laurian remained standing, and I sat on a chair, facing the *pitar*. He was wearing a white fez, and his lips were strongly coloured. A little smoke floated in the room. I recognized it later. It was *vericola*. He wanted to be sure that I spoke the truth. The only thing I could do would be to swallow an elder flower, but I was afraid he would notice. I should have found a pretext and gone out. I glanced at Laurian and realized he had fallen asleep. Perticari knew many things. He had cast open-eyed sleep over him.

The invocation was short and then he began to speak, filling me with horror to the very bones. He had the voice of my little uncle. Even though I knew well that it was the spiritist talking, I was convinced that Zăval was there beside us. I expected him to ask me my name, and I realized that I wouldn't be able to refuse. But the first question was one I hadn't expected.

'Tell me, Pâtca, who are the twins?'

As soon as I heard the question, I had no more doubts. Perticari was quite alone. My little uncle would never have asked me such a thing. As I couldn't hide, I began to tell the *Tale of the Twins*, the way that I knew it from Maxima and that even Laurian knew. And when I came to Anatol the Delicate, I was taken by a familiar smell, of fine cooking. In the pocket of his anteri, Perticari was holding a knife for Sator, even though he had told me he knew nothing. I finished the story, but the spiritist was convinced that there was a potion of the twins. He insisted, with the voice of Cuviosu Zăval, but to judge by his confidence, it was clear that the poor man had been fed a pack of lies.

'There is no such potion,' I told him, filled with the fever of truth.

'Do you know for sure?' he asked, raising his voice, and from that moment I felt the breath of Sator.

I don't know what Sator wanted to do, but I was scared. The table shifted and I had the feeling that perhaps I might have moved it, because Perticari too looked scared. Luckily at that moment, Ogaru knocked on the window, and as the priest got on the nerves even of the spiritist, Perticari hurried away quickly.

### *Cum putridis dentibus*

In the city, all was quiet. Kostas seemed to be tired or satiated, especially since Bina had left for Stamboul to dig his grave. And yet that day had an ominous, expectant air about it. I awoke with a deep apathy—the feeling that nothing was worth doing that morning. There are days like that in which you have the impression that it is better to wait, even though there is no reason. You are not enfeebled, just cautious. And it seemed as if everyone shared this prudence of mine. In the morning I took a walk around the courtyard, where the stableman was getting a carriage ready for Dubois. Cirtă Vianu's men were waiting at the Turkish *khan*. But to judge by their faces, something was not right.

Then I met Laurian, whom I no longer called Burchioiu. His father was thinking of taking over my little uncle's shop, and he would have liked to have visited Caterina, who for the time being was in charge of all my wealth. The thought of meeting that man gave me bad presentiments. I had just prepared myself to lie about how busy Caterina was freeing Dubois, hoping to postpone the meeting, when across the city the watchmen began to yell into their horns.

Everyone stopped where they were. It was the hour of noon. Out of all the dizzying uproar, I could only understand that it was something about the Greceancă. Something had happened to her. Then I understood each word perfectly.

I raced home. She was sitting on the sofa in the salon. I saw her hand first, then her face—and what I saw shocked me. Her mouth, ennobled by that proud crease, was covered in foam. She had died in agony. Her suffering could be read on her face, and my heart, which had never been fair to her, began to crack like glass touched by fire.

I scanned the room. Not far away was the table of delights, where a spoonful of sherbet lay forgotten in a glass, and beside it the drink. Darkness had fallen in the room, and I wanted nothing more than to die by her side. The bottle she had drunk from was that bottle from my first night. I recognized it by its size and by its colour, for it had no stopper. The housekeeper had bought the bottle from the grocer and, charmed by the stopper, had changed it.

Caterina had been poisoned. Like *the giraffe of Arabia*, as Zăval had written. Her teeth had fallen out. They say that life is unfair. Sometimes it is unbearable. She had died alone, without Dubois, without ever seeing him again. Without his knowing anything.

When they say that death only takes good people, it is not just a saying to comfort the bereaved. The cruelties of death are without limit. Once a man found an injured gnome in the forest. The little fellow was shivering under a red mantle. The man took him in his arms and cared for him for many days, even though the patient was full of demands. He wouldn't lift a finger himself, but he tyrannized his rescuer, criticizing his services or requesting things that the man could only procure with difficulty. He complained about whatever he was given to eat, and blamed the man for anything that displeased him. When the pretentious gnome got better, the man found out that he was Death, who had begun to cut right and left without feeling any pity. Of course, not even his rescuer was spared. Death with his fiery cape, arrogant and cold as an ice floe, kills all that appears in his way, without choice, without plan. Don't imagine that he has some list or some god that sends him through the world. Death is nothing but a heartless gnome who was pitied once by someone. And Caterina had the misfortune to be in his path.

Out of all my losses, this was the most unfair. And in time this feeling has grown in intensity. It was I that killed her. I let that bottle wander through Bucharest. It was because of me that Caterina died.

Beside the sofa was the letter, Dubois's last letter, which I have kept for a long time and which I have now taken with me.

## 1829—The Present Time

### On the Way to Vienna

Tomorrow I arrive in Vienna. I haven't felt like writing lately. My memories of Caterina's death have taken away the inclination. It is only today that I am returning to this notebook, which probably no one will read. What things can happen on a journey like this! Through the window I can see the Arnaut's calf bouncing up and down as we go. What would the soldier say if he knew what I am writing? But what if he does know? We often look with contempt at the heels of the soldiers who accompany us, judging them en masse. To judge by his appearance, he is over thirty. I can't refrain from asking: 'How old were you when the Greceancă died?'

'About seven, I think...'

'And do you remember her?'

Fortunately he's a talkative one, indeed actually keen to stand out. He moves away a little, so as to see me better without having to bend down.

'Of course, my lady,' he replies respectfully. 'I remember everyone dragging things out of the Greceanu house.'

I listen to him talking and I see his hands on his horse's harness, fingers rather fat and white. On one of them he has a ring, probably from his wife or sweetheart, or simply taken from some man he killed.

'But do you remember her? Do you still know what she looked like?'

'Not really. I know she was murdered. But as for seeing her, I only saw her flying past in her carriage. In those days I used to sit by the roadside and throw stones at the carriages. But I remember you, ma'am, the way you went about in a town carriage with a band painted around it and the Greceanu arms on the box at the back—an eagle and a lion holding a great bouquet of flowers. Sometimes I saw you leaning out of the windows of the carriage, whistling like one of the boys.

'But what about the Greceancă? What do you remember? Do you know about when her cook was taken...?

'For a long time my mother, poor thing, may God pardon her, wore a pair of slippers that she said used to be the Greceancă's. Who knows if it was true! Green slippers, of good leather. In the end I made a catapult out of them, and I was very proud of it!'

We are approaching Vienna. As the carriage flies along, I can see the Danube and I can hear a deep-pitched horn. The Arnauts spread out around me, and Sator passes through my skirts. Floating in the middle of the river is a white palace. I've never seen anything like it. Smoke is coming out of the roof through a thick pipe. If there is anything after death, it ought to be something like this, a floating beehive, from which the souls emerge from time to time to accompany Sator.

Strange that both I and this guard have kept a pair of Caterina's shoes. Of all the things worn by a person, their footwear preserves best their spirit. Every time my eyes fall on those shoes, I can see her alive. I see them climbing into carriages, sticking out like bean-pods from under her skirts, padding up the wide staircase of the Greceanu house. But all these memories lead in the end to her death and to that world being smashed to smithereens. For after she was gone, the weeks that followed were even rougher.

## 1798—Thirty Years Ago

### After She Was Gone

Dubois came round that very evening. He was pale and distraught. I remember him at her funeral, leaning on Fleury, who didn't look so well himself either. The whole city had come out into the streets, and there was no one who didn't mourn her. Even Captain Mârcă was yelling like a madman beside the bridge, so his coat was shaking on him. And all who saw him began to lament even more than he did. All the neighbourhoods were filled with pain and sorrow. Even death caused hearts to beat and yearn for change. When the cortege arrived at the Palace, Kostas came out onto the balcony and set his trumpeters to blow for minutes on end.

Then the stream of people began to jeer and to yell. There was no one in Bucharest who was not convinced that she had died on his orders. And when the people of Bucharest come out into the street, whatever a prince says turns to dung. Even Perticari had dreamed that the cook had been brought into Caterina's kitchen not for a reconciliation but to poison her. His dream had passed through every mouth, and in the end someone had put it into verses, which even today break my heart with the cruelty of the tale they tell. Inexplicably, Perticari's dream brought in Cat o' Friday too, making her a spirit nestling in the dark soul of Kostas. There were also some who believed that Caterina's husband, the one who had been killed by a wasp, had summoned her to him.

Apart from me, I don't think anyone knew the truth.

I can't remember anything else about the day of the funeral except that I was thinking of killing myself, imagining dozens of ways in which I could put an end to it all.

For the first few days I slept in the Laboratorium. When a person is at rock bottom and there is nothing to keep them alive anymore, even when they have no reason left to go on breathing, something still turns up, a shaft of light, perverse and strengthening. It is for this very reason that suicide is listed as a sin.

A few days after Caterina's funeral, Kostas confiscated her entire fortune. She had no heirs, only some distant relatives. Even the contents of the house were put up for auction, and the Gypsies, including the cook's wife, were taken by force to the market. If I had been there, they would probably have sold me too. Especially as I no longer had anyone to stand up for me. The sofa on which Caterina died was dragged out into the street, and soldiers decked their beloveds with the jewellery that she had once worn.

Now no one had any doubt about Kostas's guilt. Wherever you went in the city, you could hear details about how he had killed her, and even to this day there are those who believe that he was the killer. Meanwhile in the Palace Chronicle there is a list of the people that Kostas killed, and Caterina is at the top of the list.

# The Slave Market

The cook was yelling. Once so confident in his powers, he was now like a dirty cap thrown down by a fence. The slave market was in a valley, and all-around people were watching as if they had come to see a dancing bear. Most of the slaves were Gypsies, brought in from estates, runaways, or, in the present case, being auctioned off, at low prices. The cook's wife was in a cart with bars, and she was calling to her husband by his name. Silică had begged at the Palace, and perhaps word had got as far as Kostas, but it was to no avail. In such situations, you wonder how a ruler can be so cruel. But most of the time, terrible things happen not because the person in control doesn't know the story, but because they haven't heard it as they should.

The carts headed towards Giurgiu, leaving the sound of wailing behind them. Through the bars you could see nothing but mouths howling. Silică's fez had rolled in the grass, and the little bell that he was so proud of was glinting in the harsh autumn sunlight. The cook felt guilty and kept repeating to anyone who would listen that he had opened the door to the real guilty person, who was Cat o' Friday. And the spiritist backed him up, so that many people had started to talk about the *Book of Perilous Dishes* too.

'Cuviosu Zăval is to blame! He put the book in my hand, and since that moment everything has gone to pieces!'

He looked at me with miserable eyes, which he seemed not even to have the strength to cast upwards, as he used to do.

I had thought he didn't care at all about his wife. But over time I have seen that many men who are never at home, who spend their time seeking pleasure with their mistresses, seemingly casting their wives aside like dirty dishcloths, are, in a crisis, capable of jumping into fire for them. And in the case of the cook there was more to it than that. He didn't just feel guilty because he hadn't been able to save her, but he had got it into his head that my recipe book had invoked a demon. With every dish he prepared, he was convinced that he had also brought into the city the dreadful being that Cat o' Friday was for him. The cover, with its drawing of a cat, had encouraged him in this belief, but in reality, it was Perticari who had put it into his head. For years people have talked about Cat o' Friday, to the point that I too began to think of her as a figure with no connection to me. Whenever I recall someone from the reign of Kostas, Cat o' Friday turns up too.

Miserable and full of regrets, the cook had begun to let his food burn.

By the side of the road, crows had gathered, and to me it seemed that they were bringing a sign from Maxima. But the evil was not yet over. The red mantle of death hovered over the city.

## Napoleon

A few days later Bina came back. He hadn't got as far as Stamboul. The Kapudan Pasha had filled him in on what he was to do. And for everything that happened after that, Napoleon was the one to blame. It was through him that the real terror started. The city buzzed with the news that Napoleon Bonaparte's arrival in Egypt had enraged the Sultan.

Ismail Bina took his men, including the ever-present Cirtă, and entered the French Consulate. Fleury was taken out in chains. People had gathered in the streets, and Rigas's Greek's were chanting furiously:

> *Zito hi filoghenia!*
> *Zito hi adelfe Galia!*

Then they repeated in Romanian:

> *Long live love of nation!*
> *Long live our sister France!*

The streets were packed. Bina, with his look of a man who was simply doing his duty, escorted Fleury to Lipscani Square. Bound in chains and without his coat, the consul had completely lost his sense of dignity. Then they brought out Dubois too. He was unrecognizable. His face was swollen from weeping and his hair clung to his temples.

Despite all the protests in the streets, the two Frenchmen remained under guard.

I gathered together all the strength I could muster in myself and summoned Sator, wishing with all my heart to save Dubois. Word was that the Frenchmen would be imprisoned at Yedikule, in Stamboul, and then sold to the galleys. It didn't matter that they were diplomats. For the Turks, they had become enemies. Few people now remember what consequences Napoleon's campaign had here. But back then, in the reality of that autumn, the French general had become a sort of executioner. There was not a street corner where you wouldn't hear his name, to the point that I too saw him as a sort of eagle threatening to take the Sultan in his beak. Despite all the hopes that Napoleon would make mincemeat of the Turks, no one knew how to rescue our own Frenchmen from the Consulate.

First of all I went to Bina and tried offering him some money. In his characteristic dispassionate manner he swore at me in Turkish and made a sign to me to clear off.

Then I looked for Cîrtă Vianu. His eyes were red. He looked ill, like someone who has gone for nights without sleep.

'My heart breaks for the Greceancă!' he said. 'She didn't deserve such an end!'

Forgetting for a moment who he was talking to, he recalled how she had helped him in the past: 'If it hadn't been for her, I would have ended up a slave or thrown across the Danube!'

Caterina had ransomed him from some Serbs.

'That's exactly why we have to save Dubois!'

'You think we don't want to? Even His Excellency, Ismail Bina, would like to see him released! But it can't be done, young lady, believe me! This time we really have no way: it's an order from the Sultan, and the Kapudan Pasha has promised to bring the Frenchmen before him. If that doesn't happen, we're all dead! And not just us, but all these folk chirping today on the banks of the Dâmbovița!'

At a glance we could both view the street that descended to the river. No one was singing; there were no happy voices. That morning nothing could be heard but a low grumbling and the odd master calling a servant's name.

'At least let me see him one more time!'

'Don't even think about it!'

All the same, Cirtă wasn't a bad man. Towards noon that day I managed to see Dubois. He looked drained and his eyes had lost their alertness. He sat huddled by the door in what had been his chancery. There was no time to waste, for Cirtă had given me just a minute.

There was no point in asking how he felt. Obviously he was destroyed.

'Do you want to die?'

He raised his eyes towards me. He was interested. He immediately grabbed the bottle, which still kept the warmth of my pocket.

'Swallow it all!' I urged him.

### The Final Attempt

Zăval's yard was deserted, as usual. I found the knife stuck in the apple tree, where I had put it. I took a few boxes of black powder too, but at the gate I bumped into Ogaru the priest. Even though I was in a hurry, he was in the mood for talking:

'Listen, if you don't wear that shawl, I'd like you to give it back to me!'

I didn't know what shawl he was talking about.

'The one I gave you, that belonged to my *preoteasă*...'

I had no idea what I had done with it either. But Ogaru wanted it right then, just when I really had to go.

In the end I got clear of him and began to hang around by the Consulate. Dubois was still inside, but the building was guarded. I sat for a long time in my carriage, thinking of Sator. Thinking of Caterina too. I saw the rescue of Dubois as a sort of duty towards her.

I got out of the carriage. I took small steps, intending to get close to the first soldier and scatter some black powder all around. Through the windows of the Consulate no movement of any kind was to be seen. An Arnaut came out through the door, but initially I didn't take any notice of him. I considered that, even if Sator was of no use to me, at least I could envelope the street in smoke. Then I saw that the Arnaut was heading straight in my direction. The next moment I recognized him: it was Dubois, in the costume that he had received as a gift from Caterina. Everything went well until he got close to me. I could hear him. In fact, I heard him saying my name. However, the soldiers weren't dozing either. One of them called out in Turkish and immediately they fell on Dubois from behind.

My carriage was quite far away, and on top of that, it was as if someone had tied me up. I didn't know what to do. I couldn't even move. I looked at Dubois, who was trying to run away, but in the madness of that morning, he was heading in the opposite direction to the carriage. I went after him, and behind me I could hear the pounding of the soldiers' feet. Now and then they swore and called out for someone to stop us. I couldn't stop myself from casting a glance behind me. Cirtă had come out of the Consulate, with the face of someone who hadn't slept. In his hand he had a flintlock, which made me hasten my steps.

And then the cook appeared! I don't know how it happened, but while everyone else was staring from a safe distance, the cook came right towards us. He was dashing along in a cart with the reins in his hand, without the little coachman who usually accompanied him. I called to Dubois, who immediately grasped what I wanted, and the next moment we both grabbed hold of the cart as it passed and heaved ourselves on. Dubois was grinning, with unquenchable enthusiasm. My potion had taken effect. Hemp mixed with a drop of wine always cuts off any dark thoughts at the root. And there was also cat's blood. I had never tried this *philtrum* on anyone before, but I can say that it had made Dubois almost a whole man. Only that he was smiling a bit too much.

The cook went straight ahead, taking no notice of us. Not that he hadn't seen us, but because he was lost in thought. Since Kostas had sold his wife, he wasn't cooking any more, but had taken to roaming the streets.

We were approaching a guarded bridge, so I made a sign to Dubois to hide among the baskets in the cart. Along the way there were groups of people. Some of them had seen the Frenchman, and now they were running to see if he would be caught.

The captain of the bridge was quite a well-known character around the town because he was always jovial.

'Where are you off to, Silică?' he asked.

'Looking for some chubby lentils, captain sir.'

'Seems they've arrested the Frenchies…'

'That's right!' chipped in some idlers standing by, who were looking curiously at the baskets to see if the Frenchman would be found out.

'I don't know anything about that, sir,' replied the cook, who was completely absorbed in his own dreams.

'Take care, Silică,' said the captain. 'The road's crawling with Turks and other foreigners!'

A multitude of voices were raised in approval, and a big fat fellow winked at me provocatively, which brought the blood rushing to my cheeks.

We kept silent to the other end of the bridge. Then we began to beg Silică to take the road to Braşov.

'Do you know who I am?' Dubois asked him, still unimaginably merry.

The cook cast a glance at him and replied with no emotion that he knew: 'You're Duba, the Frenchman!'

'I want to get to Braşov. Do you know where Braşov is?'

Silică couldn't care less where the Frenchman wanted to go: 'I'm not going to Braşov.'

I broke in and tried to explain the situation. He was going to be in trouble anyway for taking us in his cart.

'If you like, come with me,' offered Dubois 'To France! I have a palace as big as Kostas's. I'll give you money, a lot of money! Will you come?'

'No.'

'Why not, Silică? You'll be able to redeem your family,' I tried.

'I'm the cook of the Princely Court, little mistress! His Highness redeemed me from the mistress. He gave her two Gypsies in exchange for me!'

Through the cook's cart the ghost of Caterina drifted for a moment, and the cloud of guilt forced itself into my heart. I was afraid that Dubois would fall again into the bile of sorrow, so I lifted the tone: 'How much longer do you think Kostas will be on the throne? To hell with that Greek!'

Dubois had fallen into thought, but for the cook it didn't matter: 'And so what if he goes? Another prince will come! They always do!'

We went on a bit further, listening to the rattling of the cart. Then Dubois started to speak in Romanian, struggling to pronounce the words: 'What do you want most of all? What would you really, really like to do?'

'To find chubby lentils, sir. For din-dins,' he said, gesticulating at the same time to make it easier for the Frenchman to understand.

Then he took a paper from his breast, on which were drawn some beans that back then I had never seen before. Dubois knew what they were: 'Of course, I know. I've eaten them too. Come with me to France and I'll give you nothing but those! Hey, will you come?'

The cook had no intention of going in our direction and turned off beside a pond. So I began to beg him: 'Please, Silică! Please understand: if he doesn't get to Brașov, he's as good as dead!'

He continued to go straight ahead, giving no sign that he was interested. I fingered the knife in my pocket, and at that moment I felt Sator. I was enveloped in a breath of warm wind, and my head filled with dreams. I imagined Dubois's house, full of beans and money.

'Silică! Come with me and you'll be free! Like the birds in the sky!' Dubois flapped his arms: 'Flap-flap! Do you want to be free?'

'No, sir! What would I do without a master? Walk the streets with an outstretched hand?'

'But is it better,' I took my turn to ask, 'to have an idiot for a master, like Kostas?'

'Princes come and go,' he replied stiffly. 'Cooks remain!'

Dubois seized the reins, trying to change direction, but the cook was adamant.

'I thought you liked me…'

'I do like you, but you're not my master…'

Dubois had got hold of the whip too, when two riders caught up with us. One was Cirtă, whose scar made him unmistakable, and the other was the strange character with spectacles, from whom he was inseparable. Both were yelling for us to hear. It was as if a devil had got into Dubois, and the cook was buzzing like a fly.

Above me, Sator was whirling. I gripped the knife in my hand, determined to jump at Cirtă's throat. And at this point my train of thought broke. The cook pulled the reins, and the cart headed for the pond. One wheel flew off. The last face I saw was Cirtă's, landing beside my shoulder.

## Parting

When I opened my eyes again I was lying in the muddy water, surrounded by tall reeds. On the bank I could see the cook, in a heap, and a little further off, the cart, with its wheels upwards. I bent over the cook and said his name. He wasn't dead, but nor did he have anything to say to me. Dubois was nowhere to be seen. Cirtă had vanished too. I ran straight to the Consulate, where nobody seemed to know very much.

It wasn't till the next day that I found out that the Frenchmen were on the Giurgiu road, on their way to Stamboul.

'And Dubois?' I asked.

'All of them!'

Ismail Bina had left with them. Later news came that they were imprisoned at Yedikule.

I began to go around seeking information, sometimes in Lipscani Square, sometimes at the Turkish *khan*. Not much was known. Fleury had left a trunk, which Kostas had promised to send to France. I don't believe he kept his word.

After the arrest of the Frenchmen, it was as if everything started to change. Kostas nearly died because of a stew, and the blame fell upon Silică, who the next day was moved to the sties, to prepare food for the pigs. Many believed that the cook had fallen into disgrace because of Perticari, who had dreamed that he was the poisoner of Caterina and the tool of Kostas. Others said that he had lost his talent because the Greek had set him to make poisons. As soon as someone becomes the butt of gossip, everyone pounces on them. Especially in such difficult situations. When things can't be put right anyway, everyone says their piece, just to feel a little better. Kostas, I well knew, was not guilty of Caterina's death, but it no longer mattered. He was now what Burchioiu had once been for me. Perhaps that was why the banishing of the cook caused such a big stir. The market was full of songs and tales about the fame of his dishes.

After a few weeks, word went about that the Frenchmen had been sold to the galleys. The news was brought by the cook's wife, whose return aroused great enthusiasm. Many believed it a miracle.

Ismail Bina had passed by a market in Ruse, and the woman had recognized him by his carriage, which was decorated with silks and tassels of an almost mustard yellow. Her new master had just started tattooing his name on her shoulder, and she was howling with pain when she saw the carriage and started to match her howls to it: 'O noble Ismail Bina! O worthy boyar! I'm the wife of Silică—the princely cook!'

Ismail Bina stopped, and the slave merchant ran straight up to him. Caught by surprise more than anything, Bina whispered a few words to him and continued on his way.

A few days later, the cook's wife arrived in Bucharest, igniting hearts that were already over-heated. More songs appeared, telling how she was the wife of such a famous cook. Moreover, Ismail Bina himself had become the saviour of the cook's wife, while the man who brought her to Bucharest, one of Bina's men, was, for a few hours, 'the great cook's wife's saviour's warrior'.

As it was Bina who had ransomed her, she spent the rest of her life at the Turkish *khan*, even though in the meantime the Sultan's envoy had forgotten all about her.

Although few people know it, the cook's last malefic dish was made for me.

### Liquamentum cum rubeta

Through all these events, Perticari was pestering me daily. It would not be long before he found out my name. The Laboratorium was for him a sort of redoubt that had to be taken. Despite all the pain of those days, I sent Laurian to look for frogs. He was sickened at the idea and he was afraid, but after various adventures we managed to catch some tree frogs.

*Liquamentum cum rubeta* or *tree-frog sauce* is an elixir of forgetting. I was glad that Zăval hadn't noted it in the book. All the same, this dish proved to me that it is one thing to know recipes and quite another to make them. The sauce calls for great patience. First, the tree frogs are left to dream in cabbage juice. Alongside them the meats are boiled, dozens of different meats, among them dove, quail, coot wings, turkey gizzards, guinea fowl necks. But other birds too, as varied and as small as possible. Only then are some vegetables boiled in the same water. It is strained, and the stock is kept cold for an hour. The most important part is the water in which the frogs have slept. Herbs are added to it, especially lemon balm and wild rose. But also black nightshade, shepherd's purse, and amaranth seeds. The quantities are tiny, and whoever sets out to mix them must be an artist. The two liquids are put together and thickened with a spoonful of ground spirlins and mustard, and this sauce, which is neither hot, nor sweet, nor bitter, is poured over goose legs that have been kept in the oven until they become crisp.

At my first attempt, the frogs woke up, and I couldn't find two of them—they were gone and perhaps they are praising their good fortune to this day. Then I forgot the pot on the boil, with the result that the dove stuck to the bottom and turned into scrapings and smoke.

The cook had become another man. Since he had been moved to the pigs, he had become humble. He wasn't sorry that he had refused Dubois, but he considered himself to blame for other things. His wife no longer spoke to him, and he was no longer allowed to set foot in the Palace. On the other hand, he confessed that he sometimes cooked something for Perticari. This was their bond. The spiritist knew a lot too, but he needed a cook, for, as I had found out to my cost, food is difficult to make. Silică laid out a few dishes for me, and for a short time that boastful glint came back into his eye from the time when he had been the princely cook.

'And who gave you these recipes?' I asked him.

'The grand *pitar*, my little mistress!'

Perticari had read other recipes too. Fortunately, even if he had had the *Book of Perilous Dishes*, he had no idea of their uses, for Maxima had forbidden me ever to write down the effects of these dishes. My book contained only the prescriptions, and anyone with their head screwed on would have treated them with caution.

Looking at him now, I observed that the cook was cross-eyed—not much, but just enough for you not to know whether he was looking at you. That was why he kept his nose in the air: to hide his defect. That's how it is with any person—once you get to know them well, all their defects are sweetened. I thought to myself that I was the only person in the world to have made this discovery. But since then I have realized that all my life I have been changing my opinions about people.

Taking advantage of the cook's changed attitude, I said to him with much regret in my voice, for in the meantime I had learned many things: 'There is a way for you to put things right.'

'You mean to get him to take me back to the Palace?'

I was sorry for him, but I continued to lie to him, looking only into his normal eye. The rest was easy. I told him about the elixir of forgetting, without telling him what its effects were.

'If a spiritist, such as Perticari, eats this sauce made by you, in a month's time at the most you'll be back in the Palace kitchens!'

'Thirty days,' the cook said to himself, casting his glance for a moment up to the ceiling. It's not long!'

'But no one must know! Do you understand?'

The tree-frog sauce wipes away memories about a person, specifically about the person who has put a vegetable messenger in the dish. There is no one who does not have a plant as their brother. Some have the poppy, others the forget-me-not. There are delicate people for whom the lime flower is the special

216

envoy, an enveloping and charming counsellor, ready to confuse anyone's paths. In the elixir of forgetting, you must send your herb, and the person who swallows it will forget completely about you. They forget the colour of your eyes; they forget the sound of your voice. They no longer remember that you ever existed. And I wanted Perticari to forget about me.

I wasn't sure, and nor did I know whether the cook would be true to his word. So I waited with bated breath. And not just for a day or two, but for several weeks.

That winter was terrible. The Metropolitan issued a paper according to which the Brothers were to take care of me. My good luck lay with Laurian. His father bought the management of my little uncle's fortune, which implied also tutelage over me. I will not complain. He was a decent man. Even if in those days I gave him a rough time. For him, Laurian was everything, and I was part of his boy's happiness. The former Burchioiu, whom I had hated to death, was the most precious person in my life, and he too was a gift from Maxima.


## 1799—Thirty Years Ago

### The Head of the Greek

In February, just as Dudescu had predicted, Kostas was replaced by Moruzi. I cannot say that Bina did not keep his word. One morning, the sort that makes your teeth freeze together, Ismail Bina made his way up to the Palace. He had with him several Turks wrapped in furs; all you could see was their eyes. Cirtă wasn't there. I've never seen him again. They said he made a life for himself in Stamboul.

Bina opened the chamber door and took out his *ferman* from the Sultan, for this Turk was always very careful about papers and signatures.

'*Dur bre, ferman!*' he said to Kostas, thrusting the document under his nose.

However, he didn't give him time to read it, but promptly cut off his head, adding: 'That's for the Greceanu lady, giaour!'

All day long, Kostas's headless corpse lay in the snow in front of the Palace, where anyone could spit on it. How Caterina had longed to see him dead! And probably my little uncle too. The age of the cook was over, and even though people talked about it for a long time, no one showed any interest in Silică anymore.

On the day of Kostas's death, you were nobody if you didn't go to see the decapitated tyrant. I too went to see the body. I don't know for what reason, but he was undressed. The belly that had stuffed itself with so many dishes, both select and perilous, lay in full view like a lump of dough.

And then I saw Silică, at the back of the courtyard. He was carrying a cauldron full of pig swill. Through the falling snow in the courtyard, he looked like an old crow. For a time, our eyes met. He was not angry; he was not happy. Standing there, with the cauldron in his hand, he looked like a little man who was ready to accept anything. I asked him with my eyes if he had any news for me, and he made a sign that he had. I could sense in his look a sort of blame. Perhaps he had cottoned onto my lies. If he had cooked tree-frog sauce for Perticari, it would be worth paying the spiritist a visit. Although I had a great reluctance in my heart. On the other hand, it was clear that the cook was deeply disappointed. Not so much at the death of Kostas, as at the fact that he was still with the pigs. He was a man who knew the ways of the world, and from the way he looked at me, I was sure that he understood that I had led him along.

Kostas's head was sent to Stamboul, to prove to the Sultan that his command had been fulfilled.

218

## My Life Thereafter

Many were the nights in which I thought of how it would be to take the Giurgiu road in search of Dubois. I could visualize down to the smallest detail how I would put the warders to sleep with poppy smoke, and how I would free the Frenchman. I even made drawings of men condemned to the galleys. I imagined how the irons that held them prisoner might be unlocked. As I saw it, my suffering for the death of Caterina naturally brought with it the duty to save Dubois.

These thoughts never left me. Not even after I was married. Lessons in French were my only consolation. All the same, I made no move. That winter, with all that happened, took away my strength, destroyed my optimism. I was no longer what I had been. When you realize that things are changing, you start to accept, and after that comes not exactly forgetting, but a sweetish numbness that makes you just get on with your life. And mine hasn't been bad. One summer I married Laurian, who no longer had any connection to the Burchioiu that had been or to anything in my adolescence. We continued to live in Zăval's house, although there was a time when I forgot altogether about philtres and elixirs. There were years in which I didn't even remember the Laboratorium.

The side facing the church we turned into a restaurant, to Ogaru's great displeasure.

And then one day I went to look for Silică the cook. He was still there, a little man cleaning out the pigsties of the princely Palace in a leisurely way.

'Will you cook in my restaurant?'

'I knew you would need me.'

I was surprised that he wasn't angry. His joy seemed like a sort of sponge that wiped away all the bitterness between us. Then he would ask me from time to time if and when I was going back to Lipsca. His mind had become confused.

On paper he is still a slave of the Palace, but nowadays no one takes any interest in him. People still talk about that famous cook of Kostas's for whom Caterina paid fifty ducats, but if they came into my kitchen, they certainly wouldn't recognize him. He is old. His passion for cooking has died, but he has the quantities of salt and pepper in his blood. It is he who decides how spicy the food should be. And some evenings, when the sound of some old song drifts in from the street or when a wave of memories comes over him, he is caught up by the fever of old times and he throws together a dish that leaves you licking your fingers when it's finished. And after that, for a week or so, he looks young again and drunk on pleasures.

Sometimes I ask him to cook something out of the *Book of Perilous Dishes*, but just enough not to drive anyone to despair. And how could you only eat things that do you good? Now and then everyone needs a drop of bile, a dash of poison.

All the madness about Satorines and wizards has flown away. Little by little, Maxima has become in my memory just a woman with fantasies, and my little uncle a merchant who dreamed of a life of adventure. My squint teeth have lost their importance; I don't have much inclination to show them. Ismail Bina was right: I didn't really look human with them! The salves too have lost their importance. In the meantime, apothecaries have appeared with medicines that I never even dreamed of. In time, that dramatic autumn has lost its intensity, and when I think of myself, of how I was back then, I see myself with one foot pushed forward, ready to attack. I was never tall, but I had that attitude that made me forget all my fears. It was something I'd had to learn at first, but in time it had become instinctive.

One day, Laurian brought a piece of wood on which someone had painted my name. Of course he didn't know, because, even though I've lost my belief, I have kept my word to this day and I've never told anyone my real name.

'Everyone's forgotten about Kostas,' he said, 'and they've forgotten about the cook. Nowadays hardly anyone even mentions the Greceancă. But everyone knows about Cat o' Friday!'

'And what do they know?'

'She was a witch brought by Kostas, who turned into a cat when he was gone. If you meet her at lunchtime, whatever wish you make comes true!'

'That's foolishness,' I protested.

But Laurian, blushing from ear to ear, continued: 'I saw her one day and I made a wish that came true. No! Don't ask me, because it's not good to talk about wishes fulfilled! If I told you, it would bring ten years of bad luck down on our heads! But I assure you that what I want us to do will bring us good luck.'

When I heard what he wanted, I immediately agreed. Since then, our restaurant has been called *Cat o' Friday*. Sometimes, around lunchtime, Perticari turns up, perhaps our most faithful client.

But all this happened long after the death of Kostas.

That winter, while his straw-stuffed head was being carried to Stamboul, I put two things to the test: the word of the cook and the power of tree-frog sauce.


## My Dowry

The *Book of Perilous Dishes* is a relic of childhood, a sort of evidence that Maxima existed and that in the stories of my family there was a grain of truth. My faith in perilous recipes was strengthened a few days after the death of Kostas.

One day I went in through Perticari's door, which as I have said is always open. He gave me a smile at once friendly and ambiguous, as only he knows how.

'What's your name?' he asked me.

I told him about Zăval, whom he had never heard of in his life. He was the same man, well versed in all sorts of tricks, a spiritist and a skilful wizard. Only that the episodes involving me were missing from his memory. And those with Zăval. On the other hand he was still obsessed with the twins, a subject that I mentioned in passing, just to check.

'Aha, the twins,' he said, fixing his eyes on me. 'There is an elixir. You don't by any chance know how to make it?'

I immediately said I didn't, and Perticari made a confession.

'Sometimes, at night, a dead man comes to me and asks about that potion.'

'Perhaps he's not dead,' I suggested.

'But what could he be?'

We were both thinking the same thing, but I knew that Perticari didn't speak about Sator. So I kept quiet. All the same, a part of me continued to think about the Satorines, even about some who can send their voices into the ear of a spiritist. I never brought up the subject again, but it was from that day that my friendship with Perticari began. He didn't know who I was, and I could tell him whatever I wanted. The tree-frog sauce had been effective; the cook had been a man of his word.

All the same, I found out later that there had been a side effect, like those mentioned in Latin at the end of a recipe. The tree-frog sauce bound the cook forever to those for whom he had prepared the dish. Perticari, the cook, and I were to remain inseparable.

Time has passed, and over the years I have made him forget about the twins too. Sometimes I make an elixir for him, although I am not satisfied with the quality of his dreams. Perticari dreams in a muddled way, and never with a conclusion. His dreams are more like wanderings in a labyrinth too complicated for his powers.

With the melting away of each day, my dreams too have lost their colour. Dubois has turned into an ant asleep at the oar of a galley, and all that is left of Caterina is a string of pearls scattered on the stairs. My little uncle Zăval lives for me only in the mohair cat, and Maxima is just a voice that continues to speak inside my head.

Two years ago, Laurian passed on to the next world, leaving a pain in my soul that will never leave me.

One day began to be the same as another for me. Until now.

# CHAPTER VIII

# THIRTY YEARS LATER

*1829—The Present Time*

### The Letter

Then, thirty years later, I received a letter that sent me right back to the time of Kostas.

Dubois, who in my dreams had been slaving away in the galleys, that same Dubois whom Caterina had adored and with whom I had fallen in love, the French chancellor who had charmed the city, who disappeared without a trace for so many years, whom I had dreamed of rescuing, wrote to me.

The letter was not long. He wanted me to know that he was well and that he would like to talk. In fact, he didn't even say precisely that, just that if I was ever going through Marseille not to pass him by. It might have been a sentence written out of habit, just a piece of politeness, like the whole French language. But for me, that sentence came as a sign.

His handwriting was the same as in the letter that I have kept for thirty years. I opened my chiffonier and read again the lines that trembled like opium smoke. He hadn't written much, just two lines: 'Your blood and my blood will flow together until the end of the world.' What crazy things pass through the mind of a man who thinks he has found happiness! It was the letter that Caterina had read just before she died. What dreams still lived on in those words! I can't help wondering what would have become of them if she hadn't died. They would now be two old folk afflicted with gout. Or perhaps not. In any case, dead or lost, they continue to pass through my mind with the faces they had then, two figures of smoke.

And now, on my long journey, I have thought of them a lot. And not just of them. You will laugh! But out of the piles of things and people, only my buttoned boots, stolen by Cîrtă Vianu, seem untouched by time. In their heels there were four gold ducats, but I didn't regret losing them as much as I regretted losing the boots. And this regret made those boots even more shiny than they had really been. I've forgotten what the Arnaut who handed me over to Cîrtă looked like. Even the face of Bina, as it was back then, has faded. Many sufferings have quite simply disappeared. I no longer care about my squint teeth. So many desires have lost their importance, while those boots still live in my brain despite the passage of three decades. Memory has its preferences, and the soul is not always their king.

Tomorrow I arrive in Milan, and I'm going to buy myself a pair of boots.


## The Meeting

The journey to Marseille took me a month, and I lost two guards along the way in a brawl. But about the journey there would be too much to say. When I entered the city it was noon, and I stopped the carriage outside a white house that seemed perched on a rock. I climbed a hundred steps, taking care not to catch my dress in the roses that grew neatly along the edge of the stairs. When I arrived at the top I was soaked in perspiration. My dress, which was the striped one, was burning me. On the veranda, between two columns, an old fellow was dozing, like a dog that doesn't know there is such a thing as danger.

I left my servants outside and stepped over the threshold, which opened onto a large hall. Hanging on one wall, in the place of honour, was the Arnaut costume, that costume given by *her*. The costume in which he had gone away, and which seemed untouched by the passage of time. Brand new.

A footman made a sign to me to go in through a door, and before long I was face to face with Dubois. Light poured into the room, making me think I was in Lipscani Square.

He was almost old; he had lost that shine. Just as the freshness of clay perishes in time. It was him, but at the same time it was someone else, who rather kept me at a distance.

Although he seemed rather heavy, he got up smartly, and from the first words he spoke he threw me back thirty years.

First, he told me about what he had done, although, judging by the house I had entered, it was already clear that his life had been that of a successful person. The nights in which I had dreamed of how I was rescuing him were now a boulder over my head.

'How did you get away from the Turks?' I asked, while a string soaked in vinegar passed through my heart.

'I don't know how to tell you. Although that is why I wrote to you, in the hope that I would be able to tell you. You saw the old man sitting by the steps to the house?'

I confirmed that I had seen him, but refrained from saying that he looked like an old mongrel without a care in the world. Dubois made a sign, and it was not long before the old fellow came into the room.

'Do you recognize him?'

The old man gave a toothless smile. One cheek looked as if it had seen the edge of a sword. And as I looked at him, I was hit by a face coming from the past.

'It's Cirtă!'

'Yes, my lady,' the old man replied, in the same bored voice with which long ago he had sized up my boots.

The night of my kidnapping, with all its adventures, was there once again, opened up like an elder flower.

'After the cart turned over, Cirtă grabbed hold of me. He and his friend.'

'The one with spectacles,' I recalled.

'Yes, the poor fellow,' added Cirtă, letting me understand that his friend was long dead.

Dubois continued his story: 'We took a few steps, didn't we, Cirtă?'

'Yes, sir, two steps at the most. I wanted to tie you to the horse.'

'I was looking at the dusty road, the one that went round the pond,' Dubois recalled, settling himself back in his chair.

In my memory, the road had begun to wind, though I didn't know if it was the road back then or the one that I had seen hundreds of times since that day.

'So, I was looking at the road, and suddenly—pouf!—it melted away! It disappeared like a drop of water sucked up by a cloth! The next moment I was in a street full of shops. It took me some time,' Dubois continued, smoothing his hair just as he used to do, though that hair was now white. 'Well, it took me some time to realize I was in Marseille.'

In the room silence fell. Out of the thick undergrowth of my thoughts, the face of Maxima was smiling at me, and it took me too a good few moments to understand. In the end it had happened. I recalled the day of the escape, the failed escape, and out of all its details, I was struck by just two things: my hand clutching the knife, and the breeze of Sator.

I didn't know what to say. My dress was trembling, and Dubois was looking at me insistently, like someone who desperately wants to be believed.

'I don't know how I got here. I don't know what happened. I have never found out.'

'And what did you do?' I asked for form's sake, because dozens of thoughts were already whirling in my mind.

'At the time I had an uncle here, in Marseille. I stayed for a week without being able to talk to anyone. As my uncle was quite busy, I had all the time I could wish for to meditate. Then I decided to leave for Paris, but two streets away I met the two of them: Cîrtă and his friend.'

'That's how it was, lady,' said Cîrtă smiling at me. 'We thought we had landed in Stamboul because we'd been cursed by an old woman with a green face, a real spiteful piece of work, who we were both afraid of. Cat o' Friday they called her.'

I would have liked to have laughed, but it wasn't the moment. Cîrtă's friend had died, without leaving any posterity in the world, but Cîrtă had children, who in their turn would pass on my name and tales of the green old woman.

All the gates that had seemed shut were now wide open.

Dubois's testimony likewise called for another testimony. All through the night I told him. My meeting with him had had a purpose; it had been more than a landmark in my life for me. I told him about my little uncle, about Sator, about the trials for which Maxima had prepared me for so long. I told him the whole story from the beginning, things I had never told anyone until then. Not even Laurian had ever known. It had taken a long journey for me to be able to tell everything that lay on my soul.

Dubois believed me. He believed in Sator and in the power of my lineage. The only thing I couldn't tell him was my name.

'And the houses?' he asked me. 'Why would he demolish them? Something doesn't add up. How could he leave you without… without a testament, without an explanation or a key? There must be something in that laboratory!

'This mohair cat,' I said, showing him my pocket. 'Perhaps it is the key. But I don't know how to use it.' Dubois was even more intrigued than me. All his rebellious energy of thirty years ago was back in full force.

'In that secure box, what did you say there was?'

'A map.'

For a while we talked about maps and about treasures. I know Zăval's map by heart, so I drew it, writing also those unintelligible words: *Nomen nule* or perhaps *nuble*.

Dubois had no idea either.

The dawn of the next day found us still in the same room.

'And the death of the marquis?'

'After I got back to Paris, I found out that he hadn't even died. My parents had written, but the letter never reached me. Most likely Pazvantoğlu had read it, and then the Kapudan Pasha himself, only for it to end up with Mârcă, under the bridge.'

The memory of these men, now long dead, brushed away all the years that had passed. I could see him young again, in Lipscani Square, beside Fleury.

'And the consul?'

'He got back. He was ransomed by his family.'

Dubois told me about the death of his wife and I realized that it was this wound, not yet very old, that had brought to mind the events of his youth.

At last we came round to *her*. Caterina slipped quietly into our recollections.

'I loved her,' he confessed.

In his eyes I could see the suffering that he had known after her death.

'Out of all my life, the months I spent with her are the most precious. If tomorrow I had to choose… you know…'

I knew, of course. True love is for the one who is not at your side. Her smile, seductive and proud, lived on in my mind.

The time had come to give him the letter. In the wounded light of the morning, his eyes sparkled. Dubois's face was back to what it had been thirty years before. The paper was

230

discoloured by time, but over the faded handwriting there still pulsed the life of those eyes that had read it just before her death.

## The Nuns' Mill

I stayed with Dubois for almost a week. One day one of his two sons came to visit him, a man who only in his liveliness reminded me of what Dubois had once been. His eyes were caught by my map.

'What's this?' he asked. 'You want to go to Leipzig?'

'How do you know what it is?' I enquired, for his youth and the casual way in which he had looked at the map didn't inspire much confidence in me.

'Just look here,' he said, pointing. '*Nonnenmühle—the Nuns' Mill.*'

I was astounded. That *Nomen nule* was in fact *Nonnenmühle*.

'And here's the *Ranstädter Tor*—the northern gate,' he added, indicating another point on the map. 'It's where Napoleon would have entered, but that wasn't to be!'

Those last days spent with Dubois really were the last. I never saw him again after that. I left him in his white house, which seemed cut from a wall of chalk.

On my return, I took the road to Lipsca, which everyone called *Leipzig*. I really had to see the town in which my little uncle had spent so much time. I stopped at an inn and went in and out of the shops. Though they were more numerous, they were far from being as well-stocked as in Bucharest. It was then that I realized that our so-called Lipsca merchants actually brought goods from many places in Europe. The town had a quiet atmosphere that a native of Bucharest would never have imagined. I went in my carriage to the *Nonnenmühle*, which wasn't too far from the inn. From a distance I was enchanted by the lake, beyond which could be seen a forest of houses. Their red caps made them look like a group of jesters. The landscape seemed familiar to me. It resembled the picture that my little uncle had in the Laboratorium. When I got closer, I discovered the bridge too. Then I saw the Nuns' Mill. The noontide sun was shining brightly. From time to time the odd scolding voice could be heard coming across the water. At the head of the bridge I made a sign to the coachman to turn back and I stuck my head out of the window of the carriage. Then suddenly, right before my eyes and not far off, I saw a house that startled me. There were two buildings in fact. On one of them, a red turret rose proudly, embraced by a cat. I stopped and ran up to it. The gate was clothed in wild rose and honeysuckle. I looked carefully at the cat, whose eyes seemed alive. Then I read the inscription on the house: '*Cat o' Friday*'.

Through my ears the breath of Sator rattled.

The gate was locked, and the lock, covered with flourishes of ironwork, represented a cat caught in a rose bush. One of its eyes was missing. A lamp lit up in my brain. Feverishly I unstitched the mohair cat and matched the ruby to the empty eye socket. The gate gave a screech and then opened. The rest was easy. The key, shaped like a skinned rabbit and familiar to me from my childhood, had been left under the threshold.

## The Satorines

As soon as I entered the house, tears welled up. Zăval's portrait was still there, where I remembered it, just as in my childhood, which I had thought forgotten. *Little Uncle*, I used to call him. I rushed up the stairs. The bedroom doors were wide open. My parents' room was at the end, a room with green and white curtains. My heart was touched with melancholy, but without taking away my happiness.

I went up the second, spiral staircase. In the turret I was hit by an aroma of dried mint. It was as if someone had just left that room that resembled a light-filled crystal egg. Everything seemed new to me; I could remember hardly anything. All around I could see the sky, through glass that was not very clean, and by the windows was the table, piled with books, phials, and little boxes. On the cover of one large tome was written in yellow letters *The Satorines*. At last I had found them.

I looked at the wooden surface of the table, on which my little uncle's hand had drawn two twins—a man and a woman, he in flesh and blood, she like a phantom about to disintegrate. At their feet lay two symbols, the broom and the whistle, picked out in considerable detail. This was their star-sign, as brother and sister born from the same egg. The drawing reminded me of Maxima's clock, from which on the hour a man and a woman appeared, and a dragon made them embrace one another.

For a few weeks I explored the house, taking delight in recipe books, salves, and miraculous stones, among them a Dalmatian jasper which, if kept in fig wine, protects you from bad dreams and pains of the soul.

The *Book of Perilous Dishes* was nowhere to be seen, but in a drawer I came across my first recipe, *pecunia*—made from lilac flowers and fifty other plants. The gentle sunlight of my childhood shone down on me again, warming the aging paper.

One restful evening, I settled comfortably in a good place and with a silk travelling rug, and at long last I opened the great *Book of the Satorines*. As Maxima had told me, it was a sort of list, in which each Satorine was entered with their name and their value. Plus a painted portrait. Being colourful, it invited you to read it, and, as it was large, I could support it on my knees, the way I think a book ought to be read.

It began with Zăval, who bore the title *Satoris Trismegistus*. And not without cause, for it went on to describe all his qualities. He could change the direction of the wind, and determine the intensity of snowfalls and the duration of showers of rain. He was capable of transporting just about anything over a great distance, just as he had moved the houses, relying on the power of any object to seek its twin seed. *Particulae geminate.* It was not the houses themselves that had been carried off, but their spirit. This place, which he had noted with such care on the map, was what counted. Here he had buried the first brick, the cornerstone, the foundation in which dwelt his power as a sweeper of Sator, a hunter of that unseen side of the world. He held the broom and took care of the cleanness of the world.

Zăval had been a spearhead, behind whom all the others hid, over five hundred people, all with the knowledge of Sator, although some could only see him, without being able to make use of him, while others were the guardians of the principal gates. Many had learned how to hide in his shadow. And there were also some who knew how to work together with him, among them Maxima Tutilina. She tamed the paths of Sator, sometimes summoning him or making him leave. Her power was the whistle. However, together with Zăval she was capable of absolutely anything. Each of them had several pages about the special practices and experiments that they had attempted. And among the hardest was the art of merging, which made them become as one. To achieve this, four people were needed, plus a very reliable *vigilax*, a sort of supervisor of the whole practice, which lasted three hours in total. This was the *magna diada*. Wherever they were, all that remained of Maxima was a *plasma*, while Zăval functioned like a magnet. Together they made of Sator a sort of wheel, a circle of fire, whose power could shake the equilibrium of any dyad.

All that exists has two hearts and two worlds, one visible and the other—subtle. And if their fine connection is changed in any way, the world changes too.

Among Zăval and Maxima's experiments was the Battle of Kagul, where they had caused the powerful Ottoman army to be defeated. In the role of *vigilax* they'd had a schoolteacher from Manchester, who had supervised all their experiments.

A rather clumsy drawing showed them together. Zăval had a black heart above his head, and Maxima just the outline of a heart, in which two wings hovered. Under the drawing were the words *The Satorine Twins*. As usual, the whistle and the broom were at their feet.

A chapter was dedicated to the ritual knife. It was now that I found out that it was made from a mineral that could only be found in the Ilmen Mountains, in Chelyabinsk. By a laborious process, the metal was extracted, and from it a certain Ivan Grosu forged the blade, leaving room in the middle for oil of wild vine. No one can invoke Sator without this knife, which attracts like a magnet and deceives Sator's senses. Dubois had arrived in Marseille because I was clutching the knife in my hand. For it was not really a knife, but a key. If on that autumn morning, now lost among my memories, bleached white by the sunlight of other autumns, I had not had the good fortune to have the knife with me, Dubois would have been slaving in the galleys, and Cirtă Vianu, instead of sleeping by the Frenchman's stairs, would now be a doorman in Bina's house. The knife had been the god of that event long ago.

It was with that same knife that my little uncle had been killed, while he was trying to control Sator.

The book also mentioned the hilt, which was of Indian wood. It had a protective role for the hands of the Satorine, keeping Sator at a distance. Zăval's knife, with its agarwood haft, had slept for thirty years, hidden by me in the laboratory in the basement. I had forgotten about it. I no longer knew its shape. I couldn't remember its smell.

### Cat o' Friday

I read a little at a time, in no hurry, wishing to spin out the reading as long as possible. When you are reading something you like, you live with the same joy and pauses.

From the tower the lake can be seen, and, of course, the *Nonnenmühle*, and on the window ledge crows stop to rest. Although

I can hear them cawing, sometimes I have the impression that they are speaking a language that I have forgotten, but the memory of which still flickers in my soul.

Around the middle of the book I came to Cat o' Friday, a page written in purple letters, for, I forgot to say, this book is written in many hands and with many different inks.

The portrait shows me many years ago. I remember that it was done by an old painter who spoke a very mixed-up language. But in contrast to the portrait I knew, in this one I have a red eye. If I hadn't known it was me, I wouldn't have recognized myself. Cat o' Friday has something feline about her, but you can see that she is only a child.

The text is short. My principal ability is to double the value of a Satorine. And in smaller letters it says what has to be done to achieve this. On my first reading I was rather disappointed. Especially after reading what the others in my family could do. Then many episodes in my childhood began to make sense, including the rule about never acknowledging who I was.

I went back to the small letters. In order to amplify the strengths of a Satorine, I had to die. This new discovery shook me. Alive I was of no use at all! If a Satorine wanted at all cost to double their value, there was nothing for it but to bash me over the head and get rid of me! Well, perhaps not quite like that. My death had a long ritual around it. But what does it matter if you're already gone? The energy that I released in the moment of death was to go into the blood of someone else.

I also had the power of sleep. For some, more gentle, there was no need for me to die. It was enough for me to bring them a noontide sleep, full of dreams and pleasures. On waking they were stronger. Not as much as if they had killed me, but it was still something. Indeed I had tried this sleep on Perticari, but it was only now that I found out that through it the Satorine was strengthened.

On another page there was something about *perilous dishes*, but just in passing, as a sort of secondary art of mine. Then, elsewhere, under *Punishments*, I was designated as one of those whose duty it was to prepare a potion for traitors and murderers of Satorines. I had become an executioner!

I also found out that my teeth, of which I had been so proud, lost their power once I was fifteen years old. For the rest of my life they were nothing but teeth, just like any other squint and frightfully ugly teeth.

That was about all. Sometimes my name appeared again, alongside other people that I was supposed to know. But most of the names meant absolutely nothing to me.

## The Others

My mother had been a raiser of crows. That was why there were so many in our yard. I knew that from their hearts a dish was made for Satorines who dreamed. Very many had this ability, as dreamers who found out in their sleep where the paths frequented by Sator lay.

Out of them all, Iulian, my teacher in the Novus Oribasius, was a sort of encyclopaedia. Anyone who was unsure of something had to ask him. Many chapters of the book were written by him, and when I recognized his handwriting I could see in my mind his face too, from the time when he taught me the arts of transformation.

Towards the end of the book I came to Caterina's father, who had been a discoverer of treasures. He wasn't her natural father. There was no more information about him. And among those I knew, I also found Perticari, against whose name was written *Rusoris*. Immediately I thought of Rusor, the god of periodic return. It is believed that he flies, and that each of his returns raises wings of mist, which make him appear to be a sort of wanderer. When I lost something or other, a ring for example, Maxima used to say: 'Never mind, Rusor will bring it back. Don't worry!' So the spiritist must be in the service of Rusor.

The most powerful Satorine was a Pole. He could travel beyond the seen world. Sometimes he would send his voice where he wished.

In Bucharest there were another two people, both in Perticari's service. One of them was the master rumour-monger, whom I hadn't been able to sniff out.

In an appendix there was a list of helpers of the Satorines, among whom an important category was those who prepared the various potions. Silică, the cook, was a *mixtator*. That is what he had meant to say; that was the mysterious word. He was the only one in Bucharest who could cook according to the *Book of Perilous Dishes*. Not even I had that power.

In a deserted house, people forget their ill feelings. Time no longer matters. For many days I did nothing but search through the rooms.

In the cellar of the house there was, of course, a *Laboratorium*. The last thing prepared by my little uncle was on the table. The remains of a mixture. In a bowl there were some beans, which had slept there for thirty years. A book with his handwriting had been left open. I read and smiled: *The Potion of the Twins*. So it really existed! Perticari had been right. It was a *philtrum* for journeys alongside Sator. I couldn't see what use it would have been to the spiritist, who didn't have this gift! The potion is only for great adepts of Sator, endowed with the power of total evasion, capable of manipulating time and space. And for things to go well, the master of magic was to drink this *philtrum*, made in six houses during the winter. You take red wine of Drăgășani in which a bunch of young wormwood has been left to ferment for a long time, and you bring it to the boil, adding a slice of apple, honey, and a few peppercorns. At the end you throw in a sprig of marjoram too. But this potion is only to be drunk by the light of a green candle.

Further on there was a drawing of a smiling candle, and beside it instructions to take clean wax and knead it well with viper's bugloss till it becomes green, then shape it into candles using a thread of silk. These release hidden gifts, helping with visions, but especially with making contact with the dead or with other unseen spirits. For this reason, spiritists often use them, with or without the potion of the twins. Consequently, for Perticari it really was good. And I had helped him to make it without knowing exactly what its value was.

I had lost thirty years in forgetfulness. The day I set foot in Bucharest continued to be an evil one in my mind. If I hadn't stopped at the showmen, I would have found Cuviosu Zăval alive. I stopped because they were talking about me. Cat o' Friday had become the enemy of the city before I even came through the gate. Everything was connected. But somewhere, thirty years ago. The showmen—my name—the rumour-monger. These three things wandered for several weeks through my brain, until I understood who I was.

What was I saying about the sort of people who sleep in prayers and forgetting? Now I was one of them!

## My Return

And since everything has to come to a conclusion, I shall write on. Although life has shown me that any ending opens new doors.

At the end of the summer I returned to Bucharest, but I was older by a hundred years.

I have taken my yellow dress out of the chest. Although it has been modified a few times, widened and its bodice replaced, it still looks good. The yoke is now covered with a layer of silk.

A drop of carmine on my lips, a drop on my cheeks. I put on the hat I bought in Lipsca and my shoes with pompoms, and I take my sunshade.

As I leave, I grab from the larder a jar and a millet broom. I get into the carriage. Lipscani Square is roasting in the sun. On a noticeboard a street show is announced. Obviously no longer the old *Karagöz* puppets, but something new, French. All the same, the shadow of a speckled monster also rises over the square, its frightening words instilling terror, although no one can understand what it's saying.

Two streets—and I open the gate. In the courtyard, under the ivy kiosk, Perticari is puffing on his pipe. His bare feet emerge from under the silk of his robe, two paws like lily petals.

'How was the journey? Did you find Dubois?'

'I found something even better!' I reply.

I take the bottle and hold it out. The spiritist studies it for a while with his wide eyes, which, despite the passage of time, have not lost their youthfulness. When the fireflies have gone from someone's eyes, you know for sure that they are old. And it's not a matter of age, but of the passion that pulses in their blood. Perticari looks better than Dubois. His Byzantine face has never aged.

On the bottle in clumsy letters is written '*Cat o' Friday*', which makes him smile knowingly.

'Did you make it?'

I smile as if at a dear friend: 'Taste it! I'm curious what you'll say.'

It ought to have an aroma of lilac. But I shall never know. Perticari drinks the potion and shakes like a cluster of flowers. Of the tall figure of a man that he was, nothing is left but a little pile of dust, of an almost reddish purple. I sweep it up carefully, and gather it into the jar, the same jar that you can see in the kitchen of my restaurant. This is the end of the great spiritist, an end that he was certainly not expecting. But he never was all that clever.

The moment has come to enter his house. Perticari was an orderly man. I open the drawers of his cupboard, in which there is nothing but foolish things: loaded dice, tarot cards, wands that produce smoke. In each room there are chests, most of them bottomless trunks. I look for the button, always hidden under a velvet ornament, and press it. Some have a banal false bottom. Others just the odd tiny box, masked by velvet, or some hollow space covered with coloured class. His most precious things are his books. Some are packaged in leather, others wrapped up in a shawl or two. First I find the *Book of Solomon*. I am touched. Perticari's fame really had a basis, and the story about the Enei Church was true after all.

After searching for about an hour, finally I come upon the *Book of Perilous Dishes*—my first book, which the spiritist held captive for thirty years.

*

When I entered the kitchen, Silică was smiling. He didn't ask me what I was keeping in the jar, although many do ask. Sometimes I put a few grains in dishes, especially in pumpkin pies, which I call *rusoris*, in memory of Perticari. Whoever tastes of them starts at the beginning again, regardless of the plans they have made. Just so you know what may sometimes be concealed in the dishes in restaurants and inns. You think you are eating a good honest steak, but often the cook is taking advantage of your hunger.

And if you ask what motives I had for putting the spiritist in the pie, I'll tell you.

### Why

When Maxima wrote to Zăval about making the *magna diada*, that meant rescuing her from Şchei. Well, for them there was only one sort of rescue—*evasio*. Zăval and his two servants, who were themselves Satorines, made the invocation. The knife should have made Sator lift her from where she was. But they also needed a *vigilax*. And that was Perticari. The worst possible choice. In those days he had got it into his head to double his power, and somehow he had found out about me. Or not exactly about me, but about the gift that Cat o' Friday possessed. Perhaps the Pole who could send his voice anywhere had whispered to him. Or some dead person had told him, as he maintained. One way or another, the hornet of power had started buzzing in his head. But he didn't know who this Cat was. That was why Zăval had got him waiting for all the post coaches that came from Chişinău. To get rid of him and of his questions.

Not for a moment had he suspected that it was me, not even after my little uncle's death.

It had all begun with an accident, as tends to be the way of things. Perticari had come across the *Book of Perilous Dishes* and had slipped it into his pocket. Don't ask me how. By an abuse of trust. Cuviosu Zăval had probably observed that the recipe book was missing, but he was sure that it was in the hands of Kostas. That was why he wrote another, thinking that the cook would have more confidence in him than in Kostas. I might add that he had started an investigation, which he didn't have time to bring to its conclusion. He was blinded by hatred, thirsty to get rid of Kostas.

Because of the general state of agitation, Perticari escaped any suspicion. For passions do not only cloud the mind, as I have said, but also lead to irreparable mix-ups. Revolutions walk roughshod over the real joys. You will say that without them there is no progress. But real progress never comes from rebellions or from the raging of the market place. They are good only to commemorate. They are like singing for the cook. True change comes from bright people and minor conjunctures. Or from the use of Sator in a just way. Visionaries know Sator's path in advance. They are the drawers of maps. Not for nothing is it said of a person who rises above the crowd through their mind that they are quite simply bright! Not intelligent. Not wise. Not a genius. Just *bright*. Attentive, alert, and open. The memory is just a bag that intelligence shows you how to open, and attention keeps it for you, finding with ease the particular moment that your mind needs in order to know what to pull from the bag.

With his eyes on Kostas, who was not even a real embodiment of evil, Zăval failed to notice that Perticari had a small mind and great ambitions. Consequently, while Zăval was making the invocation, Perticari used his only gift. He was *rusoris*. He could wipe away Sator's path, and so was capable of turning everything upside down. There is always such an apprentice who changes the course of history precisely because nobody pays him any attention.

Zăval uttered the invocation, allowing time for the knife to summon Sator. The agarwood gave off its perfume, and the vine oil clouded over, invaded by the ghosts of other lives, from the time when it was just a dry seed under heaps of limestone. The knife, the same knife that I had gripped in my hands without feeling its hidden power, that had sent Dubois to Marseille, sparked by the unseen veins that still bound it to Chelyabinsk, had begun to do its work. Sator dozed, carried along by the flux of the knife and perhaps by the thoughts of Zăval, while Perticari sang the praises of the god Rusor, who could turn everything back on its path. Even though she was so far away, Maxima had sensed the danger faster than her brother. The proof was the haste with which she had rammed into Laurian's head all that she thought at the time was important. The two twins understood one another across thousands of cities. There is no doubt that they were telepathic. Perhaps they really could become a single person, as it said in the massive volume that I had read. But this was of little use to them. Perticari upset the ritual by awakening Sator. The knife hummed. For a few moments my little uncle Zăval knew what was going to happen—his last, grotesque moments. The blade flew in a circle and would probably have killed Perticari too if he hadn't been so agile. His art of moving like the wind saved him from death. The knife passed from one to the next. It cut the throats of the two assistants, who were also people that my little uncle had full trust in, and then embedded itself deep under Zăval's chin, leaving imprinted on his face a combination of astonishment, despair, and regret, which not even death could wipe away. At a distance of thousands of *stânjeni*, Maxima died in the same manner, stabbed by the same knife, or rather by its unseen side. She died in a crowded street, and he in his own home, two Satorine twins slain by a single hand. Zăval had lost control, and instead of Maxima being saved, they all died. Perticari, the murderer of Satorines, had four souls on his conscience.

I think another mistake of Zăval's had been to lie to Perticari. He made him wait for days on end for the coming of Cat o' Friday, and this embittered him. He spread rumours. He threw the city into the craze of predictions, which caused me to waste time. I don't know what I would have done if I had arrived an hour earlier. But probably I would have been *vigilax* instead of Perticari. Perhaps I would have died. Perfect things only happen in our imaginings, and realities are full of flaws and mistakes.

When Sator set off towards Maxima, Perticari called him back. Just for a second. Sufficient for the knife to come into Sator's power. And in that rehearsed second, in that pitch blackness of any return, Perticari became invisible. Just for long enough to pass by me. It had been *his* silk cape that had disappeared into the darkness of the street. It had also been he who hit me on the head a few weeks later. My first intuition had been right. He had deceived me with his speech, with that perfidious velvet of his voice.

The punishment for the killer of Satorines is *pecunia*, the first potion that Zăval had set me to make. And I had done so.

If you pass through Bucharest, don't forget to stop at Cat o' Friday, where you will find, among other things, a pumpkin pie worthy to go down in the history books. Should you no longer like the past and want to start over again, ask for the *rusoris* version. And if you have the good fortune to come on a day when Silică cooks, you will never forget the taste of the food. They say that some people hear his voice while they're eating, although this strikes me as improbable.

But for you to know all this, you have to get to this book of mine, which I am locking in a chest, placed in open view in our houses in Lipsca. Through someone's dreams a cat will pass, dissolved in the mists of the evening, and this dreamer of cats will be my first reader. As is always the case, there are also disadvantages. And so I give you a small piece of advice: in no circumstances is it good to sleep on Friday at noontide.

# THE VOICE OF THE COOK

My words will never be seen by anyone, for they are not for eyes. They are just in my mind and in Sator's, and perhaps for the ears of a Pole who will live for two hundred years. One day he will write on paper all that meanders through my mind, and his book will pass from hand to hand for centuries. Many will call it the *Story of the Cook*, but even more will read it as a fairy tale. And all this will happen only if I am not impelled by the great Sator to pour it into another ear.

My story begins with a leek broth that I had made just for myself. What evenings there were back then! Especially that evening, when the earth still thronged with the memory of the snow, and into our lady's palace came the great Mihalache Albu, a man so grand, the like of whom had never been seen in the Greceanu neighbourhood or heard of by anyone in all Bucharest, grand as Bucharest might be and the very navel of the earth. They said his papa had sold Gypsies like me, hundreds or maybe hundreds of hundreds of Lingurari, of Rudari, and whatever other poor wretches were for sale, and so accumulated piles of money, whence the wealth of Mihalache, who bought for himself palaces, carriages, and the rank of *vornic*. And this extraordinary man, who went about in carriages the like of which no one had ever seen, met his death in his wedding bed, on that evening on which I had made a beautiful leek broth, when the last mists of winter were rising from the earth below the kitchen windows.

Out of all the skirts in Bucharest, out of all the bosoms that had been thrust under his nose, out of all the females that spread around the warm smell of desire, Mihalache picked out Caterina Greceanu, my mistress, who wasn't to be compared with any of the bits of stuff in the city. And it was, as that old cupping-glass woman used to say, a real fairy-tale wedding! I cooked sixteen dishes. There was steak soaked in wine, thin sauces, salads, and about twenty baskets of little doughnuts, cut to shape with a plum brandy glass, just the right size to take in a single bite. And after three days of partying and dancing, when all the wedding guests were flat out, and the bride and groom had gone to bed, I went into the kitchen, which the servants had left spotless. And in the quiet of the pot lids and to the sound of the snoring sleepers, I made myself a leek broth. Because you ought to know: when I cook, I don't taste anything! I don't touch the food, because cooking isn't a job, it's a delicate way of consecrating your stomach. If I tasted something, immediately a feeling of disgust would come over me, and I wouldn't be able to stir anything else with the spoon. But after it's all over, especially once the place is cleaned up, I like to make a couple of spoonfuls of broth just for my soul, especially with orache, to take away the sickening feeling, with nettles, to enhance my taste for cooking, or above all with goosefoot, after which I always fall asleep with my eyes open.

That evening I was worn out, but also happy, because it wasn't every day that I could make those pies! But I didn't manage to fall asleep, not even to lie down, because the screaming began. I ran as fast as my legs would carry me, and on that big staircase I met the housekeeper, who was yelling. The new son-in-law had been stung by a wasp. The whole house was on its feet. The mistress was weeping loud enough to be heard from Colțea, and the little folk of the house, especially the laundry-maids, were wringing their hands out of pity for her. The handsome man who had danced at the wedding, astounding the guests with the way he strutted his stuff, had turned into a toad. When I heard of such a thing, I didn't give up till I had seen for myself. I had to shin up the curtains to get a clear view. But since no one was taking any notice, in a few moves I was up there. And it was a sight to see! His face had swollen up like a bladder, and his body had grown so big that they had to smash down the door to take him to the cemetery. The man that had thought so highly of himself and had been married for just three days was now dead.

And so there followed another round of dishes, all food for days of fasting, among which I remember boiling plums and wheat till my hips ached with all the stirring. And at the funeral supper, when they'd finishing licking the bowls clean, I found myself with Gentleman Zăval in the kitchen.

'Silică, my first class *mistator*,' he said, because that's what he called me—he had some words that no one else says, they were his words, well printed on his tongue, so that, if you heard someone else saying one of those words, it was clear enough that they had been talking with the Gentleman—'how about making a *philtrum* for Caterina, to ease her pain a little?'

As soon as I heard this, I was overjoyed, because I really like to learn recipes, and especially potions, which always give me good dreams.

'Right away, sir,' I replied, and his lordship, who was a very learned man—no one could compare with him—started to tell me how to make it.

But he wasn't the sort to get you to make something in a few words. He would tell you a whole lot of little secrets. It was from him I learned that everything is connected to a story that stretches back through all the old times and that rises like dough, and if for some reason it stops it's a sign of death, for the world isn't the world unless this story keeps growing.

'Here, Silică, some *coccinela*,' he said, holding out a few ladybirds, just right for a wonderful potion.

I wasn't surprised, because, every time those grand words came from his mouth, I knew for sure that there was nothing to be surprised about. That man would have had a fancy word even for sheep dung!

'When the moon reaches that post,' he said, pointing to one of the supports of the veranda, 'put the water on the hob! But to make this potion, which takes away the lover's pain, you must also know other threads that bind everything together better. The Red Emperor, about whom you know we have spoken before, had a daughter who knew all the arts of transformation. Her name, remember, was Paparuga Mărgăriţa. What do you think of that name?'

'It's a good name, noble sir!'

'I'm glad you like it!'

And only after he'd told me the whole story did he teach me how to make the potion and how to put it in the mistress's food. And when he left, he said: 'And Silică, take note that in the autumn that girl that we talked about is going to come.'

That night I didn't even sleep. The news that the Girl was coming left me jumping on hot coals like a mutton sausage. I can't tell you how many nights I lost thinking about the day I was going to meet her face to face. Gentleman Zăval had promised that he would let me know two or three days before. But he never managed, the poor man! And I didn't know she had come, and so I didn't even know it was her, until I found her sneaking in among my pots and pans at the Palace. In the meantime, Kostas had taken me to the Princely Court, but that was also through the intermediary of the Gentleman, who had told me not to leave it whatever happened: 'You see, Silică, even if your mistress calls you or the Metropolitan begs you, don't leave here, because your greatest role is to make food for the most important bellies. It depends on you! Only you can make the world that we dream of! The great decisions of the country don't come from the ruler's head, but from what he stuffs in his belly!'

Not even if the Girl tried to push me was I to give up. And she really did appear one day!

Like me, she was rather short, but white in the face, the way Romanian girls are. And she had such devilish eyes you never saw the like: they looked like chestnuts just taken out of an oven. From under her fez came I think about ten pigtails plaited with striped silk, and because of that she looked, I don't know, like a sort of wild creature with puffed out feathers. Not to mention that on her feet she wore tall boots, like the Germans who came here in the wars!

As soon as she came in, she laid into me and, because I had heard in the marketplace that she had likely killed Zăval, I got a bit scared. And what a tongue she had!

'Don't you on any account make that rose cake, or the Devil take you!' That's how she spoke!

But there was nothing I could do about it, because the Gentleman put the *Book of Perilous Dishes* into my hands, and I had to follow it word for word. Just as he had said, the Girl wanted me to take her to Murta Street. And she wasn't the only one, because Gentleman Perticari kept going on about the same thing: 'As soon as the Girl comes, be careful to take her to Murta Street and let me know straight away!'

But, frightful as she looked, she was right, because that rose cake made all hell break loose. How I hunted for her all through the Palace and how hard I searched till I found her! But in the end she made a fool of me, because her cure for laughter wasn't at all good. And it very nearly finished me off! The Girl knew a lot, and, just as Gentleman Zăval had told me, she was a witch. I shouldn't have judged her by how she looked!

And then I had Perticari always on at me to take him into the Vodă's chamber. And in the end I took him, right after I made the plum pie, and although he promised me two ducats for doing it, he only gave me one.

I had more trouble on account of the Girl too. She talked her way into the mistress's good books, and they say that the mistress

251

gave the noble Bina fifty ducats to have me kidnapped. But I don't believe that story. Gentleman Cirtă even said to me on the way: 'Don't you worry, Silică! After His Excellency Ismail Bina leaves, you can go back to the Palace! There's nothing anyone can do to you! You're the princely cook, with papers to prove it! Just don't let on to anyone that I told you!'

For me the *Book of Perilous Dishes* was the greatest gift anyone could give me. Even today I still learn something every time I prepare a dish out of it. Many of the recipes I knew before, from the time when I lived with the cupping-glass woman, even if I hadn't a clue what power they had. Bread with mushrooms was her favourite. Of course I didn't know it was called *crumilla*. But nor do I remember it causing such a disturbance as the night when the mistress got married for the second time. But I've had some joy with that bread too. Every time I give it to someone to eat, it's as if that person loses their willpower. Some weep. Others unburden their souls to me. Once I tried it on Gentleman Perticari, because I used to cook for him too, not with much pleasure, because he was always sticking his nose in the recipe, and that filled my soul with lice. But with that bread it was all right: I got four ducats out of him. And I swear he gave me them without me even asking, without me doing anything for them!

In those days, when the city seemed to have gone mad, and the Vodă was imposing new taxes every day, I made a habit of baking that bread, *crumilla*, and sharing it around. Even though Zăval had made a point of telling me I was only to make food for Kostas. And probably even after death, he or his ghost taught me a lesson!

My first punishment was when the mistress died. I loved her! More than I loved anyone else in this world I loved her, and if it hadn't been for Gentleman Zăval I would never have left her house. She died because I made *perilous dishes* and I used them for myself. And even though I should have known my place, I didn't! And afterwards all the trouble came down on my head!

My wife, poor thing, was seized by force, all because of me. She was nothing special. And I wasn't one for marrying either. But I knew that long ago. Gentleman Zăval told me even before I grew a moustache. A cook is a celibate. In his life there are no other pleasures than the pleasure of food. Meaning not that he's a greedy-guts, just that he's a master of stocks and aromas. The cook doesn't know the delights of the bedroom. He has no family. He has no ties. When you see a fat man stirring the pot and you find out that on top of that he's got a whole pack of children at home, steer clear of eating anything that comes from his hands! He's no cook, he's just a bungler, and you should run away from him and not look back!

After the *Book of Perilous Dishes*, my life fell apart. The mistress was dead, and my wife was sold as a common slave, even though she was one of the house Gypsies too, not some Rudar woman brought from the estate! Although I knew well that I was to blame, all my rage fell on Kostas. I only wanted to see him dead. Gentleman Perticari knew a lentil, which he called *chubby*, and he drew it for me too: 'Look, Silică, if you can find this lentil, I'll teach you how to make a dish that, if you give it to Kostas, will make him do what you want!'

I was trying to get to a man I had heard of who had that bean, when there was all the business about the Frenchmen getting arrested. The Girl got involved in that. She was sorry about the mistress too, and she wanted to save Duba from the fury of the Turks. As for me, I never trusted that Frenchman. If you made me choose between him and the Greceancă's first husband, I'd go for Mihalache any time, even if his father did sell Gypsies! But the Frenchman—how should I put it? There was something glassy in his heart, a hard core that would never have melted even under the sun that shone in the Greceanu courtyard. That's why I had no inclination to do my bit to save him from the galleys. Even so, at the end of the day, if the Girl had kept on at me, I would have taken him on the road to Braşov.

However, my head was full of the Vodă, whose ugly mug was turning my days dark. There was no one left in the city that was on his side.

While the Frenchmen were on the way to Giurgiu, I was hard at it boiling the beans, while that trickster Perticari's eyes were shining. Not for a moment did he think of Kostas, still less of me. He wanted a dish for himself and for his delights, and what those were I don't know to this day. But I did get my revenge a little, by giving him a tree-frog sauce to eat, which the Girl had asked me to make specially for him. I didn't believe it for a moment when she told me that I'd be called back to the kitchen again. In the meantime, Kostas had cast me off, because of a stew in which, like a fool, I had put too little poison.

In the end I did something that I also knew from my poor cupping-glass woman: I cut off the head of a snake and boiled it well in wormwood, and, one night, when the whole Palace was asleep, I threw it at Kostas's door. And it worked, because exactly the same happened to him as to the snake: two days later, Ismail Bina cut off his head.

But these things don't matter anymore. Out of all the dreams of my youth, I'm left with only one. Among the many things Zăval put into my head, there is one that I still haven't forgotten, and sometime soon I might tell it.

'Take note of this, Silică. The Girl will leave on a long journey. When you hear this, go and ask her if she's leaving for Lipsca, and when she returns, all you have to do is to look well into her eyes. If they are shining, there will be no more need for you to do anything. She will put on her yellow dress and go out of the door holding a jar under her arm. Then you can sleep peacefully. For you, all duties will be over.

'But if she returns with her eyes dusty and shuts herself in her chamber, then you will knock on the door and you will tell her word for word what is in my letter:'

My dear niece,

When you listen to this letter, I shall no longer be, for, if I had lived, I would have told you everything from my own mouth. And if you have read the *Book of the Satorines* that I left for you at Lipsca, it means that the cook has misread your eyes.

You were the dearest person in my life; in you I placed all my faith.

Your mother was not the daughter of Maxima. None of us had children, for a Satorine is never a parent. All the same, your mother was one of the family, the daughter of a cousin of ours who could not feel Sator. She was just a *mixtator*. This grandmother of yours, a somewhat scatterbrained woman, was born in the Greceanu house and died young, leaving behind two children: your mother and Silică. I expect you will not be pleased. But remember one thing: blood is not only thicker than water, it has the power to link minds one to another. Silică was fathered by a Gypsy, who is also dead. Do not fear! Blood has no colour. And nor does it choose in which veins it flows. If you look carefully, you have a lot in common. You are his only kin...

# ROMANIAN
# PRONUNCIATION GUIDE

Spelling in Romanian is much more regular than in English, so it is easy to pronounce most words if you know what sounds the letters represent. The following is not a complete guide to Romanian pronunciation, but it should be enough to help the reader to handle the Romanian names and other words that appear in this book.

## Consonants

*c* – before *e* or *i* as in 'church', otherwise as in 'coat'
*ch* (before e or i) – as English *k* in 'king'
*g* – before *e* or *i* as in 'gem', otherwise as in 'goat'
*gh* (before e or i) – as English *g* in 'get'
*j* – like the sound represented by *s* in 'measure'
*r* – always pronounced, slightly rolled.
*s* – as in 'seat' (never as in 'rose')
*ş* – as English *sh* in 'cash'
*ţ* – as English *ts* in 'cats'

## Vowels

*a, e, i, o, u*: similar to Italian pronunciation, apart from the following:
- final *i* is generally almost silent (as in *Perticari*, pronounced *perrtee__carr__* with just a hint of a *y* sound at the end).
- *i* before another vowel sounds like English *y* and *o* before *a* sounds like English *w* (as in *Mogoșoaia*, pronounced *mogosh-__waya__*)

*ă* – like the *a* in 'about'

*â* or *î* – something like the *i* in 'fill', but with the tongue a little further back in the mouth

## Stress

It is not always predictable where the stress will fall in a Romanian word, but in longer words and proper names, it is generally safe to guess that it will be on the last syllable if the word ends in a consonant (*Ză__val__, Iu__lian__*), and on the penultimate if it ends in a vowel (*__Pâ__tca, Cate__ri__na, Si__li__că, O__ga__ru*...).

### Turkish letters

Five letters specific to Turkish appear occasionally in the book in the names of characters and other words:

In *Pazvantoğlu*, the letter *ğ* has no sound of its own but it makes the preceding *o* longer;

in *Küçük*, the letter *ü* sounds like German *ü* or the *u* in French 'tu', and *ç* sounds like *ch* in English;

in *mayın*, the letter *ı* sounds like the second *e* in English 'seven';

in *Karagöz*, the letter *ö* sounds like the *u* in 'fur'.

# GLOSSARY

*Agie*—police headquarters

*anteri*—a long robe, worn by men and women alike

*Arnauts*—guards in the service of the prince of Wallachia, originally Albanian mercenaries

*ban*—a small unit of currency in Wallachia (and still today in Romania)

*berat*—a document of investiture issued by the Sublime Porte

*boyar*—a nobleman of Wallachia or Moldavia

*brașoveancă*—a large carriage or covered wagon

*caro impudica*—'unchaste flesh' (Latin)

*comis*—commander of the Palace guard

*conscientiae labes*—'the stain of conscience' (Latin)

*dragoman*—official interpreter

*Dur bre, ferman!*—'No one moves! I have a *ferman* (an order signed by the Sultan)!' (Turkish): the standard formula for announcing that a prince of Wallachia was about to be put to death on the orders of the Sultan

*Dura's Lake*—today the Cișmigiu Gardens, Bucharest's oldest park

*giaour*—a non-Muslim, particularly a Christian subject of the Ottoman Empire

*Girin!*—'Come in!' (Turkish)

*Hominum Sator atque deorum*—'creator of men and gods' (Latin)

*impetu magis*—'under an impulse' (Latin)

*imprecatio*—'curse' (Latin)

*kalimavkion*—the cylindrical cap of an Orthodox priest

*kavuk*—a cylindrical, flat topped hat

*khan*—an inn of Middle–Eastern type, with the rooms around a central courtyard

*lefta* —Greek coins

*Laco Fulvus*—red Lacedaemonian (or Spartan) dog (Latin)

*Lingurari, Rudari*—Roma (Gypsy) tribal groups

*mahut*—a kind of dark felt

*musahip*—a close adviser of the sultan, here serving as the sultan's special envoy

*para*—a unit of currency in Wallachia

*pater veneni*—father of poison (Latin)

*pervane mayın*—'my butterfly' (Turkish)

*Phanariot*—a Greek from the Phanar district of Constantinople (Istanbul); Phanariots held important positions in the Ottoman Empire, including ruling the principalities of Moldavia and Wallachia from 1711 and 1716 respectively until 1821

*pitar*—a court official of boyar (noble) rank responsible for supervising the palace bakeries and ensuring supplies of bread

*plerophorize*—a very rare English word, used here as an equivalent of the Romanian *pliroforisi*, meaning 'clarify, explain' (a word borrowed from Greek in Phanariot times, now also very rare)

*preoteasă*—the wife of an Orthodox priest (Romanian)

*Saxon*—a Transylvanian German; early in the story Pâtca's Transylvanian city clothes lead some people to assume she is a Saxon, although in fact she is not.

*Şchei*—the Romanian district of Braşov (which at the time was predominantly a German city)

*Skatá skatá sto thirío*—'Shit, shit to the beast!' (Greek)

*Stamboul*—an older form of *Istanbul*, as the Turkish capital, then the capital of the Ottoman Empire, is known today *stânjen*—an old Romanian measure of length, at the time of the story approximately equal to two metres

*strigoi*—in Romanian folklore, either a dead person returning from the grave or a living person born with devilish qualities and powers

*Sublime Porte*—the government of the Ottoman Empire

*tezkere*—travel permit (Turkish)

*thaler*—a silver coin of the Austrian Empire

*Vlach*—a member of one of the various minority groups in Greece and other lands south of the Danube who speak Latin-derived dialects closely related to Romanian

*Vodă*—a title given to the prince of Wallachia

*vornic*—a boyar (noble) rank, with administrative and judicial responsibilities

*Walachisches Tor*: the 'Romanian Gate' (German); the entrance to the Șchei district of Brașov

# LIST OF CHARACTERS IN ORDER OF APPEARANCE

Pâtca (or Pâtculița) – narrator of the story

Maxima Tutilina – Pâtca's grandmother

Sator – the central force of the universe, whose energies the initiates of the Satorine cult seek to harness

Burchioiu (Laurian Burcu Podaru) – Pâtca's neighbour in Șchei

Zăval, known as *Cuviosu* (pious) Zăval – Maxima's brother and Pâtca's great uncle

Kostas – Prince of Wallachia (known to history as Constantine Hangerli)

The Metropolitan – the senior Orthodox bishop of the Principality of Wallachia

Silică – A slave/cook to Caterina Greceanu and Kostas

Caterina Greceanu – the richest woman in Bucharest

Johanna – Pâtca's three-legged cat

Perticari – a Wallachian boyar, famous as a spiritist

Captain Mârcă – a madman who thinks he is a captain and acts the part

Simon Schuster – a shoemaker in Șchei, Pâtca's neighbour

Cirtă Vianu – right-hand man of Ismail Bina

Pazvantoğlu – rebel leader, controlling territory to the south of the Danube

Husein Küçük, the Kapudan Pasha (grand admiral of the Ottoman navy), commander of an army sent to defeat Pazvantoğlu

261

Ismail Bina Emeni – envoy sent by the Sultan to Wallachia

Ypsilanti – a possible replacement for Kostas on the throne of Wallachia

Master Iulian – Pâtca's teacher in Șchei

Văcărescu's Gypsies – singers in the street announcing the news

Dubois – Chancellor at the French Consulate,

Gentleman Ispas – Burchioiu's father

*Comis* Dumitrache Banu – commander of the palace guard, interrogator

The Great Selim – Sultan Selim III of the Ottoman Empire

Nețu Birt – leader of a revolt in the Șchei district of Brașov

Papuc – Caterina Greceanu's housekeeper

Ogaru – Priest

Dudescu – a Wallachian boyar (nobleman)

Fleury – French consul in Wallachia

Green Old Woman (also known as 'Craiova') – accused of being Cat o' Friday

Syrka – female magician

Napoleon – French general

Moruzi – another possible replacement for Kostas on the throne of Wallachia

Ivan Grosu – a blacksmith

Mihalache Albu – Caterina Greceau's first husband